Adam and Evil

BY GILLIAN ROBERTS

Adam and Evil

AN AMANDA PEPPER MYSTERY

Gillian Roberts

Ballantine Books • New York

This book is dedicated to all the librarians who
have so enriched my life, especially these wonderful
people at The Free Library of Philadelphia:
—William Lang, Karen Lightner, Jim O'Donnell,
J. Randall Rosensteel, and Connie King of the Rare Book
Department. I send my lasting gratitude for your amazing
knowledge and expertise—and for your patience and
graciousness in the face of my complete lack of same;
—and most of all, Bernard Pasqualini, inspiration and
lifeline, who not only suggested that I commit (fictional)
mayhem at the library, but then made it possible that I do
so with his patient, perfect, personalized research assistance.

Adam and Evil

One

ODD is not a useful definition when referring to adolescents. It's hard differentiating between a teenager with problems and one whose only problem is being a teenager. It's nearly impossible for an English teacher to know if a sulky withdrawal is a sign of depression that requires attention, or a fit of I-want-to-die grief because the team lost a game.

I'm supposed to develop language skills, not psychoanalyze students. Besides, I play a tiny role in their life and consciousness. A pie chart of the teenage brain reveals that 54 percent of that organ is devoted to tracking the state of their hormones, 21 percent does play-by-play analyses of their mercurial moods, and 10 percent is given over to calculations: what music they desperately need, what movies they'd die if they didn't see, and what items of clothing everybody else has but they don't. Another 8 percent debates how to fill time when school is out; 4 percent charts who did or didn't look at or speak to them in the manner they desired; 2 percent critiques the personal lives and wardrobes of their peers and anyone in *People* or *Entertainment Weekly* magazine. The remaining 1 percent of attention is divided among whatever academic subjects they like.

These proportions fluctuate under the pressures of momentous life events, such as attending a prom, being admitted to college, or getting a zit. But by and large, this is the adolescent brain, and there is precious little place in it for either me or my course of study. I stand outside, arms waving like semaphores, trying to wedge my message into whatever space is left in there for rent. They hear nothing, and see only a rapidly aging pest with style-challenged hair (too long, too brown), boring clothing, a pathetic (I gather) sense of humor, and a love life that annoys them because they don't understand the status quo. Neither do I, but I can live with that.

Working under those conditions gets old, and it doesn't allow much time or scope for meditations on the class population's mental health. That's how it always has been.

Until now, when it's gotten worse. Kids today aren't what they used to be, which was predictably, but nonlethally, weird. Just as we'd relaxed, adjusted, listened to experts' explanations, and accepted teenagers' peculiarities, they upped the ante. Headlines erupted with stories about teens who expressed their moodiness by blowing away their classmates, teachers, and whoever else peeved them.

Lately I've found myself thinking about their teachers. Sympathizing with them. Wishing I could have talked to them—before their students killed them. Wondering if I'm destined to be one of them.

Reflecting on those news stories in a school full of adjustment problems must be like living on an earthquake fault. You know the danger's there, but if you think about it too much, you'll go crazy, which is just as fearful a prospect. All the same, if you're sane, you note seismic activity and stay aware of how extreme classroom tremors become.

Adam Evans registered a 10 on my Richter scale. I hoped my machinery—not his—was malfunctioning, but I didn't think so.

Because of him, I feared that I'd overdosed on teenagers in general. But whether or not I had, Adam Evans was a puzzle I couldn't solve, and he'd been a worry the entire academic year. I never felt sure of myself when it came to him. Never could even determine to my satisfaction whether our problems were his or mine.

Now, eight months after Adam entered my class for his senior year, I was still in the dark. All I knew for certain was that he was a royal pain. Philly Prep runs a high percentage of royal—and commoner—pains. They are, in fact, our specialty, inasmuch as we appeal to those (sufficiently affluent) youngsters who have a difficult time in larger, more standardized schools. Our mandate is to ignite a spark in the insufficiently fueled.

This was what I was trying to explain to my near and dear ones on a Sunday afternoon in late April. My sister, Beth, her husband, Sam, and their two children were visiting en route to a party nearby. This was in no way a typical experience. Beth and Sam were the ultimate suburbanites. Sam rode the Paoli Local into the city each day to his law firm, but then he hurried back out to Gladwynne. And Beth behaved as if coming to the city were the equivalent of going on safari without a guide. So this visit was an event. We drank coffee and caught up on our lives.

I talked about teaching, my growing ambivalence. I talked about Adam. I wanted sympathy, I wanted compassion. Often, lately, I wanted out. "I'm afraid for him," I said. "He doesn't seem in complete control. The other day, I was sure he was going to hit someone. I had to physically restrain him. And then he freaked. Acted as if touching him was a crime." Beth looked aghast—her suspicions about people who lived inside the city limits were proving true. I shook my head. "I'm making it sound worse than it was. He stopped as soon as I touched his arm. He hates being touched. It's part of what's abnormal about him. Anyway, I didn't have to wrestle him down, he didn't hurt the other kid, but he did overreact to both that other boy and then to me. He's off center. I can't explain it, but I worry about what he might do to somebody else—and I worry about what he might do to himself."

From atop a ladder, C.K. Mackenzie grunted, acknowledging that he was listening. Of course, he'd heard this before, so his real attention was on a painting he was hanging. My brother-in-law partnered in this endeavor, standing nearby, reading a J. Crew catalogue, ready to hand up a tool if needed. Male bonding. They didn't look at each other or communicate. They were both very happy.

I pulled Adam's paper out of the pile on the oak table. There were always papers needing marking. That, too, grew old. "Tell me this isn't peculiar. Quote: 'I will learn to harmonize with the song of my follicles.' End quote."

"You'll do what?" Mackenzie swiveled and endangered his perch. Sam dropped the J. Crew catalogue and rushed to the rescue, grabbing the sides of the ladder, steadying it. The women made sounds of alarm, the men made sounds indicating they could take care of anything.

"Not me. Adam." I repeated the sentence. Mackenzie shook his head, as well he might. "I've asked for a conference with his parents," I said. "There are too many strange things like this about him lately. He should be evaluated, get some help before . . . I don't know what. He's off somewhere, can't concentrate, reacts bizarrely with inappropriate laughs or no emotion at all . . ." My words dribbled off because I had so little confidence in my own opinion. I had a strong sense that Adam was having mental and emotional problems, but he'd done reasonably well on his SAT exams, and that piece was such a bad fit with the rest of the puzzle, it worried me, made me think perhaps I was being too harsh on the boy.

"It must be difficult trying to teach writing," Sam said in his calm, ultrasane manner.

"It's impossible." Writing logically requires thinking logically—and how can you teach that? But—speaking of logical thinking—how can you not try to? "So what's your take? Is that follicle thing as weird a concluding thought as I think it is?"

"It's, um, interesting. Really. I don't know about poetry, but I kind of liked it," Beth said.

"Imaginative," Sam said.

"Vivid," Mackenzie said. "Singing follicles would sound way better than a Walkman."

The children, in bright plastic smocks I'd surprised them with, continued playing with modeling clay, also an Aunt Mandy treat. They did not participate in the Adam Evans follicle debate.

Another reason to love being an aunt. I can be generous for very little outlay, endearing in short spurts, and incommunicado the rest of the time. And they don't leave me with papers to grade.

"Really?" I asked. "Interesting? Imaginative? Vivid? That's what comes to mind?" Maybe Adam was taking a creative leap, in which case, even if I personally felt he fell flat, I should encourage him.

My sister glanced at her watch. "Let's clean up," she said. "The party's already begun."

"Why don't you go ahead?" Sam suggested. "The kids and I will pick you up in an hour or so. I'll stay and help . . ."

Neither he nor Beth knows what to call my significant other. I call him C.K., but they're taken aback by his remaining a set of initials. "Call him Chico," I said.

"Wrong," Mackenzie said.

"I meant Czeslaw. I always mix those two up."

Beth meanwhile aimed peevish looks at her husband, who ignored them. She switched her attention to me. Earlier she'd tried to sell me on this party giver, one Emily Buttonwood, a soon-to-be-divorced, newly relocated-to-center-city friend of hers. She'd been adamant about how we just had to meet and become new best friends. I'd redirected the conversation to Adam, hoping it would convey an inkling of why my life was sufficiently congested and chaotic without becoming a city guide to one more bewildered former suburbanite. I'd done it twice so far for Beth, with time-consuming, dismal results.

"Reconsider, Mandy, and come with me," Beth said. "You'd just love each other. You have so much in common—she's a book lover, like you. In fact, she's so down on people, books are about all she loves these days—with a few exceptions. She needs people like you. Single, interesting people."

Flattering, but no cigar. A depressed, bitter, people-hating new friend. Precisely what I needed to round out my life. "I'd love to, of course," I lied. "But I have these papers to finish, a lesson to prepare, and . . ."

Beth looked downcast. Then she brightened. "I nearly forgot. Emmy would be perfect for your women's book group. I told her about it, and she's really looking forward to it. Will you give her a call? Or should I give her your number?"

"They just voted to close membership. It was getting too large and unwieldy. No time for everybody to speak up." All true, but it nonetheless left me with the sense I'd failed Emmy Buttonwood in her hour of need, without ever having met her. Somehow I now owed her. I wasn't sure how my sister had so effortlessly instilled guilt about negligence to a stranger, but she had the gift. She has inherited my mother's tenacious nagging skills. Both of them should have been CEOs of major corporations. Instead they apply their formidable powers to those who need to be brought into line: preschoolers and me.

I wasn't eager to join forces with another of Beth's displaced friends. Not with anyone, in fact. I was already drowning in too-muchness, and my current fantasies were of silence and solitude. I wanted a Georgia O'Keeffe life, as long as it didn't require artistic talent. Few possessions and fewer visitors to my plain white space. No teenagers. No sisters with dull, sad, and needy friends.

"I'll try," I said. "I'll ask the group next time we meet." They'd be annoyed with me—they'd settled the issue at the last meeting. I could only hope Beth would quickly forget about her relocated friend. Out of sight and all that.

"What do you think of our expanded view?" Mackenzie asked. The wall now appeared to have a barn window, through which we saw a vista of fields and grazing cows, the latter suspended a few feet above the painted pasture. We city dwellers living several stories above street level had found the floating bovines funny. I, for one, was in great need of funny.

Also, the painting filled a whole lot of wall. Judged by price per square inch, it had been a bargain, as my mother would say were she not safely several states due south in Florida.

"I think it's straight," Sam said. I wasn't as sure.

Beth fussed with her children. "You realize you're going to upset that boy's parents," she said to me.

"Adam's? About the conference?"

"I'd be. And if it's true, wouldn't they be the first to notice?"

At which point silent Sam surprised me by voicing an unsolicited opinion. "Be careful about your actions," he said. "It's hardly what a parent wants to hear, and given the fact that you have no background in psychology, no credentials in that area . . ."

"I'd like them to have him evaluated. To get him help if he needs it. It isn't as if I'm accusing them of something or libeling them."

"His parents might not see it the same way, is all I'm saying. Think twice."

We were all expected to listen to Sam's advice, which was always wise and always conservative, and for which he charged others big bucks, but he was annoying me. What had happened to the concept of being a decent human being? Love thy neighbor. Good Samaritanism.

"When should people intervene?" I asked. "At what point should somebody stick her neck out and try to help? Shouldn't we try to prevent things? Or should we wait for a TV crew to arrive so we can say, 'I noticed he was behaving oddly, but . . .' I'm mostly afraid for Adam. Do you know the statistics on teenage suicide?"

"Mandy!" Beth said, with a fearful glance at her children. "Sam, I think we should all go to Emily's."

I got the sense that Sam most definitely did not agree, but after hosing down the kids, many farewells, and a further warning from Sam about intervening in a child's personal life, they went off to their party.

Even with the ladder put away, Mackenzie fretted about his handiwork. "Not sure it's straight," he said. I pointed out that we lived in the oldest part of the city. In a former factory. The floors weren't straight and neither were the walls, and there probably wasn't a ninety-degree angle to be had, so how could one tell about a painting in the middle of a long, unstraight wall?

"The appearance of straightness, then," he said.

Kin to the appearance of mental illness. "I don't care what Sam said," I told Mackenzie. "If I don't put out an alert about the boy, who will?" I was convincing myself because if my sister and brother-in-law were correct, I was about to kick up a lot of hard feelings, and in truth, I still couldn't decide if Adam's essay contained brilliant imagery beyond my puny comprehension, or lunacy. Or whether I'd become such a grumpy, burned-out case that I was looking for trouble, scapegoating Adam Evans.

"Tell me about the kid." Mackenzie stared at the wall, tilting his head to the left, obviously still deliberating the painting's straightness or lack thereof.

And there you had the problem. I shouldn't have needed to tell him about Adam. I already had. Lots. He didn't listen. He divvied up his attention and deeded me almost as little conscious brain space as my students did. Was he listening now as he squinted and realigned himself and paced in front of the wall? Maybe my tales were too thin a gruel for Mackenzie's daily diet. Compared to a homicide detective's, my deviants from the norm must seem amusements.

But Mackenzie's are either dead or in hiding. Mine are right in my face.

"He smells, for starters," I said. "Remember? I told you. I think he's stopped washing. Permanently. A few months back. Always wears black—black everything, including a long scarf no matter the weather—so the dirt doesn't show, but he is fragrant. His hair's greasy, and it's sometimes hard to be close to him." I hated how superficial, unsympathetic, and narrow-minded I sounded, and I knew all the counterarguments. A seventeen-year-old boy is bound to assert himself, and annoying the hell out of his elders is a prime method. If cleanliness was valued at home, then keeping dirty would work. If nobody objected to either long or short or completely shaved-off hair, then how about stringy-greasy-smelly? I knew all that, but the sense of wrongness persisted. "He behaves . . . inappropriately. I can't define it."

"Bad?"

"Not really. Not what you mean by that."

"Disruptive?"

"Sometimes. But more like off-kilter."

"Did you ever think that maybe . . . well, this is difficult to suggest, but maybe this kid, for whatever reason, annoys the hell out of you, pushes buttons you aren't aware of, and maybe you overreact to what wouldn't bother you about somebody else? Did you ever consider that you might be . . . oh, what's the technical word for the process . . ." He looked ceilingward, as if searching for inspiration. "Ah, yes, *picking on* him?"

How dare he? To suggest that I—a seasoned, semi-idealistic, underpaid, overworked teacher, champion of the underdog—was not playing fair? That I, despite all I knew and had learned and believed in, was nonetheless prejudiced against one of my own students?

Of *course* I was. But it was still rude of him to suggest it. "I read an article about the boy who killed those people at the clinic. He was an undiagnosed schizophrenic, and the way he acted for a long while before then—it sounded like Adam Evans. Isolated, withdrawn, unkempt . . ."

"Hey," Mackenzie said softly, finally turning his back to the painting and sitting down at the oak table, across from me and the

9

stack of essays. "That describes half the world's population, including supermodels and kids on TV. The thing is, you're not equipped to diagnose—"

"I know that. I keep saying that. That's why I want somebody else to evaluate him. Somebody who does know how."

"Do his other teachers feel the same way?"

He had a blue-fire stare that reflected all the way to eternity, and at the moment I did not enjoy being the subject of it. "Are you interrogating me?" I snapped. He looked surprised, confused, and worried, all in one blue blink. As well he might. I sounded less mentally stable than Adam Evans ever had. "Okay, I'm sorry. He's been cutting a lot of classes, and yes, he's considered a problem."

"What kind of problem? Academic, or as potentially dangerous a one as you . . ." He searched for a noninflammatory word. I had made him uncomfortable, and now we were talking as if through a translator, to avoid further conflict. I felt ashamed, yet determined not to yield an inch. "As you . . . fear?"

Good choice. "I don't know. I only know what I'm seeing. I've talked to the counselor, but nobody else yet. I'm sure they're all worried—how could we not be? All those news stories about kids going nuts at school."

"Does he talk about causing harm, doing something stupid, killing people, the way those kids are said to have?"

I shook my head.

"Singing hair follicles aren't the scariest image I can think of." Mackenzie's expression was kind, sympathetic, and . . . pitying?

I knew what he was seeing—a biddy, a schoolmarm straight out of mean-spirited cartoons and the classrooms of his youth. The teacher who'd decided he was trash and treated him like an interloper because the Mackenzie family was large and forced to make do and he wore patched hand-me-downs.

I'd become an evil stereotype. Somewhere between winter break and early spring, under the pressure and trivia of the daily teaching load plus the additional reams of college recommendation letters I'd agreed to write for students who didn't deserve admission to those schools—somewhere in there I'd lost my elasticity, my ability to empathize with the thousand variations on the theme of teen weirdness, my perspective. And the headlines about killer teens hadn't helped.

"Singing follicles would be like wiring implanted under your scalp," he said. "Great audio."

I checked to see if he was joking, but he meant it. Given his line of work, you'd think Mackenzie would be the one to despair of humanity, but he's found a balance I sorely lack.

"If Adam turns out to be an eccentric genius, he'd better come up with a discovery or piece of art worth the stench." Even his handwriting annoyed me, running off the lines, changing direction, turning corners, and managing to make even ballpoint ink splot. "I've spoken with Rachel Leary—"

He looked confused. He never, ever truly listened. "The school counselor," I reminded him. "She's also meeting with Adam's parents."

"Then she agrees with you?"

"She doesn't have him in class. She knows his grades are down, that he's cutting. She knows that kind of thing."

"But you said he did well on his SATs."

"Way better than I would have thought. He's smart. I know that—I never knew why he was at Philly Prep. But lately something's gone wrong. He can't concentrate lots of the time."

"For your sake, let Rachel bring up the topic of mental illness, with a professional reason backing up what she says."

"They live with him, they have to have noticed. . . ." I saw it in my beloved's eyes. I was a zealot, a lunatic insisting on saving a world that had not put in an SOS.

"The painting's crooked," I said. "It lists to the left." On that issue, Mackenzie took me seriously. As soon as his blue-ice eyes were refocused on the landscape, I locked on my teacherly mask and returned to Adam's essay. But a shudder raced over my skin, a skittering creature terrified by where it was and where it was heading.

11

Two

HAVE never seen a woman sit as straight as Dorothy Evans. If I didn't know better and hadn't seen her enter the room, I would have sworn she was suspended by a thread set into the center of her skull.

She was a diminutive woman, but her posture turned her into a spear, and made her height quite enough. She seated herself at the far end of the small couch in Rachel Leary's office and folded her hands on her lap. She might have been made of poured concrete.

If I'd met her rigid self earlier on, I might not have pressed for this conference. In fact, everything in me increasingly wanted out, but having set things in motion, I was stuck in a crowded counselor's office, with two hostile people on a love seat across from me.

Actually, *love seat* seemed an inappropriate term for the duo's perch. Mr. Evans sat as far away as possible from his wife, nearly on the armrest. I knew from looking at Adam's records that the senior Evans' first name was Parke, but he didn't care to share that with us.

From the moment the Evanses reluctantly, belligerently entered Rachel Leary's rumpled and comforting counseling office, I knew nothing good would come of this. I wanted to bolt, shouting apologies, admitting that this was a major mistake. Our meeting became a confrontation before a single word was spoken.

Speaking didn't improve a thing. Not even when done in the gentlest of ways. Rachel has the ability to project sympathetic vibrations without necessarily feeling much. As a point of fact, I knew that all she currently cared about were her internal organs and their new tenant. Rachel was in the early stages of her first pregnancy and surprised, she said, to be behaving like Scarlett O'Hara. "I thought I was peasant stock who'd breeze through this and have the baby in a field between appointments. I thought women didn't do this anymore." Nonetheless, she had morning sickness—and afternoon and evening sickness—and this Wednesday morning she was in a state of quiet terror, fearing that she was about to experience conferencing-with-the-Evanses sickness. "It would probably seem unprofessional to throw up on his polished shoes," she'd said to me a few moments before they arrived. "Even though I don't like the guy. He's hellbent on having his son achieve some undefined triumph that will blaze both their names across the sky. I will never lay that on you," she promised her queasy midriff.

"Why'd they send Adam here? Was he always a problem?"

"I don't think so." Rachel shrugged. "My theory? Parke Evans decided that Adam had the best chance of shining in these dim halls of learning. Here he could have been valedictorian, best in his class. I know that sounds cynical, but Mr. Evans provokes such thoughts. He's completely competitive, and you'd better not best him. I wouldn't put it past him to pick—forgive me—a loser school so his son would have better odds of being a winner."

"Adam's mother?"

Rachel shrugged. "She barely spoke. Just vibrated. Tense creature."

The truth was, the old Adam could have done well anywhere, and would have definitely taken whatever honors Philly Prep distributed. His father's Machiavellian school selection would have proven accurate, if only Adam hadn't swerved off into a parallel universe.

Now Rachel leaned toward the couple and in a silky, sympathetic voice that held no trace of her dislike said, "I know you're busy people, and it's lovely of you to have responded so quickly."

To underscore her observation, busy Mr. Evans checked his watch.

Rachel cut to the chase. "We're concerned about Adam."

"What does that mean?" Mr. Evans demanded. "I came here because I am concerned about *your* concern about my son. What right do you have to be concerned?"

He made concern sound like a weapon that only he was licensed to use. Rachel and I were usurpers, concern thieves. And I made sad note that Mr. Concern himself wasn't speaking about a boy named Adam but about a possession—and one he had sole title to. "*My* son"—only his, as if Dorothy Evans was a passerby, a curious onlooker.

"Maybe this is about his college admission process?" Mr. Evans said. "He hasn't heard from everywhere yet. Hasn't responded to the one that accepted him. Is that what's bothering you?"

"*Concerning* us," Rachel repeated. "Don't worry about the schools. There's time." She swallowed hard and looked as if she'd ingested a green-gray dye.

"Adam's behavior concerns me," I said.

"You!" Parke Evans looked ready to explode. There was so much fury in his voice that I actually turned to check whether Satan had just blown through the door.

14

I had wanted Rachel to present the problem in suitably professional terms. Perhaps to show a graph or bar chart of what's normal and what is not. But she looked as if she were going down for
the count, so I plugged on. "He's changed dramatically and isn't the
boy I taught a short course to when he was in ninth grade. He was
so attentive and involved then. Now he's—"

"Ninth grade! The equivalent of a lifetime ago to him! He's a senior in high school now, a whole different stripe of animal. Why
would you expect him to be the same?"

Parke Evans was like a relentlessly yapping dog. I compensated
by making my voice even softer. "I remember how outstanding his
work and attitude were, I remember his personality, and now—"

"This is appalling. This confirms everything I thought—you
know *nothing* about teenagers," Mr. Evans said. "But it's supposedly your business, isn't it? Both of you?" He looked from me to
Rachel. "That's your expertise? That's why this fancy high-priced
school has you on its faculty?"

Neither of us chose to reply. Rachel was busily taking deep
breaths while I was wondering whom I could call to have a conference about Mr. Evans' behavior. One of the items on the mounting list of things I did not love about my job was parents who
considered me hired help. I had never thought about dealing with
parents when I'd thought about teaching. Goes to show what I
knew then.

Mrs. Evans stared straight ahead, the tight line of her lips cross-
ing the one her spine made. She was all T squares and right angles.

"I sell appliances," Mr. Evans said. "Have for . . . yap, yap, yap . . .
that's *my* expertise. I wouldn't drag you in for a conference because
ovens get hot and refrigerators are cold. They are what they are.
Teenage boys are what they are. I also have expertise there. Expertise as Adam's father. Seventeen years of observation." He sat back.
Case closed.

"Excuse me!" Rachel bolted for the door.

The Evanses looked in the direction of where she'd been, then
looked to me for an explanation. I didn't feel like giving them one.

"I am indeed familiar with teenage behavior," I said. "That's why I'm so alarmed about Adam's."

"Drugs? Is that what you're saying?" Parke Evans demanded.

"I don't honestly know. It could be." My gut feeling was that while drugs were possibly, maybe even probably, part of the problem, there was something else, too—that *x* factor, that wrongness. But even if it were "only" drugs, shouldn't the Evanses be more concerned? "He's withdrawn, his hygiene, his work habits, his grades are suffering—"

"He's a kid," Parke Evans said. "Why make an issue of it? It's the end of his senior year. Why bust a gut? Basically, all he needs to do is pass, so what is this fuss about?"

"I'm aware of that, believe me." I was the one who had to keep my students from slipping into comas that last semester. "That's not what I'm talking about."

"He is not on drugs," his father said. "I read the literature, looked for the warning signs. He comes right home, doesn't have suspicious friends, doesn't go out on strange errands." He shook his head. "No drugs."

The boy went to school in center city and didn't have to sneak out to bad neighborhoods to make a buy. He didn't have disreputable friends because he didn't have any friends. But why waste my breath? "He's withdrawn," I repeated. "Doesn't socialize with—"

"This is a difficult time for him." Dorothy Evans sat even straighter, although I would have thought that impossible. She darted a look brimful of malice toward her husband and waited.

He said nothing.

"Difficult how?" I prompted.

She tightened her features and faced me with barely seeing eyes, a woman applying maximum force to pressures that otherwise were likely to explode out of her.

"If you don't want to talk about it, let's not," I said. "We still have this problem at school."

"*You* have a problem, Miss Pepper," Mr. Evans barked. "We don't."

"His father and I are divorcing," Dorothy Evans blurted out, still not meeting my eyes. "It's not . . . it's been . . ." She looked up at the ceiling, her hands still tightly folded. "A stressful time. That's what I meant."

"However," her husband said, "that has nothing to do with what we're talking about. Next you'll blame the hole in the ozone on me! Besides, Adam doesn't have a problem. He's a *teenager.*"

"Adam and I are close," Dorothy Evans said. "He's worried on my behalf. About the future. About what will become of me. About whether there will be money for his education. About whether his father and his father's girlfriend, who is four years older than Adam, will have time for him at all. About—"

"Enough, Dorothy! Please, let us behave like adults and stick to the topic."

"The topic is Adam!" Dorothy cried. "The topic is the stress that boy is under!"

Mr. Evans looked at me as if his wife's words were so much dust clouding the atmosphere and would I please wave it away? And then his expression soured as he remembered that I was part of the problem. "Adam's a gifted boy with his whole future ahead, and if his home isn't as calm as it could be, well, these things happen, and he'll develop the grit to get through it."

"Couldn't wait, could you?" Veins protruded on Mrs. Evans' thin neck. "Not a few lousy months until he graduated. Couldn't wait and see him through. Now look what you've done."

"Please," I said, "could we—I asked you to come today because I think Adam might benefit by seeing somebody."

"*Dating?*" Mrs. Evans looked horrified. "Why? You're like his father, thinking a girl can solve anything."

"Not that kind of seeing someone. Seeing a counselor."

"Well, Mrs. Leary doesn't seem to want to be seen." Mr. Evans gestured toward the empty chair.

"If he's on drugs," Dorothy Evans said, "if that's what . . . a treatment center, you mean?"

"We don't know that. That's just it: We don't know why he's behaving—"

"We? Speak for yourself. He's my son, and I know precisely why he's behaving as he does."

"Is he bad?" Mrs. Evans asked.

"I couldn't call it bad because it doesn't feel deliberate. It feels as if . . . as if messages aren't getting through. As if . . . well, I have his latest essay with me, and maybe that'll make what I'm getting at clearer."

"What do you mean, messages not getting through?" Mr. Evans demanded. "You make it sound like Adam's crazy!" He half rose from his perch on the arm of the chair.

If only Philadelphia had volcanoes and had one now, with lava pouring toward us. We'd race away—separately. If only a gigantic hole would swallow the school and me with it. If only I'd heeded Mackenzie's warnings, and my sister's and her husband's and Rachel's, and had given Adam a lower grade and moved on.

But here I was without hope of natural disaster, and I didn't think it would work for me to say "never mind," get up and leave. I understood now how all those kids who marched around announcing their demented and destructive plans were ignored until they actually killed somebody or themselves. I saw how tempting it was to become the next adult who stayed uninvolved. "I would never use a word like *crazy*," I said softly. "Or think it. Or mean it. But it feels important to have Adam tested or evaluated."

"You think he's disturbed?" Dorothy Evans said. "I'm a bad mother, is that what you mean? That's what they say, isn't it? It's always something the mother's done."

"Not at all. There are illnesses that typically start at this age. There are medications, really helpful treatments . . ."

They stared blankly, severely, an urban, tailored version of *American Gothic*. In lieu of a pitchfork, a briefcase and a designer handbag. I waited for Rachel to return and say something clinical and illuminating, but she remained in absentia, wresting with her own child-related problems. "I'm fearful for him," I said softly. "I want to make sure he doesn't harm himself." *Or anybody else,* I silently added.

They stared at me with unreadable expressions. Finally the mister spoke, his voice dripping icy stalactites. "I think something is seriously wrong with *you,* Miss Pepper. I think, in fact, that you are out of your mind. What do you have against me or my son? What possessed you to make such a suggestion?"

"Honest concern." I could barely force the words out. A typhoon would do, I thought. A tornado. Aimed right at this room. Nobody hurt—just blown away, never to see each other again.

"You are a single woman, aren't you." Not a question.

I nodded anyway.

"Childless," Dorothy Evans said. "You've never been a mother, have you?"

I shook my head.

"I knew it. Women like you . . . you're frustrated, jealous—"

"No," Parke Evans said. "I know why you brought this up. Very clever, you think, but it won't work, so forget about your smoke-screen. Trying to get us before we get you."

"Excuse me?"

"The assault! The battery! Don't think I don't know that you molested my son!" He half stood, his face an angry mauve.

"I never—"

"You hit him! Grabbed him and assaulted him, and we are not about to let that pass. Very clever to create this diversion, but it won't work."

I hit him? I hit a student? That was the most ridiculous— "You can't mean—" They couldn't mean. It was too insane. "The other day I had to restrain your son, stop him from—"

"Restrain, hah!" He'd gone from yaps to a bark.

"He was about to hit another student. I put my hand on his arm to stop him. That's all."

"Save your story for court," Parke Evans said.

All the air in the room was gone. My story? Court? These words did not compute. Language had lost all sense.

But not for Parke Evans, who was back on the scent. "What about his college applications? Have you gone after him there, too? Did you put your insane suspicions on evaluations? Adam trusted you."

I refused to be dragged down to the level the little dog sought. "I asked you to come here today to talk about finding a way to help your son."

"I'll bet you did, or you want to now. You get your way and it'd look really good on applications, wouldn't it? Dear school, by the way, Adam's under psychiatric care, on medications or whatever else you dream up!"

"You don't like him, do you?" Dorothy Evans spoke with vigor, her voice matching her ramrod posture. The lioness was guarding her cub. "He told me you don't, that none of you teachers do. I thought it was all youthful exaggeration, but he was right. You don't like creativity. You treat originality as a problem. You must really hate him if you're trying to derail him at this point."

"We don't think you're fit to be in a school setting," Mr. Evans said. "You're dangerous to children."

At least he was now talking in terms of *we*. They were showing a unified front. If this went on much longer, they'd reconcile right here in the counselor's office.

"What is Dr. Havermeyer's position on your accusations?" Mr. Evans demanded.

"Nobody's made accusations," I said. "Please, can't we help Adam instead of . . . of whatever it is we're doing?"

"You haven't answered my question," he snapped.

"Dr. Havermeyer doesn't . . ." The last presence I would have willingly invited into the room, even if only in name, was my headmaster, to whom the only sin was upsetting a tuition-paying parent. "It isn't procedure to keep him informed of every conference as it happens, although of course there will be a note to that effect in Adam's folder."

"You kept this secret from him. This is a personal vendetta with you, isn't it?"

I had no intention of responding to his nasty, bullying tone, but it didn't matter, because he didn't require a response.

"This doesn't end in this office," he added. "You're a hazard, Miss Pepper. A fanatic. How many young lives have you destroyed already? And you don't have one iota of concern. I may be just an appliance store owner because I didn't have advantages growing up, but I've made sure Adam has everything I didn't. That's why he's here—to grow his own way. This school says it's for the unusual student. The one who isn't standard issue. You should be ashamed of yourself." He stood up, smoothing his jacket and trousers and waiting until Dorothy stood as well. "I've been advertising on TV and radio for twenty years," he said. "I have friends in the media. This is not going to be a quiet episode you can all ignore so you can go on smacking kids around and wrecking their lives."

"I want to help your son." I watched my words fly, fall, and burn. Kamikaze hopes.

Mr. Evans paused at the doorway. "I'll have your head for this."

Rachel appeared behind him and stepped aside as he and his wife stalked out. "Ouch!" she said. "If looks could kill—what happened?"

"Basically, they did to me what I assume you did to the toilet bowl."

She sighed and gathered papers and a booklet from her desktop. "I could have predicted that."

"They did a you'll-never-work-in-this-town-again thing. And an I'll-have-you-arrested thing. I am now a hazard to children's health. A batterer. Parke Evans has been generous to the school. I am disposable. He's not." I hoisted my briefcase strap to my shoulder. "I've managed to make things about as bad as they can be."

Wrong again.

Three

LEFT school quickly, avoiding the office and the agitated conference between the Evanses and Maurice Havermeyer. By beating a quick retreat, I might hang on to both my head and my job a while longer. I wasn't as sure about maintaining my sanity.

I was so overfull of boiling emotions, there was steam on the windshield as I drove home. If only Adam's parents had said, "Oh, that kid. He's been that way since infancy." Or "Adam is already seeing someone and working through these problems." Or "Did you ever notice how Adam's prose gets odd whenever he rereads

Finnegan's Wake?" Anything to make me think they knew what I was talking about. But they were forcing him to stumble on alone, and I knew of nothing more I could do to help him. Not that I'd helped him at all so far.

Would his parents tell him about our meeting? What would they say—and what effect would that have on the explosive, unpredictable boy? I'd know soon enough—his class was meeting at the library the next morning. It was a way to entertain the seniors and perhaps entice them into doing a bit more work before graduation. Maybe Adam would entertain the troops with a tirade against me. And maybe that would be good—would show he still understood cause and effect, a sign of mental health.

Halfway home, during the hourly news break, the radio newscaster said, "The Vermont high school that was the site of last week's tragic massacre that left two dozen injured and two faculty members and four students fatally wounded during a schoolwide assembly program, today held a memorial service in the same auditorium, to begin the healing process, according to Principal . . ."

"You see?" I demanded. I couldn't have said to whom I addressed the question or what, indeed, I expected them to see. What, in fact, did I supposedly see? Maybe the Vermont shooter had nothing in common with Adam Evans. There'd been so many stories, maybe I was imagining a homicidal youth behind each desk.

Watch—Adam would turn out to be one of those geniuses who in years to come would lambaste the provincial twelfth-grade English teacher who'd suggested that he was mentally ill. I'd be a literary laughingstock. She who taught great literature but was blind to greatness when it was alive and in front of her face. *Pepper* will come to mean artistic ignorance and lack of foresight.

"I wasn't happy," the Vermont boy had said by way of explanation for his killing spree. *Disturbed,* the announcer called him, a word that conjured up a more gentle image than that of a killer with a baseball cap on his head and a semiautomatic in his hands, spraying his schoolmates to death.

"Neighbors and classmates characterize Todd as a quiet young man who made up elaborate fantasies and wanted to be a computer-game designer. He had, according to several classmates, changed lately. 'Maybe as if he was always playing one of his games, a war game,' one has been quoted as saying. 'Kind of creepy, to tell the truth.' "

"*You see?*" I pounded my fist on the steering wheel. Had his teacher tried to talk to his parents? And had she been shouted down? Threatened? Do kids have to kill a dozen people in order to jump-start interest? "*Why doesn't anybody see?*"

I pounded my steering wheel so hard the side of my hand hurt, so hard I was shocked into hearing myself. I was becoming un-hinged, an ironic result of concerns about somebody else's mental health.

I simmered down, but Parke Evans' stony expression stayed with me, as did the force of his vast disdain in that barky terrier voice of his. No wonder nobody intervened when the boy in Vermont grew ever more weird. Why subject yourself to accusations, sneers, and unemployment? Why feel this awful mix of rage, worry and despair?

I couldn't stop hearing Parke Evans' voice, accusing me of twist-ing the truth, of maliciously tormenting his son.

One of my better students, Lia Jansson, was translating Henry James' *The Turn of the Screw* into a play, starring none other than herself, and I'd been rereading her notes on the novel so I could discuss her adaptation. Now the story felt terrifyingly close to my present reality—or at least to Parke Evans' vision of my reality. Was I that governess? A woman who saw ghosts, who knew the children were possessed by them, whose hysteria led to the death of the boy in her charge?

Of course, maybe there really are ghosts. James' governess goes on to be a fine teacher to other children.

I was making myself crazy and making nothing else better. I had to put all this behind me and get on with my life.

I parked the car and felt a pang of fear at the thought of joblessness. Then, oddly, I wondered whether that really would be so dreadful. Or whether I secretly craved an excuse to move on, find something new. The idea was staggering, but there it was, feeling comfy, as if it had been hanging around awhile, waiting to be noticed.

Testing, one, two: goodbye, Philly Prep.

It sounded appropriate, as if the time had come. It sounded wonderful.

I was appalled. But it felt great—as if a permanent vacation had been offered. I'd never meant to stay in this job. I'd taken it after several disheartening attempts to find a use for an English major, and I'd intended it to be short-term, after which I'd go back to school and train for something else.

I rode the elevator up to the loft, apprehensive—and giddy.

Anything was possible, if I opened myself to it.

Anything.

WITH CONSUMMATE BAD—or perhaps good—timing, my mother called an hour later. Not that her calls are so infrequent that this marked an occasion. In fact, she calls too often, at any hour, now that telephone companies offer flat rates, and the pattern of her calls is appallingly predictable. A bit about her and my dad's life in Florida ("pretty much the same" is her nearly unvarying news flash), health reports, the digest of her phone calls to relatives and friends, which always includes a lot of medical and marital up-dates, and then she cuts to the Message. She varies her approach, embroiders the idea with different designs each time, but strip away the anecdotes, the suggested reading list, the homey exam-ples, and it's the same mantra: *My daughter is single and I wish she were not.*

My moving in with Mackenzie had changed her lyrics but not her aria. We troubled her because we were spinning our wheels on the road from single to married. There wasn't even an engagement ring after all this time, she was wont to mention. She was right. I suspected that Mackenzie was just as fearful as I of the briar patch we'd enter when we did broach the subject. Neither of us thought the combo of homicide detective and high-school teacher sounded brilliant or even possible for the long haul. He couldn't help but be unreliable, unavailable, and preoccupied. I couldn't help but wonder what would be the point of being hitched to someone like that. There were reasons why police divorces were statistically more predictable than movie stars'.

For example: Where was he now, when I needed to talk through this terrible day? As fine a specimen of manhood as C.K. Mackenzie might be, what would be settled about settling down with someone occupationally incapable of being around when it was important to be around? The only way I could guarantee his attention and presence would be to become a corpse.

I never discussed my reasoning process with my mother, nor did she ask, but she saw the end result, and she did not approve. Surreptitiously or openly, subtly or with the force of a sledgehammer, she did not approve.

Today I had good news—I was most likely being fired. In her peculiar logical system—and I suppose now in mine—if I were unemployed, I could no longer complain that C.K.'s job and mine were incompatible. Bag ladies' hours were about the same as cops'.

Those were my thoughts when the phone rang. I'd been popping off the tough ends of asparagus stalks, slicing mushrooms and carrots, mincing garlic, and cubing pork tenderloin. We were having company over, or I'd have switched to a comfort menu, ice cream and mashed potatoes.

Our dinner guest, C.K.'s buddy Andy, was further proof of police-related marital spoilage, as he recuperated from his second divorce. We were also hosting his most recent acquisition—someone named Juliana, who obviously didn't believe in statistical probabilities.

Her impending presence triggered some female Og response to provide something elegant. For Andy I could have made sloppy Joes, or even takeout, and we'd have laughed, had fun, and been satisfied. But for Juliana, or because of her—or, more honestly, because of me—I was making pork stew with polenta and asparagus in orange vinaigrette. Sorbet in a fruit sauce. Doing a Martha Stewart, female muscle-flexing, implying this was the normal run of things up here in our loft. That I didn't come home bone tired and footsore, burdened with papers to grade, grudges to obsess over, and nothing in the house to cook.

I didn't even know Juliana. And I hated that I was playing a role out of some repugnant lizard-brain reflex. But that didn't stop me from whisking the orange vinaigrette.

Maybe I'd study psychology when I was a woman of leisure. Find out what made me brown meat when all I wanted to do is sulk. That's when the phone rang. Mackenzie, I hoped. Mackenzie with time and a desire to listen and be incredibly sympathetic, and about whom I'd only have good thoughts from now on.

My disappointment must have been audible. "Everything's fine," I lied into the phone. "I sound funny because I'm chopping onions, that's all. I'm having company for dinner, so I can't talk too—"

Of course she wanted me to go through the menu. I didn't altogether mind, because Having People Over was on her short list of good things to do, so I recited ingredients and what I was doing with them and how everything was homemade, even the centerpiece. I awaited a round of applause.

Instead there was a moment's silence followed by a wistful, vaguely disappointed-sounding sigh. I was so stunned, I nearly cut myself with the bread knife. "You know," she finally said, "I'll be sixty-five soon. It's made me do a lot of thinking."

Never a good sign with my mother, who functioned best on automatic pilot. What would her birthday prompt her to say about my unmarried status? Because that's where all Bea's roads lead. I waited to hear something like how fervently she wanted to be young enough to be a real grandmother to my children.

That wasn't where she was going at all. "Here I am," she said, "but where have I been? What have I seen? Where did my life go?"

My mother depressed? Introspective? Talk about a terrifying personality change. "Mom, you sound sad."

"I'm not. Just . . . seeing things differently. When I look at Beth, I see somebody following in my footsteps."

Another lecture on why my sister was the good daughter and I was not? Beth: devoted wife and mother of adorable children. Good gardener, cook—and always Has People Over. It sounded a little like an epitaph, but it was Beth.

"It's too late for her."

"Too late? For what?"

"To take chances, explore, see the world before she settles down into one little piece of it."

"She never wanted that. That isn't Beth. She's a happy woman."

"My point exactly."

I made a mental note to check my horoscope in the paper, and see if there'd been any warning that this day was going to be like no other, and that very little about it would make sense.

I held the phone on my shoulder as I sliced the baguette, then fussed with the fruit and vegetable centerpiece I'd created. And waited, wondering how my mother was going to drag this around to my unmarried state, for surely, despite the detours, she would.

"You," she finally said. "You, on the other hand, used to have plans, remember? To be a lawyer, or get a master's in journalism, and once for a while I think it was social work. You wanted to travel, live in other places, see the world. And I kept saying there's no place like home, settle down, home is where the heart is—whatever. I kept saying it. And I'm afraid you listened. There you are, with a job that doesn't pay enough, Having People Over. Making polenta and centerpieces. Okay, you aren't settled down exactly the way I settled down, but still . . . you're settled. But . . ."

When is he going to marry you? The muscles between my shoulder blades tightened.

"It's not too late for you."

"Too late? Not?" Her message was running in reverse, or my mind was.

"It's not the best idea on earth to close any doors too soon, Mandy."

When she talked about closing doors, it was in order to avoid drafts and head colds. She couldn't mean what it sounded like. She couldn't mean . . . life.

"Take your time."

"I really don't under—"

"It's important to be able to admit it when you're wrong, so I'm admitting it. I'm afraid I always said no, or 'That's a bad idea,' but you know what? I was wrong. There. I said it again. Those were good ideas you had. You were right. You're young, the world's a different place than it once was, so Daddy and I want to help you start fresh. We want to pay for graduate school. Give you the chance. Anywhere you want to go, anything you want to study. We could do the tuition."

"Mom! That's—no, I couldn't let you. I don't even know what—I don't even know if I still—no. That's so sweet of you, but—"

I hadn't mentioned losing my job, had I? My brain felt as if somebody had reached in and squeezed it. All in one day—the facts of my life turned upside down.

And her idea—so heretical. So appealing. Reinvent myself. Have a chance at a different career, different everything.

I got a grip on myself. "Thanks, and I love you for offering it, but I couldn't," I said. It wasn't as if my parents were wealthy and could or should subsidize my overlate adolescence.

"Right. So think about it. After all, I would have liked to have given you that money as a wedding present. I would, in fact, have liked to have made you a wedding, but since it doesn't look like that's about to happen—or am I wrong? Is it?"

She was wavering. Reverting. Back to normal.

"Have I missed something?" she asked.

I considered the missing something, now one hour late. "Nope," I said softly. "You haven't missed a thing."

"Then why not? Why not go for it?"

ANDY AND JULIANA CANCELED because Andy was on a case that kept him in the Greater Northeast. Mackenzie, the missing something, was two and a half hours late. He'd grabbed a sandwich by the time he came home, and he was so exhausted he fell into bed before I could tell him about even a piece of my day.

I sat at the table, the overplanned, show-offy dinner embalmed in plastic containers, and I poured myself wine and thought about my job, about Adam and his parents, and about me, and how I was living my life, sitting alone, drinking. My parents' offer sounded like that of a genie with uncanny timing.

How many more signals did I require from the cosmos that I had come to the end of a chapter? Perhaps of an entire volume.

I poured another glass of wine and searched for one good reason why I shouldn't wipe the slate clean and start all over.

For the life of me, I couldn't come up with a single answer.

Four

IN the exuberant second decade of the twentieth century, Philadelphia, flushed with civic pride, decided to break free of the modest and tidy grids of William Penn's Greene Towne. A celebrated French landscape designer, Jacques Auguste Henri Greber, was asked to plan a series of grand boulevards. Ultimately the city's budget didn't match its ambitions, so only one of the boulevards was constructed, the Benjamin Franklin Parkway, the city's own Champs Élysées, which cuts a diagonal swath from City Hall to the Art Museum at the edge of Fairmount Park and is lined with civic buildings that were copies of châteaux and palaces. These include the main library and its double, the Family Court,

31

clones of the Hôtel de Crillon and the Ministère de la Marine, which are themselves twin palaces on the Place de la Concorde.

I like the idea of creating a palace for books. I wished my students felt the same way, but, with rare exceptions, they never would. This is likely a glimpse of the future, when books will have become relics of another era, a fact that makes me feel both stodgy and sad. But I understand that books are no longer pragmatic. Most likely the library's seven stories' worth of information could fit into a laptop computer, but I don't care. I love the shape and feel and heft of books. Thinking about the potential waiting for me in any library fills me with joy—even more so when I enter this magnificent one.

I stood near the entrance, on a pattern of dark and light marble tiles, below high carved plaster ceilings, as my seniors arrived one by one. We'd arranged to meet here rather than at school so that our tour could begin as soon as the library opened and so that I didn't have to herd them here. Although I hadn't known this when we made our plans, sidestepping the school had the added benefit of sparing me contact with Dr. Havermeyer. I could remain in the dark about my employment status for another day. Even in a temple of wisdom, some ignorance can be bliss. Or as close to bliss as I was likely to get these days.

Nearby, a bearded man wearing jeans, flannel shirt, and Phillies cap stopped a woman who'd been passing by him. He looked like an Old Testament prophet—if they'd favored plaid flannel—and, cradling a stack of green pages in his arms, he gesticulated, elbows, flyers, and all, pushing pages toward the woman, who shook her head. "It's information!" he insisted. His voice was loud and odd—as if pebbles lined his throat. "Don't thwart me! You act like a roadblock, and it's information!" She murmured something. "It *is* about the library!" he said more loudly than necessary, given that he was perhaps four inches from her. "A library's more than stones and books—it's people! Our coalition—"

I couldn't hear her answer, but I definitely heard him call her "bitch."

32

The man seemed unhinged. I should call for help or intervene. Then I squelched the impulse. I had to get over this urge to butt in. Nobody wanted me to. The Samaritans were extinct—probably clubbed or sued to death by Evans ancestors who didn't think their meddling was all that good.

Besides, the uniformed guard at the entrance didn't seem worried, so why should I?

Adam was the last to join the class. He looked as if finding us there was an unhappy accident. Lately he always seemed surprised and not overjoyed that the rest of us existed.

The sight of him, the memory of his parents, the overtones of what the conflict might mean to him and to me made me too raw-nerved to endure somebody else's rant this particular morning, and I moved my group away from the flannel-shirted man and tried to tune him out. The woman—library staff, I assumed— looked terminally unhappy, almost doomed. She must face countless such people. The library was the petri dish for ideas, and for people culturing them. Some of the idea bearers had to be perched at one or the other end of the bell curve.

I pulled out my attendance record, ticking off names. All eighteen accounted for, and time therefore to begin the spiel. "As soon as our guide arrives, we'll start," I said. Their expressions were resigned and impassive. I hadn't expected them to cheer. I wouldn't have minded it if they had, but I hadn't counted on it. I decided to believe that their passivity was not apathy but a conviction that they had to be silent in a library.

In order to get them and their teachers through the senior spring semester, the art teacher, history teacher, and I had devised an interdepartmental challenge. That sounded better than *assignment*. We were attempting to seduce Philly Prep's finest into using the library's special collections to create and pitch a time-travel movie to imaginary producers. They were to write a plot synopsis, create storyboards, design costumes, and provide a list of required props. For extra credit, they could show a short film clip—a video, made at school, of a scene from their proposed work. Their characters could visit wherever they liked in the world, real or imagined, except the United States since 1950.

The teacher troika hoped they wouldn't notice they were doing historical research, creating art, and using writing skills.

The students had found the idea interesting enough to show up this morning, which more or less meant we'd tricked them into reactivating their brains although they didn't have to. The only pedagogical weapon left in our arsenal would be to fail them, not allow them to graduate. The kids knew that this option was excessive and took advantage of the fact. Besides, they terrified the staff with the possibility that if flunked, they'd show up in our classrooms again.

The flunking option was not used except in the most horrific situation.

Which thought pulled me back to Adam. Was he the horrific situation—or was his father right, and he was simply performing a baroque version of the senior goof-off? Even now he wasn't a participant. He stood at the fringes of the group, dressed too warmly in a sweater and the long black scarf, which, as far as I could tell, never left his body. He scanned the walls, the plasterwork ceiling, the glass special-exhibit cases, the staircase at the back of the hall, his eyes alighting on everything except the people in the lobby. It was not altogether peculiar behavior—the impressive building was unfamiliar, while I was all too familiar, as was the information I was reciting. I'd already given it to them back at school. Teachers and newscasters say everything three times. Once as advance warning: "This is what we're going to do/learn/see—film at eleven." Once as full-fledged presentation. And then to ram home what's been said: "To recap today's headlines . . ."

I was undoubtedly boring Adam. Still, his architectural surveillance went on too long, too continuously, too incoherently. What he saw apparently didn't register, so he had to constantly revisit and recheck it. My Adam-anxiety level rose. It was becoming a chronic condition, infecting everything else in my life until I no longer felt at home even in my professional role.

"For example," I said to the less-than-wide-eyed faces, trying not to notice Adam anymore than I was noticing the plaid-flannel man who still agitatedly harangued the woman, "if you wanted to know whether cars had windshield wipers seventy years ago, there's an enormous automobile reference collection. If this interests you, maybe your hero will be a mechanic. Or an inventor. Or you could find drawings of eighteenth-century buildings in the art department and use them for your settings. Or if your hero is a singer or music teacher, you might need something in the Drinker Collection of choral music or the Fleisher Collection of orchestral music, or old programs of what orchestras played." I was doing what I hated having done to me—reading them what they could read in their brochures themselves. But on I went, to keep them feeling like a class and to discourage wandering. From the corner of my eye I watched a security guard approach the man in the flannel shirt, who became even more agitated at the sight of him.

"The newspaper center has papers going back to the seventeen hundreds," I read from the handout. "Braille books. And the print and picture collection has enormous possibilities, as does the theater collection, which'll help you with motion pictures, TV, and radio. There's a map collection, which will tell you how the world looked whenever, or how people imagined it. Or how about information on the occult in the children's books from the last century or earlier, or . . ."

We would tour the potential sites, then set them free to forage, to stumble over something worthwhile, discover a bit of the value and possibilities of research, and even have a good time. Plus get a day off from school. In exchange, they'd get credit from their art and history teachers along with me.

The security guard had calmed the plaid-shirted man enough so that the woman, looking grateful to be freed of him, headed toward us. The man in the flannel shirt started to follow her but was gently detained by the guard.

"Hi!" Her voice broke in the middle of that single syllable, like a pubescent boy's. She coughed, then repeated herself. "Sorry!" she

35

said in an overbright, hard tone. She looked as twitchy facing us as she had while dealing with the bearded man. She was not going to be fun.

She glanced at a paper in her hand. "Let's see—you're Philly Prep, right? Seniors?" My group nodded glumly. "I'm Ms. Fisher and I'll tour you around, but first let me tell you a bit about the Free Library." She spoke quickly and without enough inflection, had obviously memorized her lines, and was interested in something besides us. She wasn't a particularly good actress, but I hoped the kids didn't notice.

Which showed how deluded I was trying to be. Of course the kids would notice. Kids' radar is astounding, a survival mechanism. It's only when we age that we dumb down and pretend clear evidence isn't so.

We followed Ms. Fisher to the base of the stairs. "Originally libraries were by subscription only. That meant you had to pay in order to borrow books."

A blond man in a pinstriped suit race-walked through the entry hall toward us and detoured at the last moment around the group and up the stairs, double time.

Ms. Fisher gasped and moved sideways, as if to clear a path for him, although he'd been nowhere near her. He half turned, then shrugged and continued up. The man was in too much of a hurry to care why someone had gasped.

Ms. Fisher behaved as if she'd been accosted. She inhaled fiercely, fussed with her hair, smoothed her skirt, double-checked that her blouse was tucked in all around, and finally pointed at a bronze statue on the landing above us.

"I—I was saying, um . . . I've forgotten. I lost track and . . ." She blushed, put her hand up to her mouth. I realized that she wasn't much older than I was—thirty-six, thirty-seven, max, only five years ahead of me—and that she'd be pretty if she'd loosen up. Even the muscles of her face were straining, each and every visible one. In fact, all of her looked too tightly strung, about to pop.

"About how people used to pay for books. That's what you were saying." That was Cassie, one of the sweetest young women ever to grace a desk. Not the sharpest, by a long shot, which combo of sweet, trusting, and dim put her in my kids-to-worry-about category.

"Thank you," Ms. Fisher said. "Yes. I was going to point out Dr. William Pepper, there."

A bronze statue of an unsmiling man in judicial-looking robes sat at the top of the flight of stairs, on a landing that was lined on each side with another flight of stairs.

"He was provost of the University of Pennsylvania in the eighteen eighties," Ms. Fisher said, "and he convinced his uncle, Dr. George S. Pepper, to provide funds for a free library. His uncle bequeathed a hundred fifty thousand dollars plus some of his estate to establish a free library with no rental charges. As large a sum as that was, especially more than a century ago, Dr. Pepper knew it wasn't enough to build the sort of institution he imagined, but he hoped it would encourage other Philadelphians to endow the place. And as you can see, that's what happened." She was back on track, chugging ahead too quickly with her memorized spiel.

My kids eyeballed me at the mention of those illustrious Peppers— those students, that is, who didn't start humming the Dr Pepper jingle. I let them speculate about family ties between their English teacher and Peppers who could toss around sums like that. Maybe they'd treat me with more respect if they believed I was an heiress, teaching for the sheer larkiness of it.

If only.

I allowed my thoughts to sidle back to Mother Bea Pepper's amazing philanthropy. It was not good to set the idea free where it could spin around my brain the same way as it had all the previous night. I tried instead to listen to our guide, who was explaining that this impressive building was not the first home of the newly created Free Library, but that when it was built in the Twenties, it was the most modern library anywhere, and the most fireproof.

"And now," she said, "to the jewel of the holdings, a special place for all you book lovers."

To whom did she think she was talking? Had she not noticed the glassy-eyed faces surrounding her? Wasn't knowing we were from Philly Prep enough? Maybe the woman had a truly dry sense of humor.

We divided in half for the ride up in the surprisingly small elevators. "I love this part of the library most of all," she said when we all emerged on a balcony on the third floor. It faced a twin balcony across the way, and between them, a long drop down to the wide staircase, stories below.

Ms. Fisher's smile looked almost sincere. "There are true treasures here."

"That why the place is sealed off?" That was Joey Nickles, who seemed always to be calculating the net worth of anything presented to him. "Like glass doors on the entryway. None of the other places have them."

Ms. Fisher nodded. "Treasures," she repeated.

Adam was wandering again, although there wasn't much room or opportunity to go anywhere. Once you were off the elevator, you could walk into a wall in a sort of elevator vestibule, or you could go to the right, at which point you were on the balcony, with no exit except a return ride down the same elevators. What looked like it might once have been an alternate exit had an enormous wrought-iron gate sealing it off.

Ms. Fisher buzzed us in, and once we were inside, her speech resumed its hurried, nervous tempo, again sounding rehearsed. "This is a special place," she began, shepherding us past closed cases filled with luxuriously bound books, and a case displaying etchings. I wanted to ask about the grandfather clocks positioned at each end of the entry hall, but she moved too quickly. "We have a priceless collection of books going back to 3000 B.C.," she said, and then she paused, waiting for a reaction. I could have told her she'd get none, but she handled it by behaving as if she had. "Ah, yes," she said, guiding us toward a cabinet, "you are of course skeptical of a book from 3000 B.C., but that's because they don't look like the books you read today. Such as these records, which are in cuneiform." She unlocked a narrow drawer and lifted out a pinkish-yellow disk. "These are clay tablets with symbols pressed into them." The students were shown a variety of tablets, some coin-sized, others fragments of larger pieces.

Adam stayed on the fringes of our group, now and then checking out what we were watching. I looked at him as he edged down the passageway, heading toward a chic—and possibly myopic—woman studying the contents of a display case. She bent over it so closely, her necklace was on the glass. When she became aware of Adam, she straightened up, looked at him, possibly caught a whiff of him, and backed off. Her fear seemed palpable. Her skin looked particularly pale against her black silk shirt, the black and gold scarf she wore dramatically slung over one shoulder—something I've always wanted to do, but can't bring myself to dare. But before I could discreetly get to either one of them, she turned and made a rapid exit. I was sure she hadn't been staff—she'd looked too elegant, with her hair pulled back like a Spanish dancer, and jewelry I immediately coveted—chunky gold earrings and the necklace that was intertwined with the scarf—a long gold chain interset with gold-edged black stones.

Adam had driven out a library patron. I sighed. I'd probably have run, too, if I'd seen him staring at me in his intense yet disoriented style.

He continued to hover at the fringes of the group as we went into a room lined with glass shelves and a few books on display on a table. Ms. Fisher showed us a stunning illuminated manuscript that royalty or an extremely wealthy family had owned.

Most of the class, except for the terminally bored, looked sufficiently intrigued, catching a sense of the history of a different time and place through the manuscript, perhaps even of how rare, valuable, and treasured books had once been.

Except for Adam, who stood apart, head tilted as if listening to a separate source of sound, frowning. It was hard not to think about

Adam, yet thinking about him caused pain. I couldn't help him and he couldn't help me. Still, he seemed stranger than ever, dully agitated. I wondered if his parents had compounded matters by overreacting to our meeting the day before.

"Young man!" Ms. Fisher's voice was painfully sharp. "You!"

Adam didn't respond.

"Adam," I said softly. "Adam." He turned.

"Please stay with your class! You're not permitted to go off on your own."

"That lady did," he said. "That lady was alone."

Our guide frowned. "I don't know who you're talking about, but if someone was alone, she had permission. You don't." She turned back to the group, thereby missing Adam's furious scowl. She spoke again, missing as well Adam's growled mutters.

From that point on he never strayed and never stopped glaring at her.

"Our holdings include a collection of over eight-hundred incunabula," she told the group. "Anybody know what that means?"

"Demons," somebody suggested.

Sounded right to me.

"Books printed before the year 1501." She showed the class one that included ornate illustrations, mostly, it appeared, of naked young women politely covering their private parts. I didn't have a chance to ask why they were naked in the first place or what the book was about. I was too preoccupied with willing myself away. From the Rare Book Department and Adam's nonstop glower. From my students. From being their teacher.

Ms. Fisher introduced another librarian, a large, pleasantly shambling man whom it was easy to imagine hunkering down in a room filled with ancient volumes. He was bespectacled and well dressed but rumpled. I knew without looking that his tie would have a stain on it.

The new speaker, introduced as Mr. Labordeaux, thanked her, and as she tagged along behind him he launched into a description of the special room we were about to enter, William Elkins' library. Not just its contents, but the library itself—walls, floor, ceiling, and furnishings—had been relocated to this place. I'd been here before and remembered the astounding paneled Georgian room.

It had, in fact, given me an idea for Mackenzie's birthday gift. He was such an avid student of history that I thought I'd search for a (less) rare book of American history for him. Start his version of the Elkins Library, I suppose. The Mackenzie Library. So far it had turned out to be a bad idea, since I couldn't find anything both aesthetically and financially acceptable. A price tag of a few thousand dollars was not in my league.

"This room is over sixty feet long," he said, and once again I wondered what the rest of his house had looked like if this enormous room was its library.

"About these books you're showing us," Linda Saylor said. She was one of our brighter students, although her forte was math and science, not books. I was momentarily delighted that she'd been sufficiently involved to ask a question. "Are they valuable?"

Labordeaux took on a grave expression, and Ms. Fisher watched him intently. Their reverential air made it clear these books were obviously worth a fortune. I could see my students' collective interest level rise.

"All our holdings are valuable in one way or another, because they are rare and unusual. And of course they vary, depending on just how rare they are, their condition, the fame of their authors, whether they are inscribed, if they have historical significance—lots of factors."

"Like what? Like what are they worth?" Linda had been born with a twenty-first-century mind, and high tech was as natural to her as breathing. I could imagine her deciding how best to sell off the contents of the room and replace them with on-line versions.

"These books aren't for sale," Ms. Fisher said sharply.

Labordeaux was silent a beat too long, as if waiting to see if she was going to interrupt again, then he took a deep breath and continued. "They're not for sale, so all this is hypothetical," he said, "but currently, in the auction market, a single volume of Poe can sell for a hundred thousand dollars. And in fact, one page of the Gutenberg Bible—one single page—sells for fifteen thousand. If that doesn't impress you enough, then consider this: There is a copy of Chaucer's tales published by Caxon that is for sale now for between three and four million dollars. In short, you are surrounded by irreplaceable works of artistic or historical significance."

My kids nodded approval. At least they understood that somebody somewhere valued these books. Imagine the worth of these rooms!

Ms. Fisher, on the other hand, scowled. She and Adam could pair up and become the inappropriate-expression twins. I had theories about what was wrong with Adam, but why was that woman miserable looking? So sharp in her responses, so tense? Was she jealous that Labordeaux had taken the reins as they entered the room most likely to engage visitors? How petty that seemed.

But of course she'd looked stressed by the man in the flannel shirt and by Adam, who hadn't been all that much out of line. Even with the man on the staircase, who'd done nothing whatsoever. The woman had problems.

". . . collection of Dickens' works, some in their original serial form, plus about a thousand letters of his." Labordeaux took a box out of a glass-fronted cabinet and withdrew pamphlets from its back. The original *Pickwick Papers*. I was impressed. I don't think I can say the same for the kids, although they did perk up at the sight of the manuscript of "The Murders in the Rue Morgue." Maybe they were Poe fans, or more likely they remembered that Labordeaux had mentioned Poe's very high worth. As for me, the Luddite, I thrilled at the sight of a handwritten anything in this computer era. What would future collectors save—printouts? Floppy backup disks?

Once we were out of the Elkins Library, the baton passed back to Ms. Fisher, who resumed her rundown of the collections, with reliable names like Shakespeare and the Magna Carta and George Bernard Shaw and Mark Twain and even an enormous stuffed raven that had been Dickens', in its pre-stuffed incarnation, and which may have inspired Poe's famous poem.

So far so good. I speculated about what might emerge from this. Perhaps the cuneiform tablets would have struck a spark and we'd be pitched a film about a Babylonian shepherd. Someone would be fired up by the children's book where the frontispiece that had been printed with GOD BLESS GEORGE III had been edited by a patriotic young hand to read, instead, GOD BLESS GEORGE WASHINGTON.

And cows—aside from those on my wall at home—might fly.

We regrouped outside the Rare Book Department, on the balcony. Troy Bloester—of course his classmates called him Blister—declaimed Juliet's speech from the balcony until I shushed him, mainly because he hadn't even gotten the words right. Not that anyone was on the balcony across from us, although it held desks and looked as if it was often occupied. And not that I thought anyone below would hear us. They couldn't see us, either.

It looked to be two or three normal stories till the next landing, and I saw only a statue of a reader nestled in an impressionistic tree. No annoyed living readers. I remembered coming here when I was small, when the area below was a smoking lounge, and the big kids—the ones in high school—took study breaks in clouds of blue exhalations. Today the area was pristine.

Ms. Fisher led us back onto the elevators up to the fourth floor, although not yet for lunch in the cafeteria. At this point we were allowed a quick peek at the theater collection, squirreled away in a narrow vertical space, and then we rode down again to the collections on the second, first, and ground floors. I straggled along, trying to make small talk with Ms. Fisher. It seemed what civilized women did in this situation. "Must be a pleasure to work here," I said.

She nodded. "Mostly. Of course, I'm new. Fairly new. And

only part-time so far, but I do love working in the Rare Book Department."

"Oh," I said. "I thought perhaps you were a docent."

She shook her head. "No docent program yet, but they're hoping to. But not me."

"So then, your title is . . . ?"

"Library assistant. I have my degree, but they didn't have a full-time opening or a librarian's opening. Someday. I'm taking courses, starting with one on computers. A lot has changed, moved forward."

She was good enough about answering questions, but each answer was a closed end with nowhere else to go, and she didn't offer anything on her own. Didn't ask me anything, either.

"So, ah, what kind of things do you do up there?" Maybe library science would be my next field.

"Whatever they need. Like this. Help with inventorying—a lot of the collection hasn't been inventoried yet, help with the special exhibits, things like that."

"Must be hard caring for such old books. I guess there's lots of work for the bindery."

She stopped in midstride and looked at me as if I'd crawled out from a rare book I'd chewed. "We do not rebind rare books," she said. "They are *rare*, you see. We don't *change* anything about them."

As soon as she began her answer I realized how dim my question had been. Of course you wouldn't repackage an illuminated manuscript. Not even a leather-bound book from the last century. You wouldn't remake a historical object. But she didn't have to have brimstone coming out of her nostrils. I'd been trying to make conversation.

"We *conserve* our books," she said, resuming her brisk pace. "Special, highly trained people who know all sorts of things about paper chemistry work to *conserve* what is there, not to replace it."

Damned if I'd try any further communication. She was a

boorish woman who didn't understand the social norm. As in normal.

Normal. That word was appearing in my vocabulary too often lately. I was defining it too often as well. For me, this was not at all normal.

In any case, from then on, the two of us made neither large nor small talk. She retreated inside herself and left me to resume my personal and varied worries.

I bided my time until after lunch, when the students would be let loose and I would skim Lia's annotations on Henry James, then find out what I could about grad schools. It wouldn't hurt to browse, to check out requirements—even though I still didn't know what I wanted to be when I grew up.

Ultimately my students, from whom I could almost physically feel myself dissociating, were wandering and burrowing all over the building in a fine imitation of scholars, and I was on my own, too, in the Education, Philosophy and Religion Department, browsing through the ultimate smorgasbord—a guide to 1,600 institutions with graduate programs.

"What are you interested in studying?" the librarian had asked when I made inquiries about finding information.

"Well, that's just it," I'd whispered, ashamed of myself. "I don't know. Is there anything that lists everything?"

There was, so I speculated and dreamed my way through programs in the humanities, and, in another volume, business, information science, law, social work . . . I also periodically checked up on Adam, who was across the room.

Libraries being no longer silent, I sat cocooned in the soft buzz of voices. Time blurred pleasantly, grew soft around the edges; and I wandered in my future.

Until all daydreams and sense of security were shattered by a shrieking—an electronic, intense alarm that pierced the skull and left shrapnel in the brain. I looked around at the other people looking around, as if we were all searching for a leader.

Finding none, and no explanation, deafened by the screaming alarm, we stood, scraping chairs and feet, and headed for the exit.

Adam was no longer among us. I had no idea when he'd left.

I broke into a run, trying not to imagine what had caused the alarm to ring. What had happened. To whom. And I hoped—I hoped so desperately I could taste it—that I didn't know, couldn't name, whoever'd caused this outrage.

Five

RAN down a wide hallway, around a corner, past a bank of computers, and joined the crush of people converging outside the social sciences room, at the top of the broad, divided stairway. Voices blurred, piled one on the other, all asking what was going on and what we were supposed to do.

"I heard a shout, Ms. Pepper. A weird noise." I turned and saw a subdued Troy Bloester. "I was near the computers, I mean, I was doing my project and all—"

"Yes," I said, encouraging him. "Speak up. That alarm—"

"I heard this noise," he said, his cheeks reddening with the effort to out-decibel the alarm. "Before the alarm."

"Where? Where did the sound come from?"

He shook his head. "Hard to tell. Maybe . . . upstairs? But I don't know."

"What was shouted?"

He shook his head. "Nothing. No words. It was like a horror-movie sound. Like a monster. It didn't sound human."

"It was, Troy," I said. "That much I'll guarantee."

He actually looked relieved. I wished such a simple truth could ease my rising anxiety, but it didn't. Human wasn't enough. Or rather, human was enough. Enough trouble.

The library was busy with people, but all I cared about was finding my charges, and finding them safe—the selfsame group of young people I'd been trying to purge from my mind and heart. All I could imagine was one of them hurting, in terrible distress, if indeed alive. So much for pulling away and not caring.

What had happened while I studied grad schools in the hopes of escaping from them? It felt tawdry, shameful—like having a secret tryst while your mate was in danger. I couldn't handle the guilt. Even though I knew I couldn't have monitored the whereabouts of eighteen high-school seniors doing independent research, I also knew I could have done more of it had I not been busy looking for my own private exit.

The alarm stopped. The sudden silence was almost painful, and then it was filled with overlying voices, questions, statements—everyone, including me, milling, looking up and down, finding nothing and no one to say what had happened.

I finally spotted some of my students in a protective huddle and headed toward them, beginning a head count. Sam and Melody and Tara and Nikki were safe. And over there was sweet, dim Cassie and with her, four others.

Counting my flock took a while, but after some time I reached sixteen. Two Adams missing—Adam Evans and Sarah Adams.

Only then did I notice the sculpture of the reader in the tree. It sat where it had been, the stylized branches like hands, reaching.

But one of the "hands" had caught something. A blotch. A dark bird that had alighted there. Or something else, familiar.

Fabric, bunched, dangling. Woolly and fringed. Black. A winter scarf on an unseasonably warm day.

It looked as ominous as a corpse would have. Full-throttle fear possessed me.

Had it been tossed up onto the sculpture or dropped from above? And where was the boy who was never separated from the scarf? Why wasn't he retrieving it?

I looked up, heart racing so hard I could barely catch my breath, but the balcony wall was too high. I could see nothing above except the pink reflection of light on its curved ceiling. But I could see the scarf, and something bad must have happened—or why the alarm, and why this mark of Adam here, now?

My pressure-locked fear broke loose. I overreacted. I behaved inappropriately, unwisely, out of panic and protective instinct. *Where was he?* "Adam!" I screamed. "Adam, where are you? *Adam!*"

I don't know what I'd expected, if I'd expected anything—besides having people stare and back off from me. I turned toward the Philly Prep students. "Have you seen Adam?" I asked. "Do you know where he is? What topic did he choose? Maybe if I knew that, I'd know . . ."

They shook their heads and shrugged, as well they might. As the ability to think slowly returned to me, I realized how stupid my assumptions had been. Why would I imagine he'd consult with or inform his classmates of his whereabouts? Why would I imagine he'd do the assignment? Do sick people suffer sudden bursts of wellness? Would Adam have had a siege of rational behavior?

I'd asked him what he wanted to do for his project. "About an actor," he'd said. "An actor maybe in Shakespeare's time, maybe. Yeah, that's it—an actor. Maybe. Or Jack the Ripper." And then he'd sat in a department that had nothing to do with any of his ideas.

Not helpful. But I had to unfixate on him. Sarah Adams, a tiny, vulnerable-looking creature, was also not accounted for. Why not fear for her? Why think of Adam at all? Talking myself down was impossible. Months of worry had etched Adam tracks in my brain. I couldn't unthink him, unimagine him.

Troy had said he'd heard a monster's roar. Whatever it might have been, it wasn't a sound a ninety-pound girl was likely to make. But her attacker might.

I pushed through the crowd, heading for the elevator, wishing there were stairs to the next floor up, the way there were from the ground floor to this level. The elevator doors finally opened, but a man stepped out. "Please," he said to the ten or so of us who were waiting. "Access denied to the third and fourth floors right now. If you'll stay where you were, please. There's been an—" He cleared his throat. "There's a woman awaiting medical attention upstairs, and we want to keep entry open. The police will need your cooperation," he continued in a louder voice, "so please return to whatever part of the library you were at and remain there."

His words were relayed back, across the landing, down the stairs, and into the great solemn rooms ringing us. Echoes and questions came from everywhere—"Who is it? What happened? Police? Why police? Did he say an accident?"

But a woman! How politically correct was he—would he use that term for a diminutive high-school senior? "Excuse me," I said. The man looked distinctly uncomfortable with his role as traffic cop. "The person up there who needs attention—I'm here with my high-school students, and I can't account for one of my girls. Is she a redhead? A teenager? Her name is Sarah."

He was shaking his head before I had finished the question. "No, no," he said. "Relax. Not yours. Ours. We know the woman."

All right, then. Not Sarah. No reason for me to feel anything but impersonal sympathy. But my pulse did not agree. What had happened to the woman? Who'd sounded like a monster? I had to find him.

And Sarah, too, of course.

I couldn't go upstairs, but I figured that if Adam were on that off-limits turf, they'd know it and have him safely somewhere. So I went downstairs, to the circulating library, usually my idea of heaven—thousands of novels mine for the asking. But today real-life stories had taken precedence over made-up ones.

Neither Adam nor Sarah was in there. Nor were they in the music room.

Finally I found Sarah on the ground floor, in the relatively peaceful children's section, where a happy accident of floor plan had protected the youngest readers from hearing the ruckus above. The alarm must have been located at the other end of the building, because nobody seemed aware that anything might be seriously out of the ordinary.

The table in front of Sarah was covered with books. "I'm writing about an artist—an illustrator," she said. "Like a hundred years ago. A woman illustrator. That's what I want to be, too. The librarian said if I called ahead next time, she'd have lots more to show me. And then I thought I'd go to the print room and see what maybe it looked like—I think I'd like mine to be an American lady."

Sarah had been snagged. Hooked. "You have a bit more time," I said.

"My mom's picking me up at five, so I have a lot of time. I'm staying later."

Joy surged and flared in me—so I poured emotional ice water on it. Wouldn't do to get reinvolved in teaching-lust. I was about to amputate that part of me. It was dead and gangrenous and I no longer cared about it. Still and all, the thought of Sarah's enthusiasm made my walk back upstairs less hopeless.

But there was still the heavy knowledge that Adam was missing.

I stood on the second-floor landing near the statue of the reader, looking down at William Pepper's head, watching for who might ascend those stairs after I had. I'd heard sirens while I was with Sarah. Medical personnel, probably.

A man walked up the first half of the stairs, approaching Dr. Pepper's statue. I knew that back.

I felt a voyeuristic thrill secretly observing him. But the thrill was accompanied by the chilly realization that his presence meant that woman hadn't really needed medical attention. Whatever had happened to her had been fatal. And not necessarily of her own making.

If he was here, there was suspicion of a murder in the library, where it seemed especially sickening and grotesque—not only a crime against humanity, but a crime against what civilization hopes for.

In short, insane.

I told myself Adam had nothing to do with this, that it was likely that he'd left the building before anything began. He was mixed up, but a mixed-up good kid, not a killer.

Mackenzie reached the landing with the statue and walked to the side to climb the remaining stairs, facing me.

I waved.

He stopped in midstride and did a classic double take, once again demonstrating that he didn't listen to me anymore. I'd told him where I'd be.

His rating plummeted into the danger zone.

"I don't believe this," he said. "Why are you here? What is it with you and crime scenes?"

"I told you my seniors—"

He fanned me off. Once upon a time he'd listened. Really listened, with such intensity it was sensual, like a stroke on the soul, and a prime component of his charm. Now it was obvious that the honeymoon was over and we hadn't ever married.

"The body's upstairs," I said.

He nodded. "Not goin' anywhere, either. You been here the whole time?"

"Out here? No. I was back there." I waved in the general direction of all the collections, not wanting to say where I'd been or what I was doing. I hadn't yet mentioned my mother's offer. I was letting the ideas simmer until I knew what I wanted to say. What I wanted. "An alarm went off. I thought there might be a fire." In this most fireproof of buildings—but Mackenzie hadn't heard the spiel.

"Anything else?"

"I came out here, along with everybody else, and nobody knew what was going on. One of my students who'd been nearer said he heard a sound like in a monster movie, whatever that means."

A woman in a suit with a jacket a tad too tight and a skirt a tad too short, a closed book in her hand, walked by us, then doubled around and hovered, openly eavesdropping. Checking out the man who didn't listen. "Are you a police officer?" she asked after Mackenzie had said something that suggested his role there. Her voice nearly choked with adulation trying to utter the words *police* and *officer*. "I could help you."

I noticed that she didn't say in what way. I couldn't tell if Mackenzie noticed. Or cared. I didn't blame her for butting in. He's gorgeous in an unflashy way. I am not living with him as a public service. You have to give him a second look to catch the shock of the blue eyes, the good lines time had etched, the total effect with the salt-and-pepper hair, his lanky rightness. Some of his charm is built into his features. The rest takes time to discover, but the invitation to the trip is all over him.

Or maybe that's just my take on it. More likely the woman in the business suit had a thing for cops. For whatever reasons, she was enraptured by his existence, and when he nodded that yes, he was an officer, she looked on the verge of a swoon.

"I was a witness," she said.

"Ah'm to take it you saw the event firsthand?" He purposely intensified his Louisiana drawl. It should make him sound less professional, but it doesn't. It makes his listener want to provide information just to hear more of that honeyed voice. Particularly in a city with as unmelodic an accent as Philadelphia, where ears get tired and in need of a smooth infusion.

"Yes!" she said, nodding so hard her hair quivered. Then she pursed her mouth and shook her head sideways, again rearranging her do. "No!" she said just as emphatically. "But I heard the worst sound before the alarm went off!"

"Ma'am, where precisely were you at the time?"

Ma'am, tahm . . . each given at least three syllables. Assaulting an officer was a crime, so I controlled myself.

"I was walking right about here—where you're standing—and this *sound*! Like a jungle sound—a shout, but *insane, inhuman*!"

"You see or hear anythin' else that could be relevant?"

"Just that . . . I was pretty much alone out here for a minute. Scared." Her eyes threatened to take over her entire face as she searched her memory bins for something more relevant than her emotions at the time, then sadly shook her head.

"Then I thank you kindly for—"

"Don't you want my name? In case you need to follow up? Or need more clarification?"

Or need a date? A life companion? A love slave?

"Ma'am, I believe that when you leave the library, they'll be askin' for a name and number where we could contact you if necessary."

She looked saddened by this, but only momentarily. "Wait!" she said. "There was something else. I remember now. After—after the alarm went off, everybody came out here, just about everybody in the entire library was looking around and nobody knew what was going on, if there was a fire, or a robbery, and that's what everybody was saying, not all that loudly, except one person, some woman, who screamed 'Adam' over and over. I remember because at first I thought she was saying 'at him,' but then I realized it was the name."

Let him not make the connection, I begged the curlicued plaster ceiling. But the gods in charge of granting me wishes had as little talent for listening to me as did Mackenzie of late. Besides, it was a ridiculous request. Even in his worst nonlistening, Mackenzie hears incessant griping, complaining, and reiteration of a name. I speak as the complainer, griper, and reiterater.

With courtly charm he managed to detach and send off his groupie, and then he looked directly at me. "An' you, ma'am? Do you recall a woman screamin' 'Adam'?"

"I had forgotten, but apparently, yes."

"Where is he? You brought your seniors, if I recall?"

So he did listen. Selectively. That made it worse. He listened like somebody going through a cocktail mix and picking out the cashews, and most of what I said was peanuts. "I can't find him," I said.

"Why'd you scream his name?"

I have seldom felt worse than I did at that moment. I'd wanted to protect Adam all along, and it was glaringly apparent that I was instead constantly compounding his problems. "I couldn't find him, thought maybe he was hurt, hurt himself—I didn't know what had happened." Might as well, I decided. I'd mentioned Adam's daily wardrobe, and I bet Mackenzie had stored that away and would make the connection once he saw the statue. Might as well offer the information up myself. "I saw—there's a scarf like the one he wears every day on the statue over there. And I thought that if he'd tossed it up, or even if somebody else had grabbed and tossed it, he'd be here, trying to get it back, and he wasn't. So I thought it had fallen or been tossed from above, from where the alarm seemed to be coming. I don't know what came over me. It was just that he's been on my mind to the point of obsession. I've been so worried about him, and after yesterday's fiasco with his parents—"

Mackenzie looked confused. He hadn't ignored that one—he hadn't been home for the telling. I didn't know which of our problems was worse.

"I don't know," I said lamely. "Don't give it another thought. Please."

"An' the scarf on the statue?"

"Kids do things like that. I've been here when there was a bra on the statue. And once, one big clunky shoe where feet should be. It doesn't mean a thing."

"And the sound the woman said she heard?"

I shook my head. "I didn't hear it. But Mackenzie, about my calling out his name—it was nothing. A worried reflex. I would have forgotten all about having done it if that—that wretched woman, that *suit,* hadn't been desperate to impress you."

He lifted an eyebrow as I sputtered along. In my next life I'd aim for subtlety. It was too late even to hope for it in this one.

We had acquired more gapers and observers, including two of my students, and before they burst forth and captured Mackenzie's attention, I had to ask. "Who is it, can you tell me? And what happened?"

He glanced at a piece of paper in his hand. "Assistant librarian named Heidi Fisher."

"Fisher?"

"You know her?"

"A Ms. Fisher gave my class the tour." I felt nauseous. "Took us around." And chastised Adam, who glowered at her from then on. Would anybody else remember their interplay? And what should I do with my own memory of it?

"She was strangled," Mackenzie said. "Not manually. No fingerprint or nail marks on her, but no apparent ligature marks."

"Ligature?"

"The thing that strangled her. It'd leave marks, and the marks would help identify the weapon. A narrow belt leaves a different sort of mark than a wire, or—"

"Got it." Each image was worse than the one before.

"No ligature marks. Something soft—a towel, say—doesn't leave marks if it's removed right after being used." He turned his head back toward the statue in the center.

"That's a scarf," I said. "Only a woolen scarf. Surely a scarf couldn't—"

"Remember Isadora Duncan? Her scarf caught in the spokes of her car's wheel and she—"

"I know." Isadora Duncan, strangled by her own scarf. Very dramatic finale, very famous story.

I looked back at the reader in the tree on which its dark intruder, the black scarf, roosted like a bird of prey.

Six

ROUNDED up my class and made sure everybody was using the mode of transportation that their parents had stipulated—feet, bus, commuter train, car pool—all without undue conversation with anyone about today's library events.

All no longer present but accounted for. Except Adam.

Even though the police had done the same before me, more efficiently, I searched everywhere, calling for him. I commandeered a librarian as he was leaving to go home—the bespectacled, rumpled man who'd shown us the Elkins Library.

"Ah," he said. "Miss Pepper, isn't it? How can I . . . ?"

I waved in the direction of the men's room. "Mr. Labordeaux, if you'd be so kind . . ."

He looked from the door to me, then waited with a half smile. "I really don't need to . . ." he said in the sort of voice one might use with a dotty old woman. "Besides, if you're going to be making suggestions like that, might as well drop the formality and call me Terry."

"I'm sorry," I said. "I'm being—would you mind checking to see whether one of my students is in there? A young man dressed all in black. Adam's his name. I can't account for his whereabouts."

"No problem," Terry said, but there continued to be one, because Adam wasn't in the men's room, either.

I checked the ladies' rooms, just in case, and in one found a woman all but stripped, layers of clothing at her feet, as she bathed at the sink. She was shampooing her hair when I walked in, and she looked faint with fear until I convinced her I was not library personnel, and I left.

I scanned the abandoned and closed cafeteria and the conference room upstairs. Both my anxiety and my anger rose as I exhausted my patience and time searching, knowing that if he wanted to hide from me, he could do so—right in the rooms I was checking. I hadn't the time, manpower, or authority to open cabinets, enter stacks, check behind each display. And I also lacked the desire. If I found Adam, I wouldn't know what to do with him. I had just wanted to find him before the police did.

"Is there anywhere else at all?" I asked a comfy middle-aged woman who looked concerned and desperately eager to be of help— the perfect librarian. But she was also wise enough to comprehend the futility of the whole search. "There is a basement," she said softly, making it clear this was a feeble last-gasp idea, a sop to make me feel better. "But he couldn't have gone down there without somebody noticing. It's obviously not accessible. And the police have already checked everywhere."

"It's my student. I'm terrified about this. And he's—he's not the most logical kid in town." I didn't want to be any more explicit.

"How he'd get down there, I can't imagine," she said, "and why he'd want to is beyond my comprehension."

I didn't want to make her nervous by explaining that comprehensibility wasn't Adam's strong suit. "He might feel easier responding to me than to the police," I said.

"You know what?" She spoke so overbrightly that I knew she wanted me to seize whatever she was going to say and run with it. All the way out of the building. "He's a senior in high school on the verge of graduation," she said. "It isn't right, but he probably went through the same process you're going through now—searched for you, couldn't find you, and decided to leave on his own. After all, he isn't a child. There's nothing to worry about."

But of course he hadn't looked for me—didn't need to. I'd been in the same room, watching him. At least, until I was dreaming of other rooms where I could be the student, not the teacher.

Nonetheless, she rounded up a maintenance man to escort me into the part of the library that in no way resembled the Trianon. Or perhaps this is how a palace's basement looks. The guts and intestines of the building were everywhere visible, pipes and other innards jutting at odd angles. "Put in air-conditioning way after the fact," my guide said as we ducked to avoid a diagonally running duct.

This was a subterranean attic, a massive junk drawer, where lamps, tables, file cabinets, at least one piano, and lots of books looked as if they'd been tossed down the stairs to stay wherever they landed. There seemed miles of storage rooms, side rooms, rooms with doors, open spaces, all so convoluted and impossible to examine that I gave up hope. A truck could be hidden here and not be found, so it wasn't the least bit surprising that we didn't see or hear Adam.

"Is there anywhere left?" I asked. "Anywhere?"

The maintenance man was silent. There were countless places left. "There's the between floors, but . . ." He shook his head, eliminating that possibility.

"The what?"

"The between floors, storage . . . what would the word be—corridors—is that it?"

I nodded.

"They're between the floors of the building, like between the first and second floors."

I must have still looked blank, because he sighed. "Okay," he said. "You got these two–three-story-high public rooms, like, say, the lending library, right? But then, you got space behind its wall, before the room across the way actually begins, so there's these other floors fit into those spaces. Whole building's more or less lined with them. Makes my life a lot harder 'cause they're crazy, go every which way, like a maze. You go down a flight of stairs in one department and come out the other side of the building sometimes. Too easy to get lost."

"Well, then, couldn't he be—"

"The kid wouldn't know about them. And if he did—if he went into them?" He shook his head again. "No point looking. Never find him."

And that seemed that.

I left the library alone and awash in anger—at myself for letting Adam out of my sight, and at Philly Prep and Adam's parents. Why did I have a student I had to watch that carefully?

I had to notify the school and Adam's parents that he'd left the premises. I had to remember to say it that way—not that I'd lost track of him, but that he'd taken it upon himself to leave, unauthorized. All the same, and whatever I said, what I was really doing was taking my little shovel and digging myself a still-deeper grave.

BY EIGHT, not yet having heard from Mackenzie, I was bone-, muscle-, and mind-tired, tired in more ways and of more things than I wanted to admit or enumerate. The phone call to the Evans household had been frosty enough to usher in another ice age—and yet his parents hadn't sounded sufficiently concerned. As if their subtext was *You have allowed a reprehensible thing to happen and we will have your hide for it—but it's okay. We're not really worried about Adam.*

Which made me think they knew his whereabouts.

And when I'd called the school to put it on record that Adam Evans had left the library unsupervised, Helga the Office Witch didn't run for the troops and didn't rake me over the coals. Which pretty much confirmed the theory that Adam was safe, but that neither the Evanses nor Helga wanted to give me the comfort of knowing that. Need I mention that this theory, the only one that made sense, did not further endear either my place of employment or the Evans family to me?

Whatever the case, I needed to stop thinking about dead Ms. Fisher. She'd been such an odd woman—so tense and rigid. She hardly seemed the type to inspire whatever twisted passion might end in murder.

Unless the murderer was crazy. I couldn't help but keep returning to that place I didn't want to go to at all.

I turned to schoolwork for diversion. I had half prepared the props for a writing lesson later in the week, and I decided to finish that up. It was an enjoyable assignment, having my ninth graders turn into garbologists who studied the leavings of characters they'd then have to describe.

At eight-thirty I realized I'd been staring at the artifacts I'd so far accumulated, those I'd fabricated and the rest of which, to tell the truth, I'd gathered by being a garbologist myself—picking through neighboring trash cans. What I had spread out before me was supposedly the contents of an apartment discovered after its occupants had gone elsewhere—a teen fanzine, toenail clippers, a candy wrapper, ticket stubs to an action movie, half a jar of hair-restoring cream, a will-call receipt for a dress, a birthday card, a pearl necklace, men's garters, a sepia photo of a foreign-looking gentleman, a tie, old-fashioned curlers, a Bible, a raveling audio-tape called "How to Make Your First Million," and three to-do lists on different papers in different hands with cryptic notations like *h/h, btr, thurs 9?* I wanted to provide lots of options. The collection was incomplete, but I couldn't think straight enough to continue with it, or to do anything much except wait for the city's finest to come home.

I plumped the sofa pillows and picked up the novel I was reading, ready to get lost in somebody else's story. Anybody's. My own annoyed me.

When the phone rang at 9:05 and the cat leaped across me, I realized I'd been asleep sitting up, the book open and unread in my hands. I blinked and looked at the cat, who was now deciding if he'd needed to bolt in the first place. Maybe his ponder-free philosophy was correct. React. Run. Avoid. Then check out whether you were unsafe in the first place. Maybe cats have only one life. They just so often overdramatize the situation, behaving as if they'd had a near-death experience when nothing whatsoever has happened, that the PR about nine lives took root.

By the third ring, Macavity decided he'd survived another disaster and that now the coast was clear. Time to rediscover wonderful me, purring, softly bumping his head against me, licking the side of my face with his sandpaper tongue. It was a cynical show, a pragmatic investment and insurance plan, reminding me that he'd been solely my cat originally, buying protection in case Mackenzie, his late-in-life love, never reappeared. But nice all the same. I had an awful thought—if the cop and I broke up, who'd get the feline? Would we have a cat fight?

I picked up the phone, surprised when the voice on the other end was my sister's. Beth, the suburban matron who believed that calls after nine P.M. were an intrusion, an affront against civilization and family life.

"What is it?" I said. "Who? Mom? Dad? Are they—"

"Of course not. You've told me I had ridiculously early cutoffs and that you're always up at this hour, so I thought you could tell me more, tell me what happened precisely. The news—"

"What news? You said Mom was okay." My mother was the only news carrier I could think of. The only one who'd involve Beth.

"About Emmy!"

"Listen, Beth, I'm sorry, but I was asleep and I don't have a clue—"

"Emmy Buttonwood! My friend—the one who was going to be in your book group, remember? You said you'd call her."

Was it actually possible that my sister was in a tizzy because I hadn't yet snapped to? Did she have any comprehension whatsoever of what my life was like? "Calm down," I said, advising something that I was finding damn near impossible myself. "I'll call her as soon as I can."

"You can't! She's dead!"

She was dead? Dead? God forgive me, I hadn't known the woman, I only knew Beth's nagging, and I felt just the smallest wave—a ripple, really—of relief. I didn't have to meet her and make her feel at home in the big city. Didn't have to annoy my book group by suggesting they change their new rules on my behalf. Dead put me off the hook. "I'm really sorry. I know you were good friends, but why call me about—"

"I was just at her housewarming Sunday. After we left you."

"I remember." I sipped the cold tea I'd poured an hour and a half earlier, before I zonked out. "I can see why you'd be upset." But I still couldn't see why she had to involve me in it. Maybe she just needed to talk to someone. Sam was sweet, but a bit of a stick. "It's hard to lose a friend," I said, stifling another yawn.

"I'd think you'd show a little more feeling," she said. She sounded as if she'd been crying before she called. "You sound . . . you sound totally uninvolved. Like it doesn't matter to you."

What was this? Why should it matter to me? "I don't want you to be unhappy," I said. "I can hear how upset this has made you, but I'm sure your good memories will be a comfort, even though the loss of a friend is terrible."

"What's wrong with you? You're talking like a greeting card!"

"I don't know what to say. I'm sorry for you. Tell me more about her. I'd like to hear. And what . . . what happened to her? Was she ill?"

"Of course not! I went to her housewarming five days ago. She was fine. I wanted you to come with me, remember? Weren't you even listening?"

I had a vision of the whole of humanity shouting, *Helloooo! Who is hearing me? Anybody?* But I had been listening. "If *you* were listening, you'll remember that you just woke me out of a sound sleep. I'm still not awake."

"Nobody goes to sleep this early. Even I don't. You told me—"

"I've had an exhausting day. One of the worst ever. My head hurts and—"

"Well, I'm sure you have and I'm sure it does. That's why I called. The news—one of those flashes between programs—said they're looking for a Philly Prep student. And that made Sam and me remember. When we were there, you were upset about a boy with mental problems. His name was Adam, too."

"Wait—Adam, *too*? They're looking for an Adam? You heard his name?"

"They're talking like this is another schoolboy gone berserk."

"What does Adam have to do with your friend Emmy Buttonwood?"

"I don't know if he does—the police think he does. Because they were both at the library, where she works. Why am I telling you any of this? You know it all. I told you that—"

"You never told me she worked there! You said she loved books, is all. Hated people, loved books."

"Who cares? She's dead. Strangled at the library!"

I exhaled in relief. "Poor Beth, you misheard. I don't know how you confused it, but the woman who died was named Fisher. Heidi Fisher."

"Her real first name was Heidi. She never used it. She signed things H. Emily. And I told you—she was getting divorced. She must have taken back her maiden name for her new job. Her new life. Emmy Buttonwood is dead, Mandy. Murdered, and I cannot believe it. And your student killed her."

"No! He . . . of course he didn't . . ." I groaned out loud at the realization that my brother-in-law would never, ever forget what I'd said about Adam. The poor boy—I'd dug him a deep pit.

"Why would anybody kill her—and in a library! She told me she felt *safe* with books. She could trust them to be what they were, always, through time. How could anybody even think of such a thing—and how is it possible that nobody noticed? It was during work hours."

That last one I could answer. "It happened on a sort of closed-in balcony, and the only place it leads to is the Rare Book Department, which probably isn't that heavily trafficked. And you can't see up there from below, either. And nobody heard anything, as far as I know. But, Beth, I have to say I don't mean to speak ill of the . . . but I'm surprised she was your friend. The woman you wanted me to meet. She wasn't at all what I'd have expected. She was so nervous and tight, and not particularly friendly."

"I told you. She was going through this awful time. I mean *awful*. And she was worried about a lot of things. Afraid, maybe. With cause. She wasn't herself lately. But to be killed by a high-school student?"

"How do you know she was afraid of something?" Because if she was, and that was before Adam, didn't it stand to reason he wasn't the only possible suspect?

"Afraid, or really bothered by something. Sunday, at the party, she gave me a key to the new apartment. Said that if anything ever happened to her, I was to go in and clean the place out. I made a joke, but Emmy said no, this wasn't a joke, that there was nothing to worry about, she was in fine health and intended to stay that way, but just in case, ever, she knew I was a person who could be trusted to do the right thing, and she'd explain everything, only not then. The party wasn't the right time."

"She gave you a key?"

"Because she trusted me. I have an idea what I'm supposed to remove, but I don't know if I should, given that she's been murdered. She said if anything happened, but she meant being hit by a bus, that kind of thing. I'm in such a tangle, and I haven't even told Sam."

Nor would I have. Because Sam would say the obvious and logical thing: Turn the key over to the cops. Tell them about the odd message at the party. Drop back and observe.

"I think I should do it," Beth said in a whisper. "She trusted me. A dead woman trusted me."

And Adam trusted me. And because of my big mouth, he was now the prime suspect, and it made sense only because Adam couldn't make sense. So if there was something that explained Emmy Buttonwood, something that pointed in another direction . . . "How about tomorrow, after school?" I asked.

"The police will have been there by then, won't they? Maybe they'll have found whatever was bothering her. I was thinking . . ."

"Now? In the middle of the night?"

"Amanda, it's not even nine-thirty! Grown-ups are awake and about at this hour. I'm surprised at you."

I was even more surprised at her. Suburban mommies weren't tooling around now. They were making tomorrow's lunches and polishing the counters and walking the dog. At least they were if they were Beth. The settled one my mother no longer wanted me to copy. Had I become more conservative than my older sister?

"I'm leaving now—I'll be outside your house in a half hour," she said. "No traffic at this hour. I'll phone from the car when I'm a block or so away, okay? We'll go together."

I was nodding my assent and my wonderment. "All right." I wouldn't have to tell anybody. Mackenzie wouldn't be back, I was sure. But Sam—"Are you going to tell Sam?"

"Oh! No. He'd be aghast."

The exact word for Sam. Anybody else would be annoyed, horrified, or disgusted, but Sam was made of less contemporary material.

"I'm telling him you and Mackenzie had a huge fight and you're on the verge of a breakup and you need your big sister to get you through this. He has no defense against girl stuff. Just play along if he asks, or if Mom calls, all right?"

If my mother called, she'd think I'd followed her advice for the first time in my adult life. Too many roads were converging, and I hoped it wasn't into a dead end.

We hung up. I shook myself to get my parts working and went to splash water on my face, hoping that whatever Emmy Button-wood wanted removed was elephantine and its meaning blatantly obvious, or I'd miss it for sure.

Which would be a perfect opportunity for me to once again make things worse.

Seven

A s more and more of me came awake, less and less of me could believe I was doing this—and with Beth, the mistress of practical sanity. Not that we were committing a crime, I thought. It wasn't a crime scene we were violating, only a crime-scene victim's condo, and I didn't think I'd heard of a law about that.

But Beth! We'd never, as long as I could remember, had anything resembling an adventure together. We'd shopped together, visited together, shared holidays, family gatherings, and childhood memories, but nothing like this. Half the reason I dragged my exhausted self out again was for the sheer implausibility of being so summoned by my older sister, whose role had always been to re-strain, advise, warn, and stop me.

And who knew what H. Emily Fisher Buttonwood meant by "clearing out" her apartment? She most likely had underdeveloped housekeeping habits—cluttered drawers and closets, disorganized pantries, wash forgotten and mildewing in the machine. The list came easily to mind because it was my list, too. The same set of compulsions that had me cooking up a storm for the unknown Ju-liana. I had a clean-up pact, only half jokingly, with my friend Sasha, who was to save me from posthumous shame.

But if something paltry on the sin scale, like bad housekeep-ing, was Emmy Buttonwood's sin, I would really regret the sleep I'd given up for this outing. I wanted something dramatically askew about her to be instantly and unambiguously obvious, so I'd know the reason someone—someone irrefutably not Adam—would kill her.

I was conflicted in a way I'd never before experienced. Deep inside I feared and believed that Adam Evans, because of his ill-ness and mounting frustrations—some of which I'd furthered—had killed a relative stranger. But at the same time I felt awful about having that thought and fearful that, having already over-stated his case and intensified his problems, I was doing it again—jumping to conclusions and prematurely judging him. And so I managed to simultaneously believe, with equal conviction, that Adam was innocent and that Adam was guilty, that Adam was a danger and that Adam was in danger because of me. I had to find a way to get him off the hook. The one I'd planted in his soft flesh.

Of course, that hope was ridiculous. What crystalline, definitive evidence did I hope to find? Given that I knew H. Emily Fisher Buttonwood only as an efficient but humorless guide to the li-brary's collection, unless Beth and I saw a Maltese falcon sitting on the windowsill, a text called *How to Wind Up Dead on the Li-brary Floor*, or at least a list on her desk called People Who Wish I

Were Dead—something along those less-than-subtle lines—I couldn't imagine how I'd recognize a discordant element that was the key to her untimely end.

When Beth called again, from around the corner, I left a superficially honest note on the kitchen table: *Beth needed me—will call in A.M. if still gone.* Then I slipped out. Macavity seemed miffed but resigned. Cats are nothing if not pragmatic.

"This is great," Beth said by way of greeting. "Not great that Emmy . . ." I heard the catch in her voice again. "I only meant getting away from the routine, having you along . . ."

Whatever lay behind Beth's words must be responsible for my mother's change of tune. Beth must have been complaining about the regularity, the predictability, of her life. As we drove along, I asked. Beth looked blank. "Mom and I don't talk about my routines. What's to say?"

It was quiet at this hour on a weeknight, and we drove through town smoothly, passing around Washington Square, which looked mysterious and hushed.

Emmy had lived—briefly—in a brick building a few blocks south of the square, with, to my amazement, actual on-street parking not far away.

We entered a pleasant lobby, neither pretentious nor shabby. "Sixth floor," Beth said, pressing the elevator controls.

When the door opened, a tall, well-tailored blond man in pinstripes exited, carrying a shopping bag in one hand and sorting through a ring of keys with the other. Even in that position, he had military bearing and looked as if perhaps the wooden hanger was still inside his shirt.

"Ray?" Beth said. "Is that you?"

He turned and looked back at her quizzically. "Beth? Beth Wyman?" He seemed to be testing the name. "What are you doing here?"

"What is either of us doing here?" she asked with a nervous giggle. "I . . . I'm visiting my sister. She lives here. In this building.

71

Mandy. Amanda, that is." The nervousness in her voice made me cringe. "Amanda Pepper."

I wasn't sure what was going on to make her that nervous, but I was sorry she'd chosen such a transparent lie. If it mattered to anyone, it was pathetically easy to check the residents list, right next to the elevator, and see that I did not live there at all.

"This is Ray," Beth said, ever the hostess. "Ray Buttonwood. Emmy's . . ."

Now I understood her discomfort.

"Glad to meet you." He stood with military posture, unnaturally stiff, and he shook my hand without bothering to fake warmth or cordiality. "I'm sorry for your loss," I said, although he didn't look like a man who'd lost anything that mattered. He had an amazingly bland face, as if life hadn't fully happened to him. Nevertheless, he ducked his head forward in acknowledgment.

Beth stood, awkwardly, and did not offer condolences.

Ray chuckled and held up the shopping bag. "I, ah, must look stupid. Came over here after work—worked late—dinner meeting, too—because Emmy had a necklace—not valuable, amethysts, fairly old, but it was my mother's, and her mother's before her. I want our son to have it, not Helena. You know how Helena can be, don't you, Beth? I'm not saying she's greedy or grasping exactly, but . . . she's a collector, let's say. Of anything. With no clear sense of other people's . . . especially her sister . . . and Emmy would have wanted her son to have this necklace."

Why was the bland blond so eagerly overexplaining? Why a shopping bag for a necklace?

Ray Buttonwood shook his head, as if despairing, but his face remained expressionless. His sorrows were not even skin deep. Beth had said he worked with Sam and was also a lawyer, but I thought lawyers needed enough acting skill to project righteous indignation and so forth. This man was a failure at showing emotion. Even faking it. Or maybe he didn't consider us worth the effort.

"Speaking of the boy, I really must be going. Very nice to have met you, er, Amanda, and always a pleasure to see you, Beth."

After the doors shut behind him, Beth kept looking in that direction, as if to see through them. "I wonder if Emmy had made a new will yet," she said, "or if everything goes to the surviving spouse. They're still married, technically, and he'd know the law, of course."

"Why wasn't he home with his son if he cares that much?" I asked. "The kid's mother was killed today. Some father! Goes after a necklace—if that's what it really was—instead of comforting his child. I don't like him, elegant tailoring notwithstanding—" And then I remembered the man on the library stairs. "I think he was there this morning. Emmy gasped when she saw him."

"Ray? This . . . you mean at the library?"

The elevator doors shut, and we soundlessly rose. A very nice building, I decided. "Just as my class began its tour," I explained. "We were still on the stairs, in fact, and this man in that suit, with blond hair, went running up, and Emmy gasped."

"Are you sure?"

The elevator doors opened onto a carpeted square with four doors, one on each side. Beth checked their numbers. I thought about the blond man on the staircase. "I'm sure about the gasp but not about the face. I never actually saw it."

"Pinstripes are not exactly unusual," Beth murmured. "After enough years with Ray, maybe Emmy had been conditioned to feel horror whenever she saw them. Plus, if memory serves me, Sam said there was a committee meeting at the office this morning. Big doings about the practice itself. Ray's on the committee."

"Could Sam check that out?"

Beth shrugged. "The thing is . . ."

"I know. She was . . . it happened in the afternoon. Can you check both times?" I wasn't sure what a morning appearance could mean, except that he knew the way to the library. Or that he set up a later meeting with his estranged wife.

"It doesn't matter," Beth said. "About Ray's being there in the morning. If he was."

"You never know." Those three words were our mother's

settle-everything conversation stopper. She used them when confronted with logical opposition, and I saw no reason not to follow her lead.

"*Et tu,* Mandy?" Beth said. "But truly, Sam is not going to like these questions." She turned and faced me. "Hold on—Sam and Ray were taking a deposition this afternoon. I'm positive."

"All afternoon? Absolutely all afternoon? No time to take a break, get fresh air, run errands? You sure?"

Beth's expression combined disbelief, suspicion, and sorrow. "Come on—nobody rushes out for a cigarette and murders somebody instead. Especially not somebody getting ready to run for Congress, which is the rumor."

"You know how long it takes to strangle a person?"

She looked at me with mild revulsion. "Why on earth would I? Why would you?"

"Mackenzie told me. They lose consciousness in ten to fifteen seconds. Seconds, Beth. If somebody comes up from behind, it's over almost instantly. Without even marks of a struggle."

Beth spoke very calmly, as if to a small child. "So I'm to find out if Ray was missing for fifteen seconds. Plus commute time, is that it?"

"Somebody murdered your friend," I said.

"Weren't you the one talking about kids going berserk?"

"This is different. This isn't the same thing." There was a kernel of disbelief in me, a need to believe that Adam had nothing to do with it. He hadn't been angry enough, didn't have a history of aggression. I'd been more worried about his hurting himself, about the likelihood of suicide. Without those news stories, I don't know that I'd have ever thought of major violence from Adam Evans.

"I'll find out what I can," she said, "or you'll keep at me, I know. Although most likely Sam will resent the questions and clam up."

"Did she have a problem with men?" I asked as Beth put the key in the door.

She shook her head and opened the door. "Just came to prefer books. She said she wanted to read them, work with them, and save them."

"Save them?"

Beth shrugged. "I guess preserve them. That department where she worked . . ." We entered an anonymously furnished space without a hint of individuality and, given Emily Fisher's stated preferences, not even a lot of books.

Beth interpreted my surveillance. "Ray fought her to the death—" She paled. "I didn't mean that literally."

"Hope not. But it does indicate that you should check out his whereabouts."

"He fought her over everything." Beth looked shaken. "Furniture, art, books, probably every roll of toilet paper. Took everything worth anything, and that includes their son, because he stripped her to a level where she couldn't support the boy decently. He'll emerge with all the booty, plus looking like Mr. American Values, the valiant single father. You watch, he won't marry his cookie until after he's elected."

"I don't get it," I said. "How could he take it all? Her son?"

"He knew he had the—" Beth clamped down on the words and shook her head. "It's hard to divorce a lawyer. That's why we hire them to help us divorce other people. So she wound up with nothing, and it was all very legal."

I wasn't satisfied, but I let it go at that, knowing I wouldn't have to contain my curiosity for long. We were here to remove something, and I was sure that whatever it was would tell me what Beth didn't want to, why Ray Buttonwood could bully his wife into relinquishing everything she held dear.

The room was immaculate and uncluttered. There were almost no signs of actual living having taken place in it, and the same was true of the bedroom and the kitchen. The apartment could have been a centerfold for *Home Not So Beautiful* magazine. "So," I asked, "is she a perfect housekeeper—or is it just that he didn't leave her enough possessions to have a single one of them be out of place?"

The sofa and chairs were upholstered with what looked like compressed dryer lint. The coffee table had a *New York Times* book review section, a bowl with cellophane-wrapped candies, and a plaster impression of a child's hand, the sort of craft project done in nursery schools. No used coffee cups growing mold, no half-finished letters, half-done crossword puzzles, half-read newspapers, dirty dishes in the sink, unmade bed, pantyhose drying over the shower curtain, dropped clothing or towels, signs of Sunday's party. The only thing that had been out of place was her life itself, and now that was over.

I allowed myself a moment's speculation on what someone would make of me if my living quarters were taken by surprise. It wasn't a pretty picture, so my only recourse was to keep myself from being abruptly murdered.

"Sunday's housewarming was sad," Beth said, "all of us pretending this was great, that Emmy was off to a wonderful new adventure. Maybe she was, but her place was so—she couldn't afford anything better, but she could have afforded brighter. That furniture . . . it all looked to me how Emmy felt lately, like a shadow that had become detached from its real person. I mean, where is—where was—she here?" Beth's face crumpled as she slumped down onto the sofa. "Everything went so wrong for her. It was like watching somebody fall down a long flight of stairs. And now, when she was supposedly settled in, safe, with a nice, quiet job—to be murdered! In the library! And you know, she told me on Sunday that she thought she had a way out of the money problems. She thought she was going to be okay."

I patted my sister's shoulder and let her cry it through while I surveyed the room. Whatever Emmy had wanted removed was not hiding in plain sight.

She had escaped her marriage with at least three photographs that sat on the mantelpiece of the living room's gas fireplace. I studied them, hoping for a handle on the dead librarian. One photo showed a woman in Jackie Kennedy clothing and bouffant, and two little dark-haired girls. Another was more contemporary, of a boy who looked about three. I turned to Beth, holding it.

"Her son." Beth wiped at her eyes. "Gage. It's a family name. She—there was a custody battle. She lost."

"Why? I can understand the money, but why the child?"

"She'd had . . ." Beth wasn't meeting my eyes. Instead, she talked to the green-gray carpet, which looked as if it would hurt bare feet. She sighed and then looked up at me. "It was never a good marriage. Emmy was unhappy for a long time, and—you know how it happens. Eventually there was a man. She thought she was in love." Her eyes demanded that I understand. I nodded.

"He was married, too," she continued. "It was stupid, but you could see why it happened. She was so lonely. As for him, well, she definitely didn't mean to him what he meant to her. After a while he ended it, and that's when Ray struck. He'd been running around throughout the marriage, but he'd become suspicious of Emmy—maybe she seemed too happy or something—and hired a private investigator. He claimed moral turpitude, made up stories about her leaving the child for these assignations, endangering the boy. Ray even convinced his mother, who'd never been crazy about Emmy, to agree to the false claims. He exaggerated and pushed, used her affair as a wedge to take more and more—he wanted out, but wanted as much of their property as the law allowed, including his son, until after months of it she couldn't stand it anymore and agreed that Gage would be better off with his father, who had money and could provide more opportunities. That's when she decided to move to the city. Staying in the suburbs and being shut out of his life was too painful. This place is set up for visits, but basically he was to live with Ray. Which I guess is for the best now." She dabbed at her eyes again and stood up, ready to complete her assignment.

I followed her into the kitchen, carrying the third silver-framed photo. "And this? Is this her in better times?" Beth looked at a drawer with an almost empty flatware organizer, then closed it back up and checked the photo I held, the posed portrait of a woman who looked like Emmy if she'd been hand polished with optimism, smoothed with poise, straightened up with self-assurance, if she'd had the tension ironed out of her muscles and tendons, and if she'd had scarves, jewelry and better-arranged hair to set off her features. A lot of ifs, but possible.

Beth opened another drawer and closed it, looking disappointed. "That's her sister. Helena Spurry. As in Whatsis Spurry—you'd know who I mean, the zillionaire computer whiz. To her horror, she divorced him before he'd made a cent. A tiny cash settlement years ago, and that was it. Two sisters with men and divorce and money problems. And that's all they had in common."

When I looked again, I saw how different Helena Spurry actually was from the woman who'd guided me around the library. And yet the look of her felt familiar—but there the impression ended. No sense of a voice or personality. "She seems familiar," I said. "Could I have met her through you?"

"I doubt it. I never cared for Helena. She's a year and a half older than Emmy, and I swear she never got over her fury that there was another baby in the house. She's always picked on her sister, begrudged her everything she had. Consumed by jealousy, always checking to make sure she had more and better. And Emmy always gave in. When their mother was alive—she died last year—it was worse. Helena was like a well-groomed, articulate toddler screaming, 'Me! Me!' " Beth was now on her knees, opening bottom cabinets, peering inside.

"So why her photo on the mantel?"

"I just told you how *I* feel about Helena. Emmy was much more forgiving. And much more intimidated. Besides, it looked good for the housewarming." Beth laughed, a bit uncomfortably, and continued to remove every item from a bottom cabinet with such expertise and nonchalance that the inventory and search seemed second nature to her.

"A peace offering," she continued. "Helena was here, probably just to make sure that Emmy wasn't living as well as she was. The

part that infuriates me is that Helena could have made a difference. She owns an antiques store. She could have pulled a few
pieces of her inventory, given them to her sister. Brightened the
place up, made it less impersonal. She could have and should have.
It was Emmy who provided the capital that started Helena's pretentious store. Emmy loaned her most of her share of their inheritance. Poor Emmy. Her timing stunk in just about everything. She
loaned Helena the money one month before her marriage exploded and she suddenly needed it."

"Maybe Helena was going to repay her. Maybe that's what she
meant about having a way out of the money problems," I suggested.

"My foot." Beth replaced a carton of dry milk, a plastic con-
tainer of pasta, and a bottle of oil. "Helena's store doesn't bring in
a penny. Helena just insists on living as if she were wealthy, and
heaven forbid she should take a job that's beneath her imagined
status. But what does any of it matter now? What I'm saying is
that even if Helena wasn't making money, she could have given
her sister, who technically must own half the store's stock, something pretty that would have made this place more like a home."

Beth sounded ready to burst into tears again. I dropped the
topic. It didn't matter. "Is—was Emmy getting support despite this
battle?"

Beth looked still more troubled. "I'm not sure now." She spoke
slowly. "She told me nothing tangible, no details, but she was under
pressure and the sisters were quarreling about the money. . . ." She
shook her head. "I'm making it sound terrible. I'm not suggesting
that Helena . . ." But she looked worried.

"Maybe Sam could find out about the will, too," I suggested. "At
least some sense of how much was left to the two of them."

Beth sighed. "He'll hate my asking all these obvious questions.
Sam's still friends with . . . you know how couples wind up choos-
ing one or the other half of a divorce, but I can see Sam's point—he
and Ray went to law school together, worked together all these
years, were made partner around the same time. But it made it so
hard on me. Like I was sneaking around to still see Emmy, and

then to be a good wife to Sam, to make his life easier at work, I'd have to be polite and sociable with Ray when I knew what a louse he was." She opened an eye-level cabinet that had two dishes, two cups, two saucers, and two soup bowls.

"Sam didn't actually come up here Sunday." Beth was staring at the nearly empty cabinet as if mesmerized. "He walked around town with the kids, used them as his excuse, but it was really because it felt awkward to him. It makes me bone-tired. Angry, too."

The night's foray made better sense now. It was more than a final act of friendship—it was also an act of defiance. Of solidarity with a dead friend.

"So far her kitchen is pathetically tidy." Beth's voice was cleansed of its bitter overtones. She gently closed the cabinet door. "Not even a true junk drawer."

I wandered back to the living room and over to the bookcase. It's how I peg a person, and as far as I could see, it was the one place in this set of rooms where a personality might peek through. I expected a librarian to have interesting shelves.

The bulk of her library was given over to world classics, heavy on the Russians, poetry collections, James Joyce, Irish playwrights. I have almost the same titles in the same editions—or had, before my house blew up. College texts—the books she'd have brought into the marriage. Plus one title about book collecting and, next to it, a dealer's catalogue, and another that was obviously the text for the computer course she'd said she was taking. One on helping your child through your divorce. One on managing money. You could chart her life by her titles. The suburban years were represented, I suspected, by a small collection of relatively new fiction. "Hey, Beth," I said, checking, "did your book group read Ursula Hegi? *Stones from the River?*"

"About a year ago. Maybe more."

"*Cold Mountain? Divine Secrets of the Ya-Ya Sisterhood?*"

"How'd you know?"

"My group read them, too. And a few more that are here, all

separated from the college classics. Ray let her keep them even though they were acquired during the marriage. Big of him."

"Probably thought they were revolutionary. Or worse—*women's* books!"

The fatigue I'd been fighting returned in waves that threatened to pull me under, and I saw how futile and silly this outing was. I went into the kitchen. "Let's go home," I said. "This is as impersonal a place as I can imagine, so why are we really here? To annoy Sam? To prove something? Do you actually think she had anything she didn't want people to see? And if so, who are those people? And how am I supposed to find something I don't know about? I'd like to throw out all her furniture, but surely that isn't what she meant. I'm useless here."

Beth looked on the verge of tears again. "I think . . . I think she was afraid on behalf of her son. I think she assumed I understood that there were love letters. Something Ray could use to poison their son against even her memory."

"Then why the kitchen? Who'd hide love letters there?"

Beth looked surprised, then she quickly opened another door and peered inside with excessive interest, examining its contents, which were paltry and sparse.

"You? You have—you're kidding, aren't you?"

"You don't think I have a life, do you?" She turned to me, her lips pursed. "You don't think I have a personality. The kitchen's a perfect place. Everybody hides things in their lingerie drawer, so everybody knows to look there. Anybody with imagination would realize how much better kitchens are. Men almost never . . . well, Sam almost never goes into the cabinets. Ingredients don't interest him."

I folded my arms across my chest and waited. It always worked on my students.

"I use a half-full box of rice. Been using it for a dozen years. An old boyfriend had a resurgence of feeling for me about a year after I was married. I didn't answer except to say I wasn't interested, and

I wasn't—but all the same, I couldn't throw them away, either, even though I knew they'd upset Sam if he found them. And about once a year the man still writes—as a friend—but he always says that in case I've changed my mind, he's waiting." She shrugged, bit at her top lip. "I can't throw them out, but I wouldn't want . . ." And she turned her back to me and continued pulling every bottle and box off the kitchen shelves.

"So," I said, "do you want me to . . . if, say, you were hit by a bus—"

At which Beth grabbed a dishtowel and wiped at her eyes. "See? Yes. Because Emmy . . . that was the pact."

To think that for all these years a piece of my sister's heart had lived in an old box of rice. Beth had always seemed to me the one truly serene woman in the world. No longer. I'd always accepted her at face value, but several times tonight I'd seen her smoothly pave over her features, give that face its desired value. It saddened me—not the knowledge that Beth was more complicated than I'd given her credit for being, but that I'd wanted to hold on to the idea that there was a thoroughly and perpetually contented woman somewhere on earth.

"I don't think Emmy used the pantry." Beth's voice was once again smooth.

"I'll check the bedroom," I said. "That's where I'd hide my secrets, even if it's predictable and clichéd." It depressed me to realize I didn't have anything that would embarrass me posthumously except general clutter, and I didn't know if that was because I was stupefyingly boring or so far gone that I didn't give a damn.

"Have you gone through her desk yet?"

I hadn't, because it was a stupid thing—a shellacky copy of one of those rickety, undersized stations where ladies in bustles wrote bread-and-butter notes with quill pens. Its surface was uncluttered, with nothing under the unmarked blotter pad. When I pulled open its single shallow drawer, the results were equally unimpressive and predictable. Pens, pencils, highlighters, a ruler, and a notebook, which I opened.

Its contents were as close to clutter as Emily Buttonwood seemed to have gotten. The lined sheets had notes in a precise hand, the sort that would have pleased her teachers. Looking at it, though, I felt sorrow behind its tidiness, a desperate need to do this correctly. But I was undoubtedly reading into it what I already knew about her. I glanced at her notes, filled with abbreviations and signals for her computer course. I wondered where the computer itself had gone. A laptop would fit on this wee desk. And in Ray Buttonwood's shopping bag. It was technically his, too, I suppose, but he still seemed a vulture in swooping it up.

The binder paper's notes were tidy, but the rest of the binder's contents were a dramatic contrast to that tight, neat penmanship. It seemed as if every inch was filled with notes to herself on scraps of paper, some with adhesive backing, some clipped to pages, many to the front and back covers and all trivial or unintelligible. Mostly they seemed the sort of reminders meant to be chucked as soon as the chore was completed. Emmy hadn't believed in the chucking part.

She had a housekeeping flaw. I felt a great wave of relief and kinship.

I compulsively read the scraps and bits, looking at their various designs—angels and teddy bears and FROM THE KITCHEN OF and DON'T FORGET stamped across the tops. Lined and plain, pastel and deep hues.

One had a list of books to buy or check out for her son: *Cat in Hat, Pooh, I Can Read*s, and another I assumed was for Gage as well: *Trucks, esp. red.* Couldn't she remember that? Was she falling apart so much she needed such primitive reminders? I'd once read about a rare neurological disorder where the afflicted couldn't "dump" temporal information. While the rest of us park our car in a structure and remember the space only until we reclaim the car, those poor souls can't get rid of the information. They remember every laundry receipt and due date at the library until their minds must be pure clutter.

Emily's notebook seemed the written equivalent. Her notes were mundane, from recipe and dental reminders—*Moussaka recipe/Terry, 12mo, VF, dent*—to cryptic missives about friends (or at least I hoped they were friends; this woman needed people) or dates—*Clark/Shoemaker/Buck95, Bauman knows?*—to the totally unintelligible (unless this was her shorthand for CDs she wanted to buy): *CDPP, CDDC, CDEDILL.* One had been imprinted with the drawing of a finger with a string tied around it on top and, in her writing, *Check/Bauman/Sabin/leaf, gutters.* I had to assume she no longer paid the bills for maintenance on a home she'd left, so why hang on to this probably painful reminder? In fact, there were two more notes mentioning Sabin at other spots in the book. I thought of the fellow who had come up with the first polio vaccine. My aunt Lydia was convinced that Sabin, whose name was whispered reverentially, had personally, specially, saved her children from the dire disease that had killed her sister. It was impossible to visit Aunt Lydia without hearing that anecdote—Sabin hadn't saved her from being boring.

I amused myself with thoughts that the doc had given away the rights to the vaccine and had been forced to repair Emily's gutters to make a living.

Which was the point when I realized what a waste of time engaged me. No sleep, and stupid thoughts. I pulled a stickum off and carried it into the kitchen. "Does anything on here make any sense to you?" I asked my sister. The paper read *Bauman/Sabin: AL: CDPP—17K, EAPMS95K,—PMS?*—medications for it? I wondered—*CDEDil21K,* and more of the same.

She studied the paper and shook her head. "Sabin," she finally said. "He developed the oral polio vaccine for Aunt Lydia, remember?"

"Thanks a lot." Emily Buttonwood, with no sense of what was important and what was not, had been a self-stick packrat. I put the notebook back into the drawer.

This outing was my dry run for my ninth graders' garbology assignment, reconstructing Emmy from her pitiable leavings. But even though I hadn't finished, I'd already collected more for my students to work with than Emily's actual life had provided Beth and me.

Luckily, because I was fading fast, Emily turned out to be just as clichéd as I would have been. The letters were in her dresser, between slips and stockings, and tied with a blue ribbon. She'd read a whole lot of nineteenth-century novels. Too many, perhaps. "Hunt's over," I called out. "They're here."

I handed the packet to my sister. She eyed them first, and then me. "What if they're something else altogether? What if they're from her dad before he died? I feel as if I'm violating her trust, but if she'd explained herself, I wouldn't have to . . . I need to read at least one, make sure I'm not burning something Gage would want."

She sat down on the edge of the bed, undid the ribbon, and opened the top envelope. It had no return address. That was enough for me to believe they were from the ex-lover. But I couldn't have burned anything without checking, either.

Neither of us was motivated by anything as base as unwholesome curiosity, you understand.

"Oh, jeez," Beth said. "She had them in reverse order. This is the end. The last one. It's like a legal document. So cold!" She cleared her throat and read. " 'Emmy.' Just that, no salutation. Afraid to even say 'Dear'? 'Emmy, this is the only possible scenario. Mistakes were made on both our parts, but it is time to resume our lives and places and minimize the harm we hold the potential to inflict.' That's it. Not even what I'd call a kiss-off. And only an initial. *P*." She said the letter scornfully, almost spitting it out.

Living as I did with a man with no apparent first or middle name, I couldn't fault the letter writer for signing off with an initial. But I could on all the rest of his chilly, cut-the-ties-and-cut-out tone. "Know who P. is?" I asked.

Beth shrugged. "It won't help anybody to say it. His wife's a good woman who never publicly acknowledges what went on."

"But what if—"

Beth shook her head. "He didn't kill Emmy."

"How do you—"

She rifled through the packet to the one at the bottom. "Look here, he was writing to her a year and a half earlier. This wasn't a one-night thing, and even this early one is careful and chilly." She skimmed the rest of the letter, then checked the envelopes, all of which had been typed in the same no-return-address fashion. "I'm burning them," she said. "How he attracted two such good women as his wife and Emmy, I will never know."

"He's obviously heartless. Why are you so sure he couldn't have—"

"Because in truth he did have a heart, although not the way you mean. He had the one that pumps the blood around, and it failed him," Beth said. "He reconciled with his wife—they'd never separated or anything—and had a fatal heart attack three months later. Is being dead enough of an alibi?"

I nodded, sad on too many counts to list, but mostly on behalf of Emmy, who wanted to keep letters from a man as wooden and careful as that one sounded. Sad to have spent so long with him, tragic to have lost custody of her child because of that involvement. "It is something of a relief, though," I said. "I was worried that old love letters could be criminal evidence. The police would want to know about passions that might have led to murder. Actually, even if he were still alive, I guess I could imagine her killing him for writing such constipated claptrap. But not vice versa."

"I'm burning them here. Now."

"The police will notice that the fireplace has been used recently."

Beth's face was set and solemn. "So let them."

I thought she was being foolish, and I thought I'd be much better off sleeping before I faced another day, but I have learned not to argue with that jawline.

She carried the small packet into the living room. "Five minutes, then it's done. I've kept my promise." She opened the glass door of the fireplace and bent to turn on the gas flame. "The logs are fake—I hope this won't smoke up the place." It didn't. She put the letters into the flames, one at a time, and they flared and turned to carbon while she watched, stoking the pile now and then.

As she bent over, a heart she wore on a silver chain dangled from her neck, and the pose clicked on my memory. "I did recognize her," I said. "She was in the library. I saw her."

"What?" Beth asked, half turning. "What's that?"

"She was wearing a big silk scarf over one shoulder, bending over an exhibit case, near the cabinet with the cuneiform tablets. Adam scared her—he was walking toward her. When she saw him, she straightened up and left. Went somewhere else. But first I saw her necklace—" I lifted the photo from off the mantel. "This necklace, a long gold chain with black stones. It had been hanging the way yours just did, hitting the glass case."

"I don't know what you're talking about." Beth carefully placed the last letter in the fireplace. "Or who. Or is it whom?"

I watched the last letter's corner catch and glow. "Helena. Emmy's sister. The one in that picture. Helena was in the library today. In the department where her sister works. Her sister was killed right outside of it."

"Oh, Mandy." Beth's voice was rich with sympathy and disbelief. "I understand that you're twitchy, having been there and all. But first it was Ray you saw, now it's . . . Helena's never read a book, as far as I can tell. Coming to see where her sister worked doesn't sound at all like her, so why would she be there? Why on earth?"

"I have no idea." That wasn't completely true. I did have an idea. The idea that an oversized scarf could be used to strangle somebody.

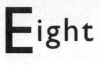

Eight

WALKED into the loft and hit the wall. Metaphorically, that is, although had there been a wall nearby, I'd have hit it headfirst. I had no more juice left in my body or brain or spirit or whatever else comprises a person. I headed toward the bed like a drowning victim spotting a distant atoll. I didn't bother to check for messages, because Mackenzie wouldn't have phoned this late. He might have e-mailed me, but in that case the message would say he wasn't here and didn't know when he would be, and I already knew that. I couldn't see the point of detouring to the computer when the bed was just over the mountain, waiting. And if my mother had called, it would be to say either that she'd changed her mind and indeed, I should immediately marry. Or that she hadn't changed her mind, and what was I doing about the rest of my life? I couldn't consider touching either one.

Getting into bed is too polite a term for what I did. Think instead of a tree with auburn hair. Imagine that final whack of the axe—and goodbye tree as it topples straight down. Two half ideas flew past my mental screen while I descended, fully clothed. One was to set the alarm clock, and the second was to find out how I could "accidentally" be in the same place as Helena Spurry of the scarves and chains. And then, not even an idea as eyes closed, more an echo inside my skull. The sound of a gravelly voice saying "bitch." Saying it to Emily Fisher Buttonwood this morning. And then all the script said was *fade to black*.

"OKAY," I told myself shortly after dawn. I said this and everything out loud, although Mackenzie was still away fighting crime. Talking to myself is a habit I like to pretend doesn't exist. It smacks too closely of my future as a bag lady. But making noise gave the illusion of company. Maybe that's why bag ladies do it, too.

"We are starting this day with a positive attitude," I told me. Instead of thinking about being jobless, out in the cold without an income or professional reputation, I'd make that damned glass be half full. I was about to have thrust upon me the chance to expand my horizons, and if I added my parents' offer, then this was about the luckiest series of events that could happen to a gal.

If I'd had enough sleep, if I hadn't been obliged to live through the previous two days, I wouldn't have sunk into smarm. But that was all I had left, so I tried to look toward the gorgeous—metaphorical again—sunrise and consider what this lucky person was going to choose to be, given that I had the option of any job in the universe.

I felt so lousy now, so besieged and put upon. I wanted something that put me more in control of my destiny, but the only job that met my requirements was that of absolute monarch of a docile but wealthy country. I wondered how you applied for that and what master's program prepared you.

I poured coffee and took deep breaths, readying myself for Havermeyer's gobbledygook. Would he, when he reached the you're-fired part, say it clearly? If not, if he hid the news in a thicket of jargon, I'd pretend I didn't understand. Only fair, because for a long time I'd been pretending I did understand.

The phone rang. "Signin' in," Mackenzie said. "You din' expect me last night, did you?"

The note I'd left was still on the oak table. "Of course not," I said as I ripped it up. "I knew where you were—well, not where, but why. And by the way, where *are* you? In the case, that is."

"Like I'd tell you of all people." He was drawling and slurring and being charming. The sleepy smile in his voice made me melt on a cellular level, but I wasn't going to cave in to this. He'd turned it on for me. I knew he used his roots—pulled sounds out of the primeval mush and covered his messages with them—to con Yankees, make them underrate him. But now it was obvious that the troops to be conquered and conned included me, and the knowledge rankled.

Rankling grew old fast. I reconsidered. Charming and conning included me when he thought I was involved in a case and might impede his work. But I wasn't going to let him know I understood. "Why not?" I asked briskly. "Afraid I'll spill my guts to my gang? E-mail my chapter of *Murder, Incorporated*?"

"Can't fool you," he said. "Not for one single minute, so here goes. No apparent motive. Nobody saw a thing. The kid's still missin', though his parents say he checked in, then left again. They say he's not runnin' from the law, and they're not hidin' him. I take it to mean they've either abandoned him to his own devices or they're lyin'."

"Isn't *on the lam* the scientific term for what he is?"

"Oh, but you're good at this. An' you? Enjoy a quiet night with the cat?"

"Mmmrph. Sorry—my coffee's too hot!" I said. I hate lying to him, but I don't mind evading the truth.

"Hope you realize your suspicions were prob'ly accurate. That boy of yours—"

"What I hope is that my stupid outburst didn't push you so hard in that direction that you aren't looking anywhere else."

"Meanin'?"

"She was Beth's friend—the one with the housewarming party Sunday. The one Beth wanted me to get into my book group, except my group was full and—" I don't know how somebody can convey exasperation over the phone without making a sound, not even a detectable heavy breath, but Mackenzie did. "Beth's friend," I repeated lamely. "So I know stuff now. Like she was going through a really mean divorce—child custody fight and all. She had an affair, and that became his leverage. And her sister—" I stopped myself. How was I going to say that Emily Buttonwood's sister had been in the library just before Emily was strangled, without having ever—legitimately—met or seen said sister? Did I want to risk Mackenzie's wrath or at least extreme disapproval by mentioning Beth and my expedition to the dead woman's condo?

"What about her sister?"

"She, uh—" What to say about this woman I theoretically didn't know about? "She, ah, they didn't get along."

He was silent for a long moment, either despairing of my mind or x-raying what I'd said in search of a modicum of meaning. "Lots of sisters don' get along," he finally said. "You mean more than that?"

My turn to be silent. What else was there to say? We were so out of sync, we could have lived in different states. I felt in danger—of what, I didn't want to think—and the silence intensified it. I wanted to shout into the phone, to say: Come home now! Let's stop this sparring, get a routine, commit to it, to us, to anything. Let's make being together one of the things I'm doing the rest of my life.

I wanted bedrock. I wanted him, but not this circling existence. I didn't want him forever elsewhere and otherwise preoccupied when I was most confused and his being elsewhere only added to my confusion.

"Gotta run," I said. I didn't want to say stupid things like that when so much more was on my mind. "I'm about to be fired for my little session with the Evanses"—not that he'd understand what I was saying. We still hadn't had time to discuss it. And would he listen, anyway? "Don't want to be late for that, do I?"

"Don' let them fire you unless you're tired of that job anyway," he said. "Not even then. Exit on your own terms. Whenever you want. You acted from conscience, tried to protect a kid, be a Good Samaritan. That's noways wrong. Stick up for yourself. Hire a lawyer if you have to. You're in the right."

He'd been listening. He'd heard things I hadn't even said. He'd thought about it. He understood. He was speaking directly. He was helping me be who I wanted to be.

I hate it when that happens. Hate it when I decide I don't need him because of his failings and he proves me a liar and does the right thing.

THERE WAS NO ESCAPING Havermeyer. The note was in my mailbox. Helga the Office Witch watched with malicious satisfaction as I retrieved and read it. In fact, she made sure I was aware of her watching me. She didn't like a single faculty member: We wanted too much, like paper, markers, the copy machine, roll sheets, and sticky tape, and we interrupted her day with questions. In short, we necessitated her actually doing her job. So why was that woman gloating? Did she think she'd like my replacement any more than she liked me?

Miss Pepper, it said on a sheet ripped from a pad headed by FROM THE DESK OF MAURICE HAVERMEYER, PH.D., *I would like the opportunity of discussing certain urgent matters with you at your earliest convenience, such as before classes begin. The office aide can cover your homeroom and roll-taking.*

Extremely ominous. Although the note could be cut and tightened (e.g., *Miss Pepper, I'm pissed, you're fired, goodbye*), it was, for Maurice Havermeyer, the essence of brevity and directness, which suggested a seriously perturbed headmaster.

And he was. "Anyone with your seniority at this position and comprehension of the unique requirements of this institution surely fathoms that establishments such as this, not underwritten by government or long-standing trusts, at the mercy of mercurial marketplaces and fluctuating economics, must have the support and confidence of its patrons."

Translation: *You know this school needs money. Why are you such a jerk as to queer it with a big donor?*

"And the irony at this particular juncture, when the school is enjoying a surge in individual and collective achievement and our student body is getting its just due, the recognition of academic progress as shown by increasingly prestigious college acceptances. Our image has been considerably enhanced of late, and our endowment fund's prospects have never been brighter."

Was he happy or upset? Yes, more of our seniors had been accepted to good colleges. The staff, myself included, took that as a sign of lowered admission standards, but still and all, it would warm any headmaster's heart. And bring in the bucks, as he'd said. Happy news. Sure, therefore, to be followed by a mighty powerful *however*. The muscles in the small of my back spasmed in anticipation.

He hadn't asked me to sit down. I bet he'd asked Mr. and Mrs. Evans to sit down. Sure, the school needed their money, but it needed teachers, too. And the students needed teachers who cared about their problems. So there. I sat down without being so invited. I had a long day ahead—unless he was going to march me off and shoot me immediately.

"Hmmm," he said when I seated myself. "Indeed. And so . . ." He contemplated me for a long moment, then sighed and sat down himself behind his oversized burl desk. "We are presented with something of a conundrum."

I said nothing. It made Havermeyer nervous as hell to have his flow of words greeted with silence.

"Mr. and Mrs. Evans, as you undoubtedly know, have been exemplary in their support of this institution, and now they are understandably distraught in the light of your hasty assumptions and your unfortunate decision to use corporal punishment—"

"I never—"

"Ah, but I believe they have proof that—"

"They can't. He was—"

Havermeyer ground on. "While a perusal of his records does indicate Adam's increasing nonconformity and a lamentable recent pattern of noncompliance with official school requirements, given the realities of understandable parental concern and the seriousness of the suggested deviations from the norm and psychomedical impairments you have raised, I must assume your actions were less than fully considered. These were rash accusations—"

"Not accusations. I thought—I still think—Adam needs attention. I think he may be in danger. I'm a *teacher*." It wouldn't be the worst thing in the world to shame him into a thought about social responsibility. "It's a teacher's role to help a child in danger." *Refute that one. I dare you.*

Havermeyer blinked.

"I could never forgive myself if I thought something was wrong and I said nothing, and then the child—something happened to the child."

"Well, of course, yes, one shares your sentiments, although surely the parents are the first line of defense, the people most familiar with their own child's—"

"In my professional judgment, not in this case."

He fish-mouthed, glubbing dry air, sucking more words out of the atmosphere.

"In my opinion," I continued, "the Evanses' serious denial is putting their son in danger." I had never before enjoyed "talking" with Havermeyer, but things were different when the pillow of possibility was there to cushion the fall. *Go ahead. Fire me. See if I care. I'll become something else—I have other options.*

"Miss Pepper." I could tell he was leaving behind the issue of whether Adam was mentally ill or needed testing. Could see him puffing out of that station into the wilds where my real sins lay. "Mr. and Mrs. Evans are eager to involve the media in this dilemma. They feel you are relentlessly pursuing their child, abusing him both physically and emotionally and destroying his future. It is possible they are motivated by psychological stress, a sense of guilt, since they are going through a difficult time themselves, but nonetheless, they perceive themselves as Good Samaritans who must alert the community to your offenses and, alas, to what they see as a failure on my part to adequately monitor and supervise my staff. This is most awkward."

Entirely too many Samaritans in town, and were we all misguided? "But—"

He put a beefy hand up. "We conferred at length and I was able to delay any such public exposure, although not indefinitely. I trust you comprehend how devastating such negative publicity could be to our entire endeavor. We are still in the enrollment process for the coming year, not to mention the possibility of current enrollees withdrawing. And with graduation approaching, the traditional time of special giving, I wish this moratorium on media involvement to continue. Although, of course, immediately after the agreement with the Evans parents, given yesterday's events, that has already not been the case."

"But—"

The hand again. "You've had an unconventional . . . well, let me say this. I'm not casting stones or blaming you necessarily, but I haven't otherwise encountered a teacher who—I have never even heard of one in the professional annals. I would doubt that among all secondary-school instructors . . ."

If only he were my student, we'd work on his communication skills. Of course, he'd fail, because Maurice Havermeyer, Ph.D., did not want to communicate clearly. If he did, his listeners might be able to see how pathetic and petty his ideas were.

". . . my observations lead me to believe you apparently have a predilection for nonacademic adventures of a counterproductive and oftentimes hazardous nature. This trait is potentially incompatible with, I believe you'll agree, and has a deleterious effect upon one's pedagogical duties."

I wasn't sure what his precise grievance was, but none of this sounded good for me. Did he mean that I got into too much trouble, created too much trouble, or what?

"Repeated instances cannot help but lead me to the opinion that you have a tendency to find yourself involved with law enforcement officials more often than—"

Than what? Than salamanders? Than normal people? Than he would prefer? I didn't feel like letting him think I understood him, and I didn't feel like letting him complete the sentence. "You're right," I said. "I am involved with a law enforcement official. I have been for several years now. Are you saying he is interfering with my teaching?"

"I never . . . I didn't . . . I'm afraid you're misinterpreting . . ." Once again I saw his engines rev up and leave another unsatisfactory stop en route. "Miss Pepper, yesterday your professional inattention allowed a child in your care to wander off. This is a serious problem fraught with both educational and legal ramifications, and although he was unharmed and reached home intact, we are gravely concerned, and of course the media—despite my earnest and previously successful attempts to prevent their presence here— the media has seized upon this."

I'd had it, whatever it might be. "Dr. Havermeyer, unless Adam is seriously disturbed and in need of special attention, as I suggested, and in which case he should not be mainstreamed in the manner he was, he should instead be under a doctor's care, and his parents' refusal to look at the situation should not be tolerated—" I not only was copying his verbosity and lack of breaks for breath, but as he started to interrupt, I put my hand up to prevent it, Havermeyer-style.

But the anger was all mine. "Unless you agree with me that he needs attention and probably medications to help him function more normally, then let's be honest. Adam is a seventeen-year-old city boy who gets himself around on his own all the time. He left the library before he was supposed to. That is all. And that is hardly a child who wanders away. We have a problem here—but with Adam Evans. Not with me."

I'm not sure anybody has ever spoken that directly or assertively to Maurice Havermeyer. Certainly not anybody who kept his job. But it felt great. Cleansing. I'd use the word *empowering* if it didn't embarrass me. I was tempted to plow on, keep the advantage and ask him questions that had been troubling me for years. Precisely what field was his Ph.D. in? How the hell had he earned it? Could I see his dissertation? I envisioned it as roughly the size of the *Encyclopaedia Britannica*, with about a paragraph's worth of meaning buried alive in it.

"The police are already here," Havermeyer said abruptly. "Extremely disruptive of classrooms and routine, although of course there is a civic duty to cooperate in such situations, still—" He looked at me accusingly. This was my fault, too. The cops were here, and I was to blame because I was a cop magnet.

"Today?" I answered stupidly. "This morning? Already?"

He nodded. "In search of Adam."

"Who is not here, I take it. Is he home? Do Mr. and Mrs. Evans know where he is?"

"May I remind you we are educators and we are not supposed to be privy to police business, despite your own predilection for such matters? I believe, in fact, that in this particular instance, the circumstance that directed official attention to our school is that Adam's name was cried out in such a public and incriminating manner as to throw him under the shadow of suspicion, to implicate him in the regrettable events in the library yesterday.

Furthermore, I have been led to believe, until otherwise contra-indicated, that you were said person who did the crying out, Miss Pepper."

"I couldn't find him. I was trying to find him." I didn't think that was the whole truth, but it would have to do.

"Do you consider that appropriate and protective behavior in regard to one of our own students?"

Yes, indeed, I thought it was appropriate when the teacher was near hysterics and couldn't find the boy whose behavior had frightened her and whose black scarf was draped over a statue while an alarm was blaring throughout the library and something was really wrong. How much more appropriate could you get?

"This . . . propensity you demonstrate for overinvolvement in criminal activities and matters that by rights concern only those entrusted to handle such matters—this is incompatible with peda-gogical responsibilities, Miss Pepper. I realize that the term is speed-ily nearing its completion. In a matter of weeks, we will all be free to engage in whatever summertime activities we so desire, and to my regret, at such time, it will behoove me to reconsider this issue, reassess the situation, and for you as well to determine whether or not you have found that professional position which most suits your particular temperament. It may be that your nervous system requires more excitement than a small secondary school can be ex-pected to provide. It may be that you would find a greater degree of self-satisfaction in a different environment."

I'd just been fired, Havermeyer-style. Murkily given notice. I stood to leave and, standing above him, could see his bald spot and how he tried to cover it with long hairs growing near his ears. I tried not to look at it because it made me feel sorry for him. It was so silly and pitiable a disguise—and for what? It made me realize what a mess of a man he was, and I wanted to think of him not as that but as my enemy and oppressor.

"In the interim," he said, "and despite any desire on your part for exposure to the media, I want this school kept out of the news-papers, unless it's to disseminate good news. I believe the popular term for the behavior I require is 'keeping a low profile.' Are you familiar with the term, Miss Pepper?"

I nodded, although I resented the implication that I was a media slut, constantly inviting the press in so I could publicize myself. I understood his plan now. He, too, would be low-profile. Just as low-profile as a snake. And when the term ended, he'd quietly fail to rehire me. No outcry, no high profile, no witnesses.

He pointed to the *Inquirer* on his desk. Emily was on the front page—and so was Adam, always referred to as "a senior at Philly Prep." "Suffice it to say, no more of this."

As if I'd murdered Emily, just to push the place where I worked back into the news. "I've never contacted the press," I said.

"Intentionally or not, you nonetheless manage to involve them. You must admit, Miss Pepper, you took your class for what in any ordinary, normal circumstances would be a quiet research outing at the library, and once again, catastrophe strikes in a garish and horrifying fashion. You must admit you have a talent for being near such events and for generating all manner of unwelcome attention to our student body and establishment. You must admit—"

"You are absolutely correct, Dr. Havermeyer," I said. "I must admit that the woman who toured us through the library was strangled, potentially traumatizing my students and, may I say, myself. I'm sure you understand the psychological necessity of talking about it, and I want to thank you for being so generous with your time and helping me deal with what I've been through. Now, I need to follow your example and extend a helping hand to my students. I assure you I'm fine, despite the trauma, and thank you for asking. Now I have to run or I'll be late for first period."

I was going to make his role in my dismissal as difficult as I humanly could. I would not accept his meaning until he said it clearly. The English teacher's last stand.

Nine

THE only thing I really wanted to talk about was the fact of my firing. Also, the probable fact of my being sued, arrested, or whatever happened when you're accused of battering a student. I wanted to talk about it with everybody I'd ever met. It would have been heartening to talk with Mackenzie—if only I knew how to reach him when he was capable of listening and in a mood to chat.

Normally I had a guaranteed fallback in my mother. She so loves a play-by-play recitation of news in the making. Her ideal daughter would wear a microphone at all times and treat her life as if it were featured on CNN. "Now, Mom, I'm bringing you this live from the classroom, where my days have just been numbered by my headmaster." But today, in her new perversity, my mother would not commiserate. She'd say Havermeyer's decision was a sign that it was time to begin her agenda for me. She was a bit of a pagan, finding portents everywhere—and, amazingly, those signs always pointed in her direction of choice.

With no one on the horizon who wanted to hear my problems, I hauled myself out of my wallow and loaned an ear to others. The first miserable-looking creature who intercepted my do-gooder beams was a senior, Daisy Rollins. "You look upset," I said. "I can understand, given what—"

"I'm upset because I can't find my backpack, so I don't have my homework because I did it ahead of time and it was in it." She looked sulky and shifty, as if she were lying—or certain that I'd think she was. Which I did.

"I'm sure it will turn up," I said, and that was it for grief counseling. Instead I held my tongue, a painful process. I was still an English teacher. This was class. I was supposed to keep a low profile. Being fired was pretty low in itself, but whining about it was apt to bring attention and further blustery wrath from my headmaster. While I was musing about this, two tenth graders, Jill Dunlap and Nancy Cain, quietly approached my desk to softly utter, almost in unison, a request for a conference at the end of the day. "We have something for the newspaper," they whispered. "Exposé. We've been working undercover again." They each took a step back and waited for my response.

I often had to remind myself that they weren't twins or a double exposure. Best friends since elementary school, about the same height and body size, both with dark blond shoulder-length hair, they were like old marrieds, finishing off each other's sentences, and sometimes, as they'd just done, actually speaking in unison.

An exposé, indeed.

"We want to write under a pseudonym," Nancy said.

"What's wrong with your names? You've used them before." So far, the fearless duo's undercover work had revealed that the cafeteria muffins were shrinking as the semester went on. Also that Lollie Jackson, the Spanish II teacher, had paper-trained a puppy in her schoolroom closet for three days. Her students had kept the secret, and even my Woodward and Bernstein waited to report it till the puppy was trained and able to stay home and it was too late to pursue either Ms. Jackson or her dog. "Come on, you've got a journalistic reputation. Don't you want to enlarge on it?"

They shook their heads at the same tempo. I wondered if they rehearsed.

"It could get us in trouble?" Jill said.

"Could we call ourselves Brenda Starr?" Nancy asked.

"That's been taken."

"Then make it Brenda Stare." Jill giggled. "The Watcher of Evil."

I promised to see them after school.

The seniors talked about the previous day's tragic events, but after a while it seemed more like tabloid TV than therapy, exploitation without catharsis, so I had them work on their projects, although I suspected that the murder had probably dampened their desire to spend lots more time at the library. I watched their glances dart to, then away from, then back again to Adam's usual seat—the way a tongue probes the empty socket of a tooth just pulled. But no one asked the obvious question—where was he, why wasn't he here, and could we take the combination of those factors to mean that he was involved in this crime?

Perhaps those weren't their questions. Perhaps only I was thinking in those terms. Once again I felt I could be the governess in *Turn of the Screw*, except at least she had the conviction of her beliefs. I, on the other hand, didn't know how much I was super-imposing on reality. Maybe everyone else thought of Adam as an eccentric goof-off and not so very different from the rest of the Philly Prep population. Maybe that's what he actually was.

I worried whether the end result would be the same, and I'd wind up inadvertently destroying someone in my charge.

Which reminded me—I hadn't finished rereading the James "nouvelle" and I'd promised to go over Lia's notes with her. Where had I put her book? I'd just been reading it, but when? Not when I'd fallen asleep on the couch the night before, so where was that book? The last thing I wanted to do was discourage a self-motivated student.

I was constantly surprised that Lia's parents had chosen our school—she deserved more academic stimulation than we could provide—but apparently it was a matter of geographic, not scholastic, desirability. We were close to their house and seemed a safe haven from their perception of the public schools.

I had no idea where the book was. No image came to mind. My stomach cramped with fear that I'd lost her labor of love.

Between classes I searched my briefcase and desk, several times, all of them in vain. And then finally I remembered where I'd last seen it—on the library table where I'd pushed it aside so I could study graduate programs. I'd forgotten all about it when the alarm sounded and I left the department.

I was so tired, so ready to go home at the close of day, but I had no choice but to retrieve it—if it was still there. If not, another teacherly failure. And what if Lia's overprotective parents complained to Havermeyer about the butterfingered teacher who'd lost their daughter's work?

Would that violate my low profile? Did news of me—bad news of me—to Havermeyer constitute being high-profile? Or did it only apply to the media? And what was a low profile, anyway? The words made me think of my headmaster's jowls.

I was carrying on about nothing. I'd find the book, complete the reading, meet with Lia, and keep myself and the school invisible to the press. Easy enough.

I had already packed up when Jill and Nancy appeared. As always, I smiled at the sight of them. They currently thought it cool—or whatever word meant "cool" now—to prowl secondhand stores for fifties garb, poodle or pegged skirts, saddle shoes, et al.

The net effect was a shabby but aching innocence. An innocence that was pure fantasy, I'm sure, as if a few decades back nobody had so much as an off-color thought.

Or maybe it wasn't mythical. Kids didn't mow down their teachers and fellow students in those days, so it truly was a more innocent time. And very long ago.

"Okay, girls," I said. They were so into their fifties personas they didn't flinch at having been called anything but *women*.

They closed the classroom door and hovered, silently deciding where to settle. I like desks in a circle whenever possible, as they now were, and they picked the two nearest me.

"We've found something like really majorly serious?" Jill said. Nancy's enthusiastic nods made her ponytail bobble. "Criminal?" Jill said. At this, Nancy's eyes widened and her expression grew solemn as her nod rate slowed down.

What could the jitterbug twins have found? More cut corners in the cafeteria? Had they perhaps confirmed my suspicion that Helga the Office Witch was secretly selling the supplies she hoarded? Black-market gum erasers?

Nancy leaned close and looked around. I was surprised the girls didn't pat me down to make sure I wasn't wired. Their paranoia and sense of self-importance were entertaining. Even when satisfied that we weren't being observed, she spoke in a whisper. "There's a big business counterfeiting transcripts and recommendation letters and having other people take your SAT exams. All over the Delaware Valley. The boss of it's here. Our school."

"Whoa! How could—is this true? How did you—on what are you basing this?" I had trouble switching gears, shifting expectations. Forget muffins. This was serious indeed. And bizarre. This was Philly Prep—who would have one of our students take their test and hope to do well?

"We're taking swing lessons?" Jill said. "Through this club my parents belong to? And this boy there goes to another school, but, like, I'm not saying he's dumb, but he's a really good golfer, so that helps with schools, but still and all—"

"He was telling this other guy," Nancy continued, "who goes to another school, about how to get in wherever. Like he had. He's going to Columbia next year. Because somebody took his SATs for him."

"Somebody who goes to Philly Prep?" It was hard keeping the squeak of disbelief out of my voice. Hiring one of our students to take a test was like hiring somebody from Clown College to perform Hamlet.

"Not exactly." Both girls said that, then Nancy took over. "What we heard is that the guy who took the test didn't go here, but he works for a guy who does. You contact the guy here and he finds the other person."

"And those other things?"

They nodded in unison. "He has, like, forms and things on his computer?" Jill said. "He makes transcripts? And recommendation letters from people who don't exist?"

If this was true, then Philly Prep had its first genius—albeit one who turned his smarts to entrepreneurial crime.

"We told you it was serious," they said.

I took a deep breath. "And . . . what do you want to do about it?"

"Write about it! It's a crime," Nancy said, in case I'd forgotten.

"Bad," Jill added, without even making it into a question.

"We have the facts. We're ready."

I barely heard them through the din in my head. If this was true, we had a major scandal. We had Maurice Havermeyer's worst nightmare, and its timing couldn't have been worse for me. I knew what the right thing to do was. But I didn't know if my system could take the results of anymore of my doing the right thing. So I hedged.

"This is the sort of story that the newspapers—the real newspapers, and the TV—are going to pick up on." They looked at each other and grinned. "This is a serious crime. You won't stay anonymous for long."

They darted cryptic signals to each another. I didn't dare think of what I wanted them to be saying in their private language. It would be so unworthy of me to wish this story unborn. To squelch it. Even to suggest that it should wait till next year. Till anytime but now. "Wait a minute," I said. "Do students here use these people, too?"

Their nod explained a lot about our improved acceptance rate—that statistic Havermeyer so adored. It probably explained Adam's good SAT scores, too. I could see the story whirling, spreading, rippling out across the Delaware Valley. "You're sure about your sources?"

"We knew the name of the guy who got into Columbia," Nancy said. "And then we went undercover, see?"

I did not, could not imagine the two of them doing anything surreptitiously.

"Pretended to want to know about doing it ourselves. He told us a whole lot."

"He liked Nancy," Jill said, rolling her eyes. "Thought she was older—in eleventh grade? He told her about two other people who'd gotten fake recommendations? We have the names and the school names. Is that what you mean?"

"I think so," I whispered.

"We know the police will probably get involved, but we can protect our sources, can't we? It's the right thing to do. Our parents think so. Don't you?"

Whistle-blowing was the ethical, moral, civic-minded thing to do. Right for everything—except me.

I wanted to crawl under the desk and hide. I had quick and searing fantasies of blackmailing my headmaster with this: *Keep me on your staff or I break the story, Maurice.* "Yes," I said. "You have to write it up." Maybe they'd do it really, really slowly. "This is awful. A corruption of everybody's standards." My sweet neophyte reporters with such a high-profile story. How many times did this happen to a high-school newspaper? "Take your time. Do a good job."

"We did. Here. Here's the story. All ready to go." Nancy handed me three typed pages headed with "The SAT Scam and Other Crimes." "You like the headline?" she asked.

"Catchy." I wanted to bang my head on my desk and cry. There was no hope left for me on earth, at least not in this school. I'd be booted out by sunset.

It was a great headline. Everybody would borrow it—the *Inquirer*, the *Daily News*, and every local TV station. With my luck, the Nancy and Jill show would go national, on *Oprah*. Making Philly Prep a household word. A household bad word.

There was no place left to hide.

Or maybe this was, indeed, what my mother would call a sign. In this case, a billboard-sized sign screaming GET OUT!

Ten

BY the time I left school to go find the book at the library—
it was probably right next to that needle in the haystack—
I felt beset. Worn down. Hopeless. Exhausted. I could
barely walk.

I had no choice. Parking around the library could be a nightmare. So I walked through a misty rain that the British tout as
producing beautiful English complexions. Cheaper than a facial, I
told myself as I inhaled pure humidity. And then I told myself to
cut the jolly crap. It didn't help. Life stank lately, and this chirrupy
voice—my sunny, platitude-spouting inner Pollyanna—just slicked
that downhill slide.

I walked through Logan Square, which is actually a circle, and which celebrates wetness, anyway. Three heroic figures represent the city's rivers, and even on a drizzly afternoon, water spouted from bronze porpoises and amphibians.

I was mildly surprised to see that the library looked its customary self, with no signs of post-traumatic shock. That's what's wonderful about buildings. It takes a whole lot—war, earthquake, fire—to mess with their integrity. Maybe I'd study architecture.

And that's what's wonderful about libraries. Their very existence suggests history and time and the idea that no matter how bad the moment may be, the collective wisdom has seen it all and survived. This too shall pass.

Maybe I'd study library science.

I passed through the line of smokers braving the wet to stare into space and inhale furiously in front of the building, and went directly to the information desk, where a good-looking man in a rumpled white dress shirt, plaid vest, and solid blue tie sat bent over a crossword puzzle. I remembered him. It was Terry Labordeaux, who'd helped tour my class, and later, at my request, had searched the men's room for Adam. But he glanced my way without a sign of recognition. That would be depressing in itself, were there room for yet another downer in my crowded collection. I cleared my throat. "Excuse me," I said. "I left a book here yesterday."

"The other library users will be grateful," he said without looking up.

"My own book, I mean. I left my own paperback. Henry James. *Turn of the Screw*. I'm hoping it hasn't been reshelved."

"Shelved. If it's your book, it never was on our shelves, so it really couldn't be *re*shelved." His nose was nearly on the puzzle as he wrote another word.

Did he have any idea what roiling wretchedness he was messing with? "Forgive my syntactical and lexical errors," I said. "I'm having a really bad day. But on the other hand, you aren't going to win any gold stars for helpfulness, either. Did you notice that this desk is placed so as to be convenient for people to ask questions?

And twenty across is wrong." I couldn't see the clues, his answer, or the numbers, but I didn't care.

His sudden smile nearly obliterated the memory of his officious nit-picking. I realized he might have been trying for humor. I also once again realized he was cute. Arrogant, but cute. I should have appreciated his gentle wordplay, and normally I would have. "Check lost and found," he said. "If whoever cleared the decks noticed that there were no call letters on the spine, it might be there."

He spoke gently, but the intellectual and professional chasm between us had widened. I was a dolt who thought a book was a book was a book, and he was a trained professional, a Dewey decimalian. *"Turn of the Screw,"* he said. "A James fan, are you?"

I shrugged. "One of my students is writing a play based on it. It's her book, actually. Annotated. The basis of her script. That's why I have to find that copy."

"That's what they all say. It's not for them, it's for a friend." He squinted at me, then pulled glasses out of his vest pocket, put them on, and looked at me again. "I know you! Pepper, right? You were here with your class yesterday. Sent me into the men's room later on."

"I didn't think you remembered me."

"Nearsighted," he said. "Very. Too lazy to put on the glasses, but otherwise—of course I would have remembered you! I must have seemed—sorry I was so flip. I'm not actually here. Well, of course, I am, physically, but only waiting for a friend. It was supposed to be a few minutes, but it's been . . . no excuse for my answering you badly, as you now know. Of course I'd remember you, that valiant soul trying to generate excitement for rare books and seeing only bored kids. Poor you." He was on the verge of another smile, but before it could truly bloom, it dimmed. "Awful, what happened to Emily Fisher."

I hadn't wanted to get back into this, just wanted the book.

"We're all heartsick. She hadn't been here long, but all the same . . ."

"She seemed quite knowledgeable."

He nodded and stood up, making this feel less an official Q-and-A. And at close range, I saw the stain I'd known would always be on his ties. A bachelor, I decided with clichéd assurance.

"A quick study," he said. "Smart. Noticed and remembered everything. Loved books and libraries, and was really motivated. Almost too much so—like this was her whole life, and maybe it was. This place was definitely her haven. At least when her husband wasn't doing his serpent-in-her-Eden act."

"He came here?"

Labordeaux nodded. "Checked up on her."

"Meaning what?"

"Apparently he didn't think she was earning enough. Maybe his support payments depended on her income, and God knows we aren't overpaid. He insisted she'd chosen to work here so she could bleed him dry—that kind of thing. He sat in the cafeteria with her at lunch, badgering her. Everybody could hear, which he knew, as if he were playing to a jury."

Ray Buttonwood sounded worse and worse. Emily's recent life was like the childhood nightmare of being sucked down the drain. "Do the police know who did it?" God knew when Mackenzie and my paths would cross again, and whether, at that time, he'd tell me anything about this case.

"That boy," he said. "That crazy boy. Your student, isn't he? Very sad. Nobody's been arrested, if that's what you mean. Can't find him, as I understand it."

I refused to insert Adam's name into my questions. "Do you have any idea how whoever did it could have disappeared so quickly? Is there a way out of that balcony? I remember it being closed off, understandably, so that there isn't easy access to the rare books. But that also makes getting away . . . how could somebody do it?"

He was silent for a moment. "There are doors. You didn't notice because they're for staff only, or as separate entrances for special receptions. Or you could take the elevator, up or down. Go up to the cafeteria, and from there, down the stairs to the theater section, although that'd be pretty much a dead end. Or you could go out on the roof terrace, even though it's not allowed," he continued. "But if you've just murdered somebody, no-admittance rules probably don't intimidate you. You could hide in any of those places and leave later. Or hop on the elevator and be down and out before anybody arrived. There was that lag time. And nobody out there except poor Emily, and she was beyond telling."

"I guess you could hide by staying right where you were. I mean, going back to some part of the rare-book department. Hide in plain sight."

"Like in 'The Purloined Letter,' which would be appropriate given our Poe collection." His expression combined both appraisal and approval of me. Maybe even something more. "With the number of people who are in here on legitimate—or at least ordinary—pursuits, nobody'd notice, long as the killer looked normal. And we have a wide spectrum of what passes for normal in the library, given our street people looking for a warm dry place, and our usual revolutionaries and counterrevolutionaries researching how they are going to tear up the world. Pretty much anything goes. Is that what you're saying? Interesting. Very interesting."

"More or less." I had a queasy and pleasantly surprised sense that we weren't really talking only about the murder. That we were, in fact, doing a peculiar, library-colored, postmodern variation on "Hi, what's your sign?"

"That crazy boy who did it, do you know where he is?" Terry Labordeaux asked me. "Do his parents? Have you spoken with them? Has he gotten in touch with you?"

"No, supposedly, no, and why would he?"

"He must be scared. Disoriented. I mean, who'd take you in if you're mentally ill and a killer? I keep thinking about him." He shook his head, as if bewildered by the idea of Adam.

"I don't know that he's the killer," I said.

"That's nice. Protecting your student. Bighearted."

We were back to using a murder as grounds for flirting. "About my book?" I gently prompted.

He looked puzzled, then smiled again. "I nearly forgot. Henry James, of course. I'll walk you there as soon as—"

"If you'll just point the—"

He waved at a small man rushing toward us, wispy hair haloing him. "Sorry," the new arrival said. "Sorry, sorry. The tires—"

My buddy waved his words away. "No problem at all. I've had charming company."

Definitely a mating dance happening here. I wished I knew if I wanted it to continue.

He turned to me to make an introduction, then stopped and produced that grin again. "Never did get your full name," he said. "I think we're beyond the Miss Pepper stage, aren't we?"

"It's Amanda."

He looked as if nowhere on earth did there exist a more splendid first name. "Amanda, meet Sandor. Or, Amandor, meet Sanda."

The little man's hand was damp with either the rain or his haste. "I've been stuck in the worst—don't even ask." As I hadn't, we let it go at that.

"And yesterday, you told me to call you Terry," I said. "Short for Terrence?"

"Short for the never-used-and-don't-start-now Alastair. My Scottish grandfather's name. Try having a French-Scots combo. Too many jokes about cheap wine." After explaining to Sandor why, after waiting for him, he wasn't going to stay with him, we walked down a flight of stairs.

"I hate to keep asking questions that are none of my business," I lied, "but do you happen to know who found the—who found Emily Fisher?"

He stopped walking and looked at me with gold-brown eyes and a solemnly set mouth. "Unfortunately, I do. I found her." He took a deep breath, his eyes focusing backward, on twenty-four hours earlier. "I ate late. Been working on the Fraktur—" He saw my frown of confusion. "The Pennsylvania German folk art collection. Lost count of time, and so I ate lunch after everybody. I got off the elevator and there she was, with the alarm going off, and—"

113

"How awful for you."

He looked at me appraisingly, as if he wasn't sure I was being honest. Then, satisfied, he nodded. "The alarm," he murmured, as if surprised. "Why didn't I realize it sooner? There's a wrought-iron gate on the balcony. Real heavy ornamental stuff. It covers the opening to a staircase—a grand staircase like the one downstairs. It was closed off for security reasons. There's a small notice on it that an alarm would sound if the gate were opened. That's been hypothetical until now. Nobody ever opened the gate—I don't even see it anymore. It's part of that wall, but that must be what happened. He opened the gate, the alarm started, he shut the gate, and it kept going."

"You're saying that's how the killer got out."

"Makes sense, doesn't it? Unless there was a Tarzan jump off the balcony, can you think of any other way out?"

"The elevator?"

He looked at me so intently, I felt uncomfortable, although I knew I was supposed to feel flattered and appreciated. "Kind of risky, isn't it?" he said. "They are notoriously slow to arrive."

I nodded. "He might have bumped into you, coming down from the cafeteria."

He slapped his forehead. "Damn—I've been so . . . well, whatever . . . this is embarrassing. I forgot to get the key, or the security guy."

"For what?"

"The lost and found. It's not exactly an official place, just an office where people toss found objects. And it's locked."

So we turned and ascended the flight of stairs, which once again would have been several flights in a building where one story wasn't actually several stories high. "Till now," Terry said, "I didn't associate the two events. I thought the alarm was a whole separate thing, a false alarm set off by Louie."

"Excuse me?"

"Louie Louie. That's his actual name, he swears it. He's an advocate for the homeless, which would be fine. You know, we have issues with people trying to use this as a dorm or public bathhouse, and things aren't always sweetness and light. Patrons had become nervous about using the rest rooms for fear of who or what they'd find . . . we had to do something. But we worked it out—until Louie declared himself their advocate." We'd reached the security guard at the back of the entry hall, and after some discussion and some obvious conflict about leaving his post, he gave Terry the key to the room that served as a lost and found. We started down the stairs again.

"Is Louie homeless?" I asked.

Terry shook his head. "But I don't know why not. Looks like he could be. He's long-haired and bearded, always needs a trim, and is definitely a little off. Also, he's here almost every morning the same time I get here, as if this is his job."

The bitch man?

"But he obviously sleeps and eats well. I assume he's a trust baby."

"That's what I always meant to be," I said. "Where did I go wrong?"

"Same place I did." Terry had a world-class smile. "Picked the wrong parents. Mine forgot to feather my nest. Do you think it had to do with having not one extra feather?"

"They probably pay Louie to stay away from them," I said. "They probably pay him out of shame for giving him that name."

"They should pay us, too, then. For coping with him. He is forever preaching, railing, making as much noise as possible. Doesn't think there should be rules, guidelines, exclusions. And of course," Terry said, "since being reasonably quiet in the library makes sense, to assert his rights and his distaste for rules, he makes noise."

"Apropos of nothing?"

Terry nodded. "Scares everybody to death, and what are we supposed to do? What crime did he commit? Disturbing the peace usually requires more than a whoop or a scream. And the times he's been escorted out, he's called the press and we've gotten more bad PR as oppressors of the oppressed. Easier to live with the idea he'll freak us out now and then. So yesterday, when I heard the alarm . . . it's actually ironic, I guess."

"Meaning?"

"Well, if indeed this time the noise was about Emily, because of her—at least, because of her death, she and Louie . . . Emily had a fierce streak when she thought something wasn't right, and she wouldn't let go of it. You could call her stiff-necked, prone to high moral dudgeon, and she thought Louie Louie was wrong. They bumped heads almost from day one."

We reached a glass-paneled door near the men's room. Finding what had been lost didn't seem a high priority at the library, and I worried about the odds of my seeing that book again. Rather than face Lia and say I'd lost it, I would be forced to commit hara-kiri.

"Why did they fight?" I asked as he opened the office door. Lost objects, including a large blue drum, which seemed as if it would be hard to lose, waited to be reclaimed from atop chairs or on the floor. There were no shelves, nothing designed for the waiting-to-be-found, none of the organization I'd expected.

"I'll look," Terry said, moving into the room. I got the feeling I wasn't to enter the inner sanctum, so I waited by the entrance. "Emily wasn't used to his commando raids and he scared her half to death first time he pulled one. She retaliated—called the cops, chewed him out, burst into tears. The works." He inspected the top of a row of lockers while continuing his running narrative. "It was on the evening news, and I have to say that for once, we didn't necessarily look bad. Here was this tiny woman crying, and this nutty-looking, wild-talking so-called advocate. It didn't hurt that one of the homeless women hugged Emily and told her to stop crying. On camera. Made Louie more fanatical. He came after Emily, harassing her until she was on the verge of getting a re-straining order. Which would have been useless. When you're nuts and the cops have a couple or three other things to do, to keep call-ing every time Louie Louie is spotted in the public library . . . In-stead we reached a truce. He'd hang around in the lobby but not go after her the way he was."

"But he was here yesterday, and I saw him stop her. I didn't know who he was then, or who she was, but I heard him call her a bitch. And say she *thwarted* him."

"He has a fine vocabulary."

"Do the police know about Louie?" I was grasping at anything, and starting to feel paranoid myself, imagining Emily-enemies everywhere—her sister, her soon-to-be ex-husband, Louie Louie. But not Adam. No. Not even if the killing had been on the balcony, from which it was logical to assume Adam's scarf had fallen.

"I have no idea what the police do or don't know," Terry said. "They asked me what I'd seen. Didn't want anything beyond that. I told them about finding her, and I pointed out the book bag on the landing, and even then, they acted like I had exceeded my bounds. They would have seen it themselves. So I shut up."

He slowly turned, double-checking all the shelving. This didn't bode well for Lia's book.

"Do you know whose bag it was?" I asked.

His attention was still on the shelves. He shook his head, then walked toward me, his expression mournful. "It isn't here. I'm so sorry. But you know, somebody might still turn it in, so why don't you give me a number where I could reach you, and I'll check every day."

I might have said no need, but there was a need, even though I wasn't sure why he really wanted that number. "Easiest thing would be to call the school. Philly Prep," I said. He looked disappointed, verifying my suspicions that he wasn't really motivated by the missing book. "They'll get the message to me."

"Can I atone a little?" he asked. "Buy you a cup of coffee? Do you have time?"

I hesitated.

"Didn't mean to give too glamorous an idea of what I had in mind," he said quickly. "Upstairs—the cafeteria—a cup of coffee? I could do with a break and," he checked his watch, "it's still open."

"Well, then, sure."

117

On the elevator ride up, he asked discreetly and I discreetly conveyed the idea that I was "somewhat involved." I heard my own voice qualify Mackenzie with that "somewhat" and realized in that instant that I wasn't one hundred percent sure how ecstatic I was about my unavailability. A man like Terry would be around when you needed him. I couldn't imagine there were many library emergencies, overtime, extra shifts. Plus, he listened. And he was, if not a C.K. Mackenzie type all-round knockout looker, sufficiently attractive in his own way. And with a smile that made the rest not matter.

As for those ties—it was obviously a case of his bad eyesight. Not some character flaw.

The elevator passed the Rare Book Department's floor. "Mind if I meet you back up here in two minutes?" I asked as we reached the cafeteria on the top level. "I'd like to look at that landing where Adam was."

He kept the elevator door open with his hand and looked startled. "Well—sure, but why?"

"Is it still open? The Rare Book Department?" I asked.

"Till five every weekday." His voice went flat, without interest, as if this were a question he was too frequently asked. "The elevator won't stop on that floor after the department's closed, so yes, it's now or never." Then he paused, and looked at me with renewed enthusiasm. "Do you want an escort?"

Maybe, if he hadn't looked so interested, or used the word *escort*, which made our encounter seem more than a casual one. Maybe, if I hadn't been as ambivalent about how casual and impersonal I wanted it to be. "Don't trouble yourself," I said. "I'll be back in a flash." He let the elevator door close.

Seconds later, I walked off into the elevator alcove, then to the right, to the balcony landing. It still seemed an impossible place for murder. The actual entry to the Rare Book Department was glass-enclosed, making everything on the balcony visible from inside, as well as from a twin balcony directly across from it.

A less than sane person might not realize that, a voice within me said. I stifled it, looked at the wrought-iron gate blocking the stairs, and with a sigh, returned to the elevator and was upstairs in the two minutes I'd promised.

"Find what you wanted?" Terry asked.

"I don't know that I wanted anything specific. I thought maybe being there, I'd figure it out, but it doesn't make sense," I said. "It's too visible a place." He was kind enough not to mention that logic and planning and even self-preservation might not have had a role in this murder.

The coffee was predictably awful, but welcome as preventive medicine for the rainy return to the great outdoors. "So," he said. "Your job. You enjoy it?"

"Sometimes. Lately, not a lot. But mention of it makes me think about my students, and I don't think you told me if you knew whose book bag it was." I was sickeningly sure I knew.

He looked annoyed. Understandably so. He hadn't wanted to talk about book bags.

"Everyone at my school carries one," I said.

"Everyone at most schools carries one," he answered. He didn't say the word *boring* but I could feel it hover in the air between us like ash. He didn't say—but I nonetheless heard—that for no apparent—to him—reason, having been ultravague about my "relationship," I was making it difficult for any serious flirtation to get off the ground.

Then he suddenly grinned. "I'll bet you got in a lot of trouble at school for asking too many questions. Am I right?"

"I'm sorry, I must be annoying—"

"No—I didn't mean that." His smile beamed on. "I just had this image of you as a cute kid with that same intent expression and curiosity."

I kept my eyes on my coffee cup. "Well," I said. "Maybe that's why I became a teacher. I get to ask all the questions I have."

His expression sobered. "I'm sorry. I didn't mean to make you feel awkward about asking whatever you like. I was . . . I thought I was complimenting you. Ask away. What was it about? Oh, yes. The book bag on the balcony."

The book bag that any kid in the city could have owned. Why was I making such a fuss about it? Thursday afternoon, the library had been filled with students, and the bag Terry found could have belonged to any one of them. I had to stop plugging in Adam's face wherever there was a gap.

"I have to assume it was that crazy boy's," he finally said. "The one they're saying did it. Who else? Adam Evans was the name in the paper, and the bag had a letter made of tape on it. That Greek thing—I should know what it's called. The Æ dipthong, where they're both one letter with the E's prongs coming out of the side of the A. That's all I know. It more or less fits him, doesn't it?"

More. Adam had written his initials that way for years. I'd thought of it as part of his interesting mind before his mind got so interesting it frightened me.

Terry's smile really was awe-inspiring. Till now, I'd thought "lights up a face" was just an expression.

"What?" I asked.

He shook his head. "Don't want to upset you."

"No, what?"

"It's just that . . . you love this stuff, don't you? Visiting the crime scene, asking questions about evidence . . . why?"

"I hate not knowing. I hate being bamboozled. Guess this makes me feel less out of control or duped."

"You've got an interesting mind. More analytical and logical than most, I guess. You're a very unusual woman, Amanda Pepper. It's quite attractive, as is the physical package, if I may be so bold." He leaned forward and lowered his head in a mock bow.

I lowered my eyes and did a fair approximation of modesty and also hoped the demure pose hid how much I enjoyed his being so bold. How grand it felt to be actively and thoroughly appreciated.

"Seriously, I can tell how concerned you are about that boy, that student of yours."

"I wish I could find him. He's out there, somewhere, and I'm afraid for him. For what people might do to him, or he might do to himself."

"Maybe I could help you find him. Not that I know how—or know him—but I'm reasonably intelligent and you could fill me in."

I experienced a jumble of emotions. Shame, that we were using Adam. Using a murder and a missing and mentally ill boy as a ruse for flirtation. Amusement, too, at Terry's transparent motives, and at the strong sense I had that he wouldn't have minded a bit if I'd told him so. He wanted me to know he was interested. I wanted him to know that I knew.

The image of Mackenzie flashed.

Right. I had benched myself from this game. I was wrong to let the man across from me think otherwise, at least until I decided whether I wanted to keep my current status. "Thanks," I said softly. "I'm not really hunting for Adam. I wouldn't know where to begin. But thanks for the offer." As if the offer had meant anything about Adam. I took a deep breath. "I'd better be going," I said. "I'm running late."

There's a male way of registering hurt and disappointment in and around the eyes. Nothing is said, of course, but the light sputters for a second. Subtly, but definitely, as it did on Terry's face. He cleared his throat and the look was gone, replaced by a hard-edged indifference.

I was sorry to have created an awkward situation. I thanked him profusely for his time, and made a hasty retreat, back out into the drizzly spring afternoon. After two years of one man, I wish I felt less ambivalent about my monogamy.

I crossed the many rain-shined lanes of traffic and walked through Logan Circle again, looking up for a moment to the Parkway, the wet flags of the world limply hanging from poles all the way to the art museum. We had all seen better times. The pinks and oranges of the newly cultivated flower beds ringing the circle were blurred and softened in the misty rain.

The square was deserted, except for two homeless men too far gone to come in out of the rain. One slept on a bench with soggy newspapers as a blanket, and one sat staring at Alexander Calder's fountain, which spouted on for its one-man audience. I knew, because Mackenzie had told me, that this had been the site of many good and bad events since colonial times, but the only one I could recall offhand was that it had once held a gallows.

I exited toward the Academy of Natural Sciences, its dinosaur and butterfly banners bright beacons against the drab day. My mind was stuck on that Æ. Where was Adam? What was he feeling? Fearing? Thinking? Had he done anything? Or in fact had I done everything to put him into a downward vortex just like the one I'd imagined for Emily Buttonwood? Next stop, his own wet bench on Logan Square. I'd been told that half the homeless were mentally ill, "mainstreamed" right onto the streets in the 1980s. Adam seemed on his way, with my cooperation.

At precisely which guilt-suffused, miserable moment, a hand clasped my shoulder, like some great judgment-day call of *Guilty!* I instinctively pulled away—or tried to, but couldn't.

"Don't!" Adam's hand was so tight on my shoulder it hurt. "Don't move! Don't say my name. Don't scream. Don't say anything."

Eleven

SCREAMED. Couldn't help it—sometimes instinct overrides everything. I screamed and turned—and screamed again, a mix of surprise, fear, shame, and I don't know what. "Adam! Let me go! Don't do this! Adam!"

"No!" he bellowed. "Stop screaming! *Don't scream!*"

The gray world around me felt ominous and harsh. The absence of anyone nearby—the homeless guys were half a block away and definitely not interested in my welfare—made the landscape desolate.

I didn't know Adam. I wanted to believe in his innate nonviolent goodness, I wanted to defend him—but I didn't truly know him at all, and I surely didn't know who he was becoming. I'd been whistling in the dark, convincing myself he was harmless. That didn't feel as much a given now with the two of us on a deserted street. I swallowed hard, took a deep breath, and nodded. "I'm . . . I'm . . . you surprised me."

"You took too long." He lowered his voice to a point midway between a mutter and a growl.

"Long what? Screaming?"

"Leaving there." He gestured toward the library, a distant pale looming mass through the trees, the dusk, and the rain.

"You've been waiting? Why?"

"I left."

"I meant—where have you been? I've been worried. Everybody was. Is."

He shrugged. "I don't like that place anymore, understand? I don't like it."

"Where are you staying? Sleeping?"

His eyes were without expression or light. He faced me, but I couldn't tell what he actually saw.

"You're wet," I said softly. "I don't want you to get sick. You need warm clothing." He swiveled his flat gaze to the bright banner announcing a special exhibit across the road at the Franklin Institute. He was wearing his customary black sweater and jeans, probably the same ones he'd been wearing yesterday, and a light windbreaker. God knew how long he'd been out in the rain. "Adam, where is your scarf? You always wore that long black scarf, and you could use it now. Where is it?"

He touched his neck as if to check, looked back in the direction of the library, up the parkway to the museum, then nodded overemphatically, his brow furrowed. "I need it. Wait—maybe—" He squatted down and opened a bright red backpack, pawing through its contents, shaking his head. His dark hair looked painted onto his forehead and cheeks.

He stood up again, lifted the open backpack off the ground, and handed it over to me, his missing scarf no longer on his mind. "No scarf."

124

The bag said DAISY in large blue-tape block letters. She'd told the truth about her missing backpack.

"That pack doesn't look anything like yours," I said softly. "How'd you wind up with it?"

"I—I got mixed up, maybe. I thought . . . I don't know, it was mine. I couldn't find mine and I needed one to put stuff in."

"What stuff?"

"*Stuff!* Whatever stuff! Backpack stuff!"

I didn't know what to do about his increasing agitation except to back off, at least metaphorically. After a few seconds of silence, Adam's temper gauge dropped noticeably.

"I don't want it. Too dangerous. Give it back." He had no apparent interest in whose backpack it actually was, whose belongings he'd just searched for his scarf. "I don't want it on me. Used as evidence against."

"Against what?"

"Me!" He shouted the word, then laughed.

"Evidence of what?"

Now he looked annoyed, as if my questions were unfair, as possibly they were. "I don't know that!" he said sharply. "I don't know them. Whatever they want. Against me. Evidence!"

"Adam," I said, "do you know what happened yesterday at the library?"

"Yeah." The voice that had just shouted, laughed, reflected agitation now went flat. "A lot of things. We saw the departments, we had lunch. I read."

"I mean about Ms. Fisher, our tour guide. What happened to her."

"She hollered at me in the library and God smote her. Fisher-lady's dead now." His voice was low, vague, dissociated. I couldn't figure out what was going on inside of him, what he felt, if anything.

"Why do you say that?"

"Isn't she? Isn't she dead? I saw."

I nodded. "Did you see God smite her?" I kept my voice as soft as I could.

He stared blankly. He seemed so changed, as if the road he'd been on had suddenly grown steep and he was speeding on a downhill curve. Two days ago his disease had been subtle enough to debate with his parents. But now, partly because of the weather and a night, I suspected spent out of doors, and drugs, perhaps, and whatever he had seen, or done, in the library—he was mentally jumbled, emotions and words fragmenting, coming out overemphatically or not at all.

"Do you remember what you saw?"

"Her. I saw the fisherlady. Not a fisherman, no. A fisherlady."

I smiled, to show I got his wordplay, and I felt a moment's painful sorrow for what was going to be wasted if Adam didn't get help. Even if help had to be within a prison system. "You could help the police, if you saw anything. Or heard anything."

He seemed to shrink within himself.

"I have the feeling you did," I said softly. "And you were frightened and still are, maybe, and it makes me sad to think about you being frightened. I think I can help you if I know what you're feeling. Did something mix you up, maybe make you run out of the library without telling anybody?" I waited between questions, watched his eyes dart off me, into space, up into the young green leaves of the trees. He didn't blink against the misty rain the way he should have. He didn't seem to feel the drops. "Did anything frighten you? Anybody? You could tell me. I'm not scary. It's the same old me, Adam. The same old two of us."

"No, no," he said. "No police, no, no trouble for me, no evidence. I didn't see anybody. Nothing."

"Not . . . God? Smiting her?"

"The dead lady. The fisherlady. I saw that."

"How did you find that out? That she was dead, I mean."

"She was there. She was dead."

"Where were you?"

He shrugged. "In where we . . . in the room up there where I was going to—the little clay things. The shepherds. The receipts."

I remembered mentally joking with myself about the odds of anyone's being interested in cuneiform tablets. Some joke.

"I went out to the balcony. I thought—I was going to go somewhere else I can't remember, but I saw her. And I heard."

"You were on the landing?"

His face went through a series of unrelated expressions, as if he were testing them. A frown, a quizzical look, an annoyed moue, almost a smile. "The balcony? Is that the same as the landing?"

I nodded, trying to hear what lay behind his words, trying to determine if that was what he'd decided was the best answer, or whether it was the truth. Or whether he could recognize what was true and what was not.

"I didn't see anybody except the fisherlady. On the floor, all . . . dead. Just dead. And there was shouting."

"You heard a shout?"

Adam looked at me intently. "I hear things. Other people are deaf. I hear it."

"I believe you."

"No, you make my head hurt."

He looked battered from inside. He looked crazy. He looked two or three minutes away from being the next denizen of Logan Square, sitting on a bench, talking to himself.

"I heard something," he said, "then I thought I should run away but the elevator didn't come, then I thought I should hide but I didn't know where, then I thought I should go look and I did and she was still on the floor, fisherlady."

I nodded. She was already on the floor. Not by his hands or doing. Please let him be right. Let him have the chronology right, and keep him coherent enough so that other people believe him, too.

"Somebody shouted. Said 'dead' or 'kill.' "

"That voice—was it a man's or a woman's?" And not in your head, Adam, please God.

"I don't know—it was too loud."

Not good. I had been hopeful for a while, but now . . .

"And then the siren."

The alarm.

"I was running."

"You opened the big iron gate? Is that what started it?"

"Then 'Adam! Adam!' "

"That was me."

"Yes."

"You knew it was me?"

He nodded.

So he'd been nearby when I called out. "I was looking for you. I heard the alarm, and I was frightened. I needed to know that nothing bad had happened to you. Where were you?"

He put his hands to his ears. "Running. I was running. Maybe the noise was inside me."

"The person who said 'kill'? Or 'dead'?"

"No questions! No noise! My scarf!"

"Adam, let me take you—"

"No! Don't touch me!" He backed away.

"Wait—" I took a scrap of paper out of my pocket and wrote my phone number on it. The least I could offer. "Here," I said. "In case. For whatever. Call me anytime. I'll help you, I promise." I found two quarters and held them out, too.

He made no move to take any of it. "My *scarf*," he said. "I need it!"

I shoved the paper and coins into his windbreaker pocket. "Don't go!" I said. "Don't—" But he was leaving for who knew where with long strides, and then a loping run. "Adam," I whispered into the rain. "Adam." He was gone. Lost.

I hoped he really did have a safe haven. I wanted him stored in a clean, dry place until some of this became clearer.

I walked slowly back to the school and my car, dredging for nuggets of fact within our bizarre, brief conversation. Had he been hearing voices or had he heard a voice? And how much of whatever it was should I relate to Mackenzie?

I saw a gopherlike image of Adam, brain aching from the scrambled bombardment of life, peeping out of the hole in the earth into which he'd fallen, searching for safety. And along I came, the great protector, taking whatever he gave me, forging it into a mallet, then hammering it directly onto his head, pounding him farther and further into the pit. Protecting him from himself.

No wonder there are no parables about my ancestors, the Unwittingly Horrible Samaritans.

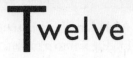Twelve

I WAS beyond tired. My marrow had dissolved. I wanted to be waited upon. Needed to be served. Yearned to be doted upon.

I wanted a mommy—a theoretical one, not my assigned one, because the latter would want answers, and currently, all her surprising largesse had done was raise more questions. I wanted a mommy who also knew massage.

I trudged toward the loft from the spot I'd finally found for my car—which, incidentally, was in as bad shape as I was, on its last legs, or bearings, but I couldn't think about that issue now.

As I turned the key I heard the faint sounds of the TV, slightly surprising, but it meant C.K. was home, so I entered, playing for my audience for all it was worth, posture slumped, head bowed forward. The picture of somebody the world had mistreated. Somebody who needed all the TLC in the world.

"Hey, hon." He waved casually from the sofa, his eyes never leaving the TV. Sprawled on a couch watching the tube in broad daylight—or at least narrow daylight, as night approached. All he lacked was the pink satin kimono, fluffy mules, and a box of bonbons.

I held the pity-me pose. He'd notice. My muscles spasmed. What was he doing staring at the tube like nobody I'd want to know?

He's tired, my inner nice person suggested. I told her to shut up. I knew he was. He'd worked all night. But in that case he should be in bed, sleeping. And if he was too wired to sleep, which happened, he should be doing something kind. Whipping up dinner or—bare minimum—turning his head away from the TV and asking me how my day had been. Being civil. In fact, he shouldn't even need to ask the question; one look at me should have summoned forth his emotional-paramedic techniques. Instantly. Had he given me one look.

I dropped the posturing—if a woman poses in the forest and nobody watches, is she still pitiable?—and dragged myself into the loft, just about commando-style, elbows propelling me across the loft floor. I might as well actually have done it for all the New Age–sensitive guyness my significant other demonstrated.

"Good flick," he said out loud, presumably to himself. "I like it every time." He noticed me staggering across the loft. "Come sit." He patted the square inch of couch he wasn't covering, ignoring the fumes coming out of my ears.

The cat, snuggled behind Mackenzie's knees, looked up balefully. I'd become not only irrelevant but a potential intruder. I ignored both of them and walked behind the couch to check the table where we tossed mail. Not that I expected anything beyond bills and circulars, and not that I was wrong.

It was a fairly good position from which to wring the man's

neck. Which thought, of course, reminded me of Emily Fisher. How had somebody done that to her? From behind? From where?

Better to think about make-believe. I checked out the TV. *North by Northwest*. I guess I should have felt relieved he wasn't hooked on a soap opera.

"Reminds me of my childhood," he said. " 'Cept, of course, they didn't have so many movies on TV then. No videos. No VCR. We went to the theater to see them, or my mother did. She adores Cary Grant. Not even his death has weakened that love. The household gods, Cary Grant and Katharine Hepburn. Anything they were in, together or apart, she'd go see and see and see. Wanted her boys to be like him, her girls to be like the great Katharine. Had an arrangement with the local theater—they did revival movies every so often—that she could have any posters that survived the showing. I remember . . ."

My world was decomposing and he was nattering about his mother's viewing habits?

"Look," he said, "here it comes—the crop-duster scene."

"Oh, of course!" I said. "It's *Cary*!"

"Uh-huh," he said.

"Not him—you! Your mother loved Cary Grant, wanted her boys to be like him—so of course—C for Cary!"

"Wrong."

I walked around the sofa and clicked off the set.

"Hey!" he said, sitting up. "Why'd you do that?" Macavity leaped to the floor, resettling in a hostile puff of dust-colored fur.

I folded my hands over my chest—primo teacher position. "Only way to get your attention, unless I get murdered."

"Dear God," he murmured.

That sort of male conciliatory behavior makes me crazier still. Conversing with the Lord about me, as if my behavior—or expected behavior—deserved divine sympathy.

"Look," he said, "I'm real sorry, but I've had a long, long time of it. I have three cases driving me silly, and I'm too wired to fall asleep, so—what's the harm in it? My favorite scene, too!"

132

"That's everybody's favorite scene. You're supposed to be different. Special. I'd think you'd be creative. Original." I had reached the refrigerator—the loft is spacious, but the living-dining-cooking area is all in one portion of it. "You're becoming a household cliché. Ordinary." I slammed the refrigerator door shut.

"Ordinary?" he echoed in a voice so low and soothing it alarmed me. That was the way you spoke to madmen. "Ordinary? Maybe I am, after all. But you surely are not, because ordinary would be now and then civil, compassionate, to her long-suffering man."

I was sorry I'd already slammed the refrigerator door. Opening it again in order to repeat the action seemed silly. So instead I snapped, "There's no dinner. I forgot to buy food and we're out of anything coherent and I don't care! I'm going to bed."

"Hey," he said mildly. "Whoa. What's wrong? Have a bad day?"

"A bad day? Bad? What is the meaning of 'bad'? How about a *pukey* day? A heinous day. A malevolent day. An atrocious day. A day that makes you not want to have any more days. A—"

He took a deep breath. "What happened?"

I struggled between the twin desires to keep sputtering and to move us on now that he was listening. To get sympathy at long last. This was my last port in the storm.

"First of all, I'm being fired."

Mackenzie raised an eyebrow, tilted his head, and shrugged mildly. "This isn't the first time."

"It's different now. Havermeyer told me as much. End of semester, end of me. And I'm not sure I care. I think maybe . . . maybe it's time for a change."

Of what, he should by all rights ask. Of scene? Of men? Or just of job?

Luckily, he didn't, because I wasn't sure about that, either.

"And they're still threatening to sue me. For battery. All part of their conviction that I'm after him."

Mackenzie looked oddly troubled by that—conflicted. Maybe even ready to react and say something, but I plowed on, not wanting to hear whatever it was. I didn't need more of his mulish attitude about Adam. That wasn't the issue at hand, and I didn't need to justify my actions with the man I lived with, of all people.

"And then two of my tenth graders overheard something at a tennis club and now—not that they're wrong, but they wrote an article for the paper about a major, major scandal at the school. A business selling substitute SAT exam takers, fake transcripts, fake letters of recommendation. They came to me because of the paper. It's just going to cap it all for Havermeyer."

"If you're already fired, why worry?"

That was not the correct response. I had said I was definitely fired, but I didn't 100 percent know that. And I didn't want to be—if I left, I wanted it to be on my terms. I wanted to call the shots. Jill and Nancy's discovery made the odds of that happening still worse. Mackenzie wasn't getting it.

"And *then*," I said, "I had to go back to the library. I left Lia's book there yesterday. The one she'd annotated and underlined, and they couldn't find it. Somebody must have taken it, and the kid's going to be heartsick. Understandably. I already am.

"And *then*, when I left, Adam was outside the library, waiting for me. Is that list sufficient to qualify me as having had a bad day?"

"Adam Evans."

I nodded. "He had somebody else's book bag yesterday. Wanted to return it." It was incredible how rational that made his actions sound, though they'd felt anything but.

"His book bag was next to the victim."

I nodded. "The librarian told me. When I was back there today." I finally sat down on a kitchen chair. "Mackenzie, you're here, you're chilling out—does that mean you have a suspect? An arrest?"

He sighed and looked at me as if he wished he were seeing something or somebody else. "We have a suspect, yes. But he's not under arrest unless you detained him and brought him here with you. This is not a subtle case. Only difficulty is findin' him."

"Adam?" I wanted to disagree, to pull out facts that would refute that, but I couldn't think of a single one.

"Where'd he go?"

"He ran off. He said he was okay, that his parents knew where he was. I have to assume he's with a friend, although he's an absolute loner at school. But I hate that he's your only suspect."

"Did he say he didn't do it? He was up there, Mandy."

I hadn't asked outright. Hadn't dared. "He said he found her. That she was dead. He may have overheard the actual killer. He heard a voice."

"Schizophrenics—some of them—hear voices. What did his say?"

I whispered it. " 'Kill.' Maybe 'dead.' "

"That's it?"

I nodded. "I think he heard himself. His own reaction to finding her on the floor."

"Or to deciding to kill her," Mackenzie said.

I hurried on to firmer ground. "I've found out a lot more about the dead woman. She's on the outs with a homeless advocate who's always there, and her sister, who was there, and her husband, who's been known to be there, and—"

"I don' get it," he said, standing up. "I don' get it at all. You're so convinced the kid's dangerous you practically accused him of murder before you knew that anybody was dead. Then—"

"I never! You're saying I made things worse for him, aren't you? Why? You've had the weirdest attitude all along whenever I even mentioned him. Why?"

His blue stare was enough to freeze-dry me. "We've been through this already," he said, and with me instead of Cary Grant in front of him, he ran out of energy.

"No," I insisted. "No, we haven't. You kept saying I would make it worse, but you didn't say why you were so sure."

"The thing is, Adam is the clear number-one suspect. All logic points to him, and so does his scarf and the book bag, and the truth is, in his case, we may not require logic. Kids in his class said he was angry with Ms. Fisher. She hollered at him—"

"She didn't shout."

"Whatever—the kids called it hollerin'. That may be motive

135

enough for him. An' he was there. He had opportunity. And the scarf . . ."

"Method," I mumbled.

He stretched, and I caught myself watching with admiration the shape of his torso against the blue shirt. Caught myself, and broke visual contact. This was no time for admiration.

"The thing also is, I'm sorry I doubted you early on. You were obviously right to be nervous about him, okay?"

"But—these other people. Her sister who owed money she couldn't repay, and her husband who wanted her out of the picture so he could run for Congress, and this advocate for the homeless—"

"Why?" he asked. "Why them? Why suddenly now? You are completely emotional about this. Back off. It's the only thing you can do. Just . . . plain . . . back off."

"You're like a posse, determined to get Adam when there's no reason to—"

"I can't talk to you anymore than I have about this case. You know that. I can only say—ask—beg you to stay clear of it. Leave that boy alone. Let things work out as they will. You aren't helpin' anybody, you're just . . ." He sighed and half turned from me. "I wish, just now and then and again, maybe once a year, that you'd listen to me. Believe that in some instances, I have experience on my side."

"About mental illness?"

"Maybe. People who kill aren't the most stable portion of the population."

"You don't trust me at all, is what's wrong. You act like maybe I'm an idiot—and as if I'm *harming* Adam, not trying to help him." Why not blame my worst fear on the man in the blue shirt? It eased the guilt—the part about Adam. Later I'd worry about the guilt of dumping what wasn't his on Mackenzie. "And you don't take my situation seriously at all. I'm being fired. And sued. All hell is about to break out at school. You could show a little sympathy! You could *care!*"

"I do," he said. "Maybe too much for anybody's mental health. I'm real tired, is all. An' I have to go back in too short a while. I'll try a nap if it's all the same to you."

It's nearly impossible to have a truly successful squabble in a loft without divider walls. There's the bathroom and the bedroom and that's it. I used to live in a tiny three-story warren of under-sized rooms. It had its problems, but you could storm off and sulk without exposure to the elements. Here it was much more challenging.

He stopped halfway to the bedroom and paused, as if waiting for me to say something or waiting to hear himself say something, but we remained mute.

Only Macavity took a stand and made his preferences clear. He checked the scene and, after a discreet moment, sauntered off with Mackenzie.

I watched the male residents, human and feline, until they were behind the bedroom door, and thought only about how closed-minded Mackenzie had been. If that was the approach of the Philadelphia police department, Adam was as good as behind bars. And Mackenzie had as much as said that my ranting about the student was part and parcel of why he was so sure Adam was guilty.

Guess I could eliminate mediation, arbitration, and diplomacy from my list of possible future careers.

Thirteen

THE weekend, at least the part of it during which Mackenzie and I cohabited, passed in a cordial chill. Something
was out of kilter and we both knew it, but neither of
us chose to look at it too closely or discuss it. We'd had another
date with Andy and Juliana, but once again they canceled out. Apparently they were having problems. So were we, but theirs were
faster arriving and out of the closet. We rented videos and sat in
parallel silences, viewing them.

No mention of Emily Fisher or Adam Evans. But twice I answered the phone to hear labored, agitated breathing and "My
scarf!" When I asked if it was Adam, when I said his name—softly,

so that Mackenzie didn't overhear—and told him to please let me help him, he clicked off.

For once, the arrival of Monday was welcome relief. Back to something, which was better than the growing nothingness at home in the loft.

I skimmed through the morning, trying so hard not to think about everything that felt truly important, trying not to look too closely, to notice the missing Adam, to spot his parents back at the school, trying not to say anything that might further inflame or upset, and most of all trying not to think about either my personal or professional life—that by noon, my jaw hurt from clenching my teeth. The weather was benign—a breeze, not a wind, sunshine and temperatures in the sixties—and the school felt anything but, so I decided to spend my lunch hour out-of-doors.

At the corner, I bought a soft pretzel with mustard, and breathed deeply for the first time that day before taking my first delicious bite. I considered my options. I could drop in on Sasha, as I hadn't seen her in a while. She was participating in an experiment at a local research lab, more precisely, a "smell" center where busy scientists and their subjects devise better deodorants and room sprays.

Her malodorous phase should have ended by now, but until I was sure, I passed on an unannounced visit. The only sense I hadn't been stifling all day was that of smell. No need to work on censoring that one, too, so instead of Sasha, I'd take care of The Birthday Gift.

Even if I was angry with Mackenzie, even though I was so disappointed in the dull distancing that had come between us that I didn't even try to look into the future, even if the entire idea of monogamy was losing its appeal, ignoring my partner's birthday would be cruel and wrong and frighteningly final. I was still fixated on the idea of a lovely old history book.

I relaxed a little with a sense of direction, a project I could accomplish. Good going, I complimented myself. With renewed energy and sense of purpose, I turned toward Locust Street—and smashed into Terry Labordeaux. He stepped back, laughed, and straightened the bridge of his glasses.

"I'm sorry!" we said in unison.

"I was hoping to find you," he said, "although not necessarily so . . . abruptly."

My sense of purpose ebbed. He'd come to see me on my lunch hour. Nice? Yes. Nice.

"Because—" He was wearing a tan raincoat that of course looked slept in. He reached into his pocket and said, "Voilà!" And there was Lia's *Turn of the Screw*.

I know it was just a trick of the sunshine through the nearly bare trees, but he was suddenly bathed in light spelling out "H-E-R-O."

"I cannot thank you enough," I said. "In honesty, after it wasn't there Friday, I never expected to see it again."

He fell into step next to me. "I believe that persistence pays," he said, putting all due spin and possible meanings onto his words. "And is rewarded with another opportunity to visit with you."

I had the fleeting idea that perhaps the book had been in the lost and found all along, but he'd decided to make it a token in the courting ritual. Then I decided that was ridiculous, and I was reading too much into his polite gallantries.

"Besides," he said, "I couldn't rest until I found out what you told your student. The girl who annotated the book."

Lia had, of course, asked about the book and I'm ashamed to say I'd danced around the truth, although I didn't precisely lie. I simply said, "Oh, no—it isn't with me." But did I have to tell this man about my weasel words? I glanced over at him, and my expression must have shown my confusion.

"Well, you know," Terry said. "Here you are. A complete turnabout. This time, the teacher didn't have her assignment. So what did you say? That the dog ate your homework? Or did your mother write you a note and say you had the flu? What?"

I grudged a smile, which seemed to satisfy him. Then he looked around at the swarms of student. "Did I interrupt you? You seemed very much on your way somewhere. Am I keeping you?"

"I do have to hurry. They don't give us luxurious lunch hours, and even with a prep period afterward . . . I'm in search of a book, a gift. If you like, come along. It's right up your alley."

"There's a bookstore up my alley?"

"There's a rare-book store on Locust."

"He looked thoughtful and slightly puzzled. "Bauman's?" he asked.

I hadn't ever noticed its name, just the books and the look of the inviting shop, but of course he'd be right. "I knew you'd know it."

He shrugged and walked beside me. "You're buying a rare book as a gift? he asked.

I knew I was supposed to explain for whom I sought such an expensive luxury. What I didn't know was how detailed a picture of my emotional life I wanted him to have. So instead of answering, I sidestepped. "I'm hoping to," I finally said. "I'm not sure how much cash 'rare' translates into. Do you know? Not the million-dollar ones you mentioned when my class was at the library."

He looked at me as if he were x-raying my brain, trying to see what and who was really inside there, figuring out for whom I was shopping and what that meant. "It varies," he said, "but more than ordinary new books cost, for certain. What sort of book are you after?"

I sighed and shook my head. "Wish I knew. History, probably. Americana. Or poetry."

His turn to sigh, for whatever reasons. He checked his watch. "I'm afraid you'll have to explore on your own. It's right over there." He waved across the street, and I saw it. "I would see you to the door, like a proper gentleman, but I have to go back."

"Really?" My disappointment was audible. Even I heard it. And then I realized he'd misinterpret it as romantic sorrow. "I was hoping . . . you know so much about this."

"Sorry," he said, his voice tight, and I knew that once again I'd managed to hurt his feelings. "I'll . . . see you."

"Hope so," I said. And meant it, which didn't help my mental muddle. "And thanks again for finding that book. Saved me from having to fall on my sword."

And he was gone. I crossed the street and entered a wonderland out of the past: a town house lined with polished wood shelves filled with gold-etched brandy and burgundy and deep green leather-bound volumes. I inhaled the place. If I could live there, I'd be able to think through all my problems and reach sane and calm conclusions. Sherlock Holmes lived in rooms like this, lined with books like these. Anywhere else, he wouldn't have been as bright. I wondered if they took boarders.

A charitable gentleman showed me volumes of Americana. Charitable because he continued to be helpful and considerate even after I gasped at the first price tag.

Mackenzie would have been in heaven there. The books were lovely to look at and hold, and their contents—firsthand accounts of early explorations and discoveries—were precisely what delighted Mackenzie's soul. The only snake I found in this bookish Eden was the realization that the less a volume has been read, the more valuable it is. A loved and much-used book with all the marks of wear and tear is devalued, but if the pages have never even been cut, up goes the price. So one might be a book lover—but not a book reader.

"This would be perfect," I said. "Absolutely perfect for him." I held a volume of verse that told the history of Daniel Boone. I was sure the poetry would be forgettable, but the combination of two of Mackenzie's passions—poetry and history—and the impulse someone had felt to combine them were irresistible. Only the price tag, somewhat over six hundred dollars, was resistible, although in this emporium, that paltry amount made it a bargain-book-table special.

"I think it's in Sabin," the kindly gentleman said, pulling out a reference book, as if I truly were about to tell him to wrap it in special birthday paper. "Possibly also Howe," he continued. "Let me look. You might enjoy learning more about it."

The book had credentials. It had a book of its own!

Sabin was one of the thousands of reference books documenting these precious volumes, the man explained. Nonetheless, the name made me think of the oral polio vaccine guy, which in turn made me feel as if I was experiencing déjà think. "Don't go to any bother," I said. "I have to work on the budget, decide whether I can manage it. I'm a schoolteacher. . . ." Maybe it was the paneling, the feel of the place, but I became a Dickens character—the pathetic match girl pressing her nose against a warm household's windowpane. I put down the book, thanked the man, and left, filled with anger at my life. Why didn't I make enough money for a gesture like that? It wasn't even a selfish impulse—I wanted to be able to give a gift I was sure would please.

I knew there were worse problems than an inability to buy rare books, but still and all, I was more depressed when I left than when I'd entered. A bad way to spend a lunch hour. Then I realized I was close to Antique Row, that street of upscale hand-me-downs—more things I couldn't afford, even if I wanted them—and among the collections there was Helena Spurry's.

I hadn't been in Traditions!, but I'd visited its neighbors with Sasha on a long and frustrating search for photo props. I'd marveled at the fine line that divides garage sales, thrift shops, and antiques boutiques, because along with finely crafted and classically styled furnishings, I'd found kitschy items I remembered from my parents' home. There are many things to praise about my parents, but a sense of style isn't on the list.

Before they moved to Boca Raton, they'd rid themselves of the selfsame googly-eyed cat clock I saw for sale on Pine Street with an impressive tag, and a kidney-shaped blond wood coffee table I saw with another ridiculous tag. My parents had put their clock and table out on the curb, free for the taking.

Nothing my untrained eye could spot seemed changed since the last time I'd looked through Helena Spurry's windows. I remembered the ridiculously proportioned and water-stained armoire and the dining room table that ran almost the entire width of the store.

I peered around the annoying gold Gothic-style lettering that screamed TRADITIONS! across the plate glass. I tried not to see the exclamation point, because it made me feel I had to, well, exclaim!

It was difficult seeing clearly into the store. It had the muted lighting of most antiques stores—a dimness that makes me suspicious. What would bright lights reveal? But I thought I could see enough to realize the store was deserted, except for someone silhouetted as she crossed a doorway at the back. Helena, I supposed.

I don't have the expertise or patience to comb through stores like this. I loved owning a few pieces of my grandmother's, because of the connection, and their destruction when my house went kaput still makes me sad. I'd be honored to have an old piece that held emotional overtones—a gift, an inheritance, a token of affection, a souvenir. But I'm stunned that people pay extra to own a stranger's crackling, peeling, fraying, or mismatched castoffs.

Or perhaps people don't. This wasn't a heavily trafficked stretch of sidewalk, and in fact I was the only one there except for two men leaning against a nearby wall discussing the coming baseball season.

Dust motes floated in the still, yellowish air of the shop. This was a place to keep its owner occupied, not a place expected to turn a profit. It gave one pause to wonder what Helena Spurry was doing with a high-end, empty shop.

And what she'd been doing in the Rare Book Department.

A check of the time—via my wristwatch, not any of the malfunctioning timepieces in Helena's window—showed that I had to be back in twenty minutes. But there was always after school. I was in no rush to head home these days. The tension floating in our atmosphere made Helena's dusty shop sparkle in comparison.

I found a working phone in only five blocks of searching, and called Sasha. "Are you still—"

"Nope," she said. "I am no longer the handmaiden of science"

"Finished?"

"Sweet as a flower once more."

"Then can you meet me around three-thirty at Traditions!, the antiques shop on Pine?"

"You sound like you're on speed."

"I respect punctuation. That exclamation point makes me crazy.

Or, rather, crazy! Anyway, can you make it? Let's pretend you're looking for props for a shoot."

"Why would we?" Then I heard a weary, ridiculously overdone intake of breath. "Don't tell me. I can't believe you! I saw your school in the paper with that murder—tell me you aren't . . . what's this about?"

"Okay."

"What?"

"I won't tell you." But I did. I briefly explained, including the part about my having unwittingly set up Adam Evans as prime suspect. "And I'm intimidated by stores like this. I don't know the language. I would seem a phony for sure. I don't know furniture makers and periods and what's kitsch instead of junk. But if you were looking for props, it'd be different. Maybe I could get her chatting, because I saw her at the library—and she was wearing a scarf that could strangle a horse."

There was an overlong silence. "This kid," she finally said. "He could be dangerous, and he's definitely getting you into trouble, so why not just back off and—"

"Never mind." Sasha was fearless when it came to the opposite sex. Stupid, to be brutally honest. Reckless and always endangering herself. But that was where her sense of adventure ended. "I'll figure out a way—"

"Oh, hell, I'll meet you," she said.

As I knew she would.

"Wanted to talk with you, anyway," she added. "I had time for a lot of thinking while I was socially unacceptable, and I decided to move."

"Why?" She lives in a luxury condo that was her father's. Between two of his many marriages, he gifted her with it—wrote it off his taxes. In any case, it allows her to live in a manner she could never otherwise afford on her uncertain and irregular earnings. Maybe she was going to rent it out and live more humbly. I could understand that.

Emily Fisher's place was available. I was ashamed of the thought.

It felt disrespectful of the dead. Nonetheless, good apartments are not easily come by. "If you want to stay on this side of the city, I know of a building near Washington Square."

"I'm thinking London."

I tried to think of what section of Philadelphia was called London. She read my mind, or rather my absent, malfunctioning mind. "The London that's in England," she said. "I need a major change of scene. I can't believe I'm in my thirties and I've never gone anywhere. I still live in the city I grew up in, even though my parents have moved on. I still see the same people. Haven't tried anything really scary, if you exempt men, and I haven't seen anything, if you again exempt men. It's time. Feels like maybe my last chance, in fact."

I was sorry I'd called her. Her words and decision made me sad. Which is not to say I didn't understand. Even my mother would understand these days. That made me sadder still.

"We'll talk," I said. "After school."

London. I tried the word out on my way back to Philly Prep. London. It sat on my tongue, melting into it like imported hard candy, tart and sweet. Now there was an idea. Cambridge, Oxford. How narrow my horizons were. I hadn't considered anything that far, that new and different. I wondered if my parents' largesse included overseas adventures or whether my mother would balk because long-distance calls would be prohibitively expensive.

I let my mind float across the Atlantic to an entirely new life, and my mood and stride lightened up. That live-in-the-moment, be-here-now credo was passé. Didn't work. My new mantra was: Be anywhere else, and be there soon.

BY THE MIDDLE of the afternoon, I decided I was having a decent day. Nobody had served me with papers saying I was being sued; Havermeyer had avoided me as assiduously as I was avoiding him; Nancy and Jill's exposé was not yet in print; Lia's book had been found; a man—Terry—had definitely flirted with me; Adam was still missing, which at least meant the police didn't have him, so there was time and opportunity for other ideas to reach the law;

and on the more ordinary, teacherly front, there were actually interesting responses from my tenth graders, whose assignment had been to write their entries for the hypothetical Philly Prep alumni newsletter of 2075. Although a few had skirted the assignment by having a classmate convey the sad news that they were long since dead and hadn't made much of their short lives, others exerted their creativity in trying to think ahead.

> Since retiring from the chairmanship of the Interplanetary Interior Designers Alliance, I've been on the lecture circuit, showing slides of my beach house on Alpha Centauri and the use of asteroidal materials in furniture construction. . . .

> I have five daughters. Two of them are Nobel prize–winning scientists, one is an Olympic skater, one is an opera singer, and my youngest plays Nana on *Days of Our Lives*. They've produced seventeen grandchildren (all girls—girls rule!). I had my family while simultaneously pursuing my Oscar-winning film career (of course, my husband helped by staying home and doing all the cooking—thanks, hon!), but I'm taking things easier these days on the other side of the screen, as a film critic on Channel Three. Not many good roles for ninety-year-old women, so instead I see every film that's made, and get paid for it. Pretty good, huh?

> I enjoyed both my terms as the first female president of the United States and want to thank my former Philly Prep classmates for their support. All your photos are in my presidential library. Come visit! And I owe all my success to my tenth-grade English teacher, Ms. Pepper, may she rest in peace.

That wouldn't get her a higher grade, but I admired her for trying.

I liked their dreams, as ridiculous as they were. Might as well reach for Alpha Centauri. I wondered what I would have written at their age, whether I had dreams I could no longer recall. Well, I decided, whether or not I did, I was going to start cultivating them right away. That very moment.

I felt a lot better about everything as I prepared to leave the building for the second time that day. En route to the exit, I checked my office cubicle and was relieved to find no summons to Havermeyer, no furious note from the Evanses. Life was giving me a break.

Rachel Leary put a hand out and touched my shoulder as I was leaving the office. "Did you hear?" she asked, making the question sound like a sigh.

There went the day. "What?"

"About him."

"Havermeyer?" I had a wild surge of elation. He'd quit. He'd been fired. He'd relocated to Bolivia.

"Adam."

"Adam what? Oh, God, what?"

Her hand flew to her mouth. "You didn't hear. I thought one of his classmates would have . . ." Her complexion was still frighteningly pale, and she had dark circles under her eyes. That pregnant glow was taking its time about gracing her. But just then she looked worse than her normally pallid self. She looked heartsick.

"He didn't . . . he didn't kill himself, did he?" My worst fear. That boy in the rain. That boy with nowhere to go.

She shook her head. "He robbed a dentist's office."

It was so ridiculous compared to suicide, I laughed out loud, imagining him stealing false teeth, toothbrushes, floss. "A sudden surge of interest in personal hygiene?"

Helga the Office Witch strained to hear. Helga was deaf to requests—but boy, could she overhear. I steered Rachel out to the hallway.

"Why in God's name?" I whispered once we were out of Helga-land. Luckily, the remaining students who milled around, heading for the street, were consistent. They'd never had and still didn't have any interest in what I had to say.

"He and this creep he's staying with stole nitrous oxide. Laughing gas. It's used at raves, those dance parties?"

I nodded.

"But it can be lethal. And with Adam's chemistry already off . . ." She shook her head again. "Somebody—I have no idea who—described him, and the police are sure it was our Adam."

I thought about it. "The police already think he's a murderer. Stealing nitrous oxide isn't going to make it any worse on him. At least I can't see how it would."

Rachel shook her head. "I meant he's playing with death. He's out on the streets, hanging with bad sorts, and he has no judgment. He could have died last night. I gather the friend dragged him home—to Adam's home—thinking he was dying. He was lucky this time."

"How'd you find this out?"

She inhaled sharply. "His mother called Havermeyer. Adam was there. Havermeyer told me because I'm supposed to know that kind of thing about the students, but I gather that everything was couched as an accusation—somehow this is all your fault. Well, a bit apparently is mine—I did inadequate counseling, hence this entire mess.

"Like dominoes, is what Mrs. Evans said. Because I did not do my job well enough, you were able to physically and emotionally attack her son without fear of recrimination, and then, mad with that triumph, you upped the ante and involved him in a homicide case, which forced him to live dangerously, on the street, associating with unsavory people, and because of that, he nearly killed himself last night."

What could I say? There was a possibility she was right. I took a series of deep breaths. "Where is he now?" I finally said.

She shook her head. "Gone again. As of this morning. Parents swear they don't know where. But listen, Mandy, there's more."

More. The more was never something insignificant, tacked on. "Something else."

Something worse. I did not want to hear. I wished I knew how to faint dead away, but I am unfortunately too sturdy for that, so I had to listen to whatever was coming.

"You're my friend, and I'd want to know if the situation were reversed. For all I know, it may be." She laughed, rather nervously.

"Rachel, this is obviously difficult for you to say, but please, please say it."

She nodded and sighed. "While I was talking to Havermeyer, he got a call, and from what he was saying, Mandy, I'm positive they're advertising for an English teacher, who will also run the newspaper, starting in the autumn."

I nodded.

"So unless they're expanding the school, adding classes . . . Is anyone in your department planning to leave?"

"Planning? No. Nobody plans. We're English teachers. We know old sayings, collective wisdom such as 'The best-laid plans . . .' "

Fired.

It had been a threat, something that I'd been sure I'd get out of—but now I was really and truly going to be history. This chapter of my life was over.

And damn, but did I have to get news of it on a day when I'd actually gotten good compositions?

Fourteen

I DROVE home fighting vision blurred by frustration and fury. Havermeyer had implied he'd wait awhile. Despite my play for sympathy with Mackenzie, despite my insistence that I'd been fired, I'd been privately sure that with some salvage work I could keep my options open.

Instead they were advertising for my replacement. How dare they!

That was it, then. I'd never darken that door again. Never come back. Not even to collect my paltry possessions. Never. I'd show them. Show him.

And then the biggest escape route I'd yet imagined came back into mental view. England. I'd go, too. I slammed my car door shut and locked up. England, I thought as I stomped toward my soon-to-be-abandoned home. London. Save money by rooming with Sasha and—

Sasha! I checked the time, ran back to my car, and drove to Pine Street, where I wound up being too late to cruise for a spot. I was hostile paying the parking attendant, slapping bills onto his hand, as if it were his fault I'd screwed up.

She was waiting. It's hard to miss a six-foot-tall woman in high heels—or high buttoned boots, as the case actually was. Sasha never differentiates between street clothes and costumes, and that day she was done up in Edwardian duds, a long skirt, those boots, and a high, ruffled blouse. The only anachronism was the camera strapped around her neck. "For effect," she said when I gestured at it. "I'm looking for props, aren't I? I should look like a photographer."

"You are a photographer."

"I should look like a *busy* photographer. And what is it I should be hunting in there?"

"Inspiration. Nothing specific, nothing she can say she doesn't have."

"Who are you supposed to be?" Sasha asked.

"Your friend. In fact, that's the only solid job classification I've got left." We were out on the sidewalk, hardly the best time or situation for major life revelations, but it was a nice day and I felt stretched as far as I could go. The pressures building inside me needed an escape valve, or the hope of one. "Sasha," I said, "would you consider having a roommate in England?"

"I don't know. My style might make a Brit uncomfortable, and I'm leery of adjusting to anybody else's, too, plus—"

"I mean me."

Her eyebrows lifted, and she smiled. "Really? Incredible! That'd be great, that'd be—" Her eyebrows lowered. "I'm talking England," she said softly. "The one across the Atlantic Ocean."

"I know. I'm talking grad school over there."

She narrowed her eyes, stared at me.

"Then maybe we should both be talking Mackenzie." They'd been at war, politely but adamantly, for a long time, but had struck a pact somewhere along the way, and now she was one of C.K.'s biggest fans. "You know, your love? Lover? Roommate? Possibly the last good man in town?"

I shrugged.

"You'd . . . leave him?"

"Don't think of it in those terms." Leaving men, or being left, was Sasha's specialty. Actually, it was a family trait and probably genetic. Generations of her family switched partners seasonally. There was no reason for her to stand on the sidewalk, gape-mouthed. "This isn't about him. It's my adventure . . . my finding something new."

"But you and—this really upsets me. What happened?"

"Nothing. Absolutely nothing. I'm just—I'm having an attack of feeling exactly the way you do. I need a change, I need to do something. I'm being fired, anyway, so I'm basically being forced to make a change. My *mother* thinks I should change, too. Grad school was her idea—well, mine, of course, originally, but now out of the blue she says she'll pay my tuition. She says I shouldn't rush into marriage. As if I were doing that."

"Your mother? Bea Pepper?"

I nodded. "That mother."

"She said that?"

"Did you answer my question about wanting a roommate?"

"I never thought about . . . well, if you were actually there and . . . sure," she said without enthusiasm. "But . . . you and Mackenzie . . . he's special, Mandy. You're out of your mind—unless there's something." She waited. "Some*body*? As in else?" She waited again. For half a second, the librarian with the gold-brown eyes occupied my mind, but—I shook my head. "Then something really bad. Something not negotiable." When I still didn't offer up a something or someone, she shook her head and continued. "Then you're nuts.

You were going to be the ones who made it, the exception to the rule. The reason hope can keep springing eternal. This is so—"

"Let's go in before she closes," I said. "It's odd that it's open at all. Given that her sister was murdered, she might have closed out of respect." I wondered when the funeral would be, whether the police still were holding the body and if so, how long they'd keep it. Mackenzie might have answered my questions, had I asked, had we attempted to stop snarling at each other.

Sasha gave a histrionic sigh to make sure I knew she wasn't finished with the subject. She even stamped one boot-shod foot. And then we entered the store, which was still devoid of customers. "Hope you don't mind if I browse," Sasha told the proprietor, who approached us with a smile tuned to precisely the right degree of intensity. Not desperately pleased to see us, simply glad enough. "I'm Sasha Berg, and I'm a photographer. I have an assignment that calls for me to create a certain ambience in the background. Can't yet define it, but I know it would be period, though which, I'm not sure. Definitely amber light and all, you see it?"

Helena Spurry, looking as chic and slicked back as when I'd last seen her, was again dressed monochromatically, this time in chocolate brown slacks and shirt. And again, she wore an oversized printed scarf—cream and caramel, this go-round—artfully draped over one shoulder. The black and gold necklace again wound around part of the scarf, and then hung below it. Obviously, her signature look—the look of a bored, Americanized matador. She harmonized perfectly with the soft yellow light and aging waxed woods that surrounded her. She ran her thumb and index finger down the chain, and I wondered whether a scarf wrapped around a chain could do its fatal damage without leaving ligature marks.

The scarf and chain apparently served her as a talisman, something to clutch when life or Sasha's remarks confounded her, as was apparently now the case. She had no idea what Sasha meant—how could she? Sasha herself didn't. But Helena was ready to help make it happen. I suspected she was thrilled to have actual people walk through her door, and I wondered what she did all day while she waited for the likes of us. There were just so many times you could dust furniture before you wore off its finish.

"This is my friend, Amanda," Sasha said. "She's helping me. She's familiar with the client's taste. She's not a pro, but she has a good eye."

I took that as a compliment and tried to assume an air of good-eyehood, landing judgmental and stern-edged glances on Helena Spurry's wares.

"Are you looking for large or small pieces? We have table settings to armoires." Helena gestured at the crackled, water-stained monster I'd noticed through the window.

Sasha glanced my way. I frowned, confused, then realized I was supposed to be helping her make these momentous decisions. I shook my head. "Not the right feel," I said. "Too intimidating. Besides, the water stain . . ." I shook my head sadly at its imperfection.

"The Johnstown flood." Helena fingered her chain. "This was in the home of the banker when the waters rushed in. I consider it a historical marker, surely not a mere stain."

"Interesting." Hereafter I would think of all splits, tears, blemishes, and ravels that way. Nothing would ever wear out. It would instead become historically marked. A good philosophy for my impending impoverished life.

Helena looked from one of us to the other. "May I ask what the product is?"

"It's actually . . . not so much a product shoot as a portrait," Sasha said. "But the subject is rather an eccentric. Happily, she can afford to be however she pleases, although it makes certain things, like this portrait, more difficult than they need to be. She wants a definite feel to her setting, her style, more or less, while she doesn't want any invasion of her privacy. We are shooting this in my studio because she does not want people—including me—trooping through her actual house. Her personal collection is quite distinctive, and much of it's museum-quality, but she never opens her house for charity and is close to being a recluse. Doesn't want anything she owns in photos, on record. Encourages thieves, I suppose. Odd, then, to want to do a portrait with props that simulate the look she loves, I know," Sasha rambled as she held up a flowered china bowl. "But still and all, not as odd as some of my clients."

Helena had no choice but to laugh along with Sasha, to act as if her client list were also chockablock with peculiar people. Both women were lying. Sasha had no stable of clients and barely scraped by—in fact, I'd have to ask her how she planned to stay alive in London before I considered sharing her flat—and Helena seemed the only member of humankind sincerely interested in the contents of her store.

I looked at the two financially struggling women and made another major occupational decision: nothing under the heading of self-employed. It might seem appealing to have no boss, no possible Havermeyer, but the downside was too frightening. With that thought, I felt as if I'd made great strides forward in one of the many upended segments of my life.

"Are you planning to buy or rent these items?" Helena asked.

"Buy them, of course," Sasha said. "And then M—my client will donate them to charity."

I was intrigued by this imaginary eccentric, although Helena's business wasn't going to improve via a figment. How did her shop stay afloat? This was the vocation of a woman who existed in a different place than Helena did. This was the comfortable retreat of a comfortable woman, but for Helena this was a fantasy, projecting an image of financial security. It had nothing to do with reality, with paying actual bills. This was indeed a catastrophe waiting to happen.

Or what had precipitated a catastrophe in the library.

"Have you—Traditions!—been here long?" Sasha asked, lifting a piece of red Bohemian cut glass. She passed it to me. I loved the way even the feeble sunbeam that made its way past the looming furniture and around the porcelain shepherds slid through the ruby glass. But as one or the other of us was going to have to buy whatever we decided would make a good prop for our imaginary friend, I twirled the glass, squinted at it, then regretfully put it down.

"Six months," Helena said.

"Where was the store before then?" I asked.

Helena looked taken aback and annoyed. "Traditions! was born six months ago."

When her sister had loaned her the bulk of her share of their mother's inheritance. And almost immediately needed it back. Had anybody believed that this hobby shop would support anyone?

I meanwhile stammered along, searching for the subtle way to ask, *By the way, did you strangle your sister with your long scarf or necklace?* "I've been thinking of opening my own place, being my own boss," I said. "How do you do it? For example, have you always collected antiques?"

"I've always enjoyed fine things, craftsmanship, beautiful objects, classic design. For myself and others, whom I help with their interior design. And I've collected through auctions and travel for years, so once I had the capital and a location, setting up was quick, but it isn't easy turning your passion into a business, no matter what anybody tells you. Of course, a great deal depends on what your merchandise is. Bagels aren't the same as heirlooms. What sort of store do you have in mind?"

"Oh, I thought . . ." I hadn't thought. I'd only spoken. I had nothing in my mind except a wish that, for once, I'd get things straight before I nattered on.

"Tchotchkes," Sasha said. "That's a scientific term for this and that. She adores stuff nobody needs."

"Don't make it sound tacky," I said, instantly defensive about the merit of my nonexistent collection. "It's . . . memorabilia. Letters, posters, the ephemera of popular culture." I had it, and I was ready to roll now. "Old magazines, original movie posters—" I was getting into it, ready to phone up Mackenzie's mother and ask if she'd like to sell her Hepburn-Grant posters. "And the prizes they used to give out, and—"

"I see," Helena said, underwhelmed.

"Of course, you could have been open for years and I'm so oblivious." Sasha to the rescue while I felt stung and sorry for myself—what was so bad about *my* things? "I'm not a collector myself," Sasha said as her thousandth lie of the day. "I inherited my furniture."

A thousand and one lies. Although who's to say that acquiring one's furniture and wardrobe from secondhand shops isn't "inheriting" it?

"Mostly I work with art directors who choose everything, so I'm not really up to date with what's around," Sasha babbled on. "Mandy, this is quite nice, don't you think?" She held up a gracefully shaped oil lamp.

I nodded, then caught a glimpse of the price tag, which had way too many digits. I said in a stage whisper, "Do you think your client wants to be identified with oil?" I kept my eyebrows up a ridiculously long time, miming my keen desire for Sasha to "get it"—or pretend there was something to get. Would Helena buy the suggestion that Pew family members would find a gilt-and-crystal lamp too symbolic of the Sun Oil foundation of their fortune, and therefore bad?

"You know what would be fabulous?" People into props and antiques, people with a good eye, used words like *fabulous*, I thought. "Something like that chain you're wearing. Elegant, understated, but bold. I can just see—ah, the client in it, can't you, Sasha? It isn't old, is it? I mean, it's a reproduction, isn't it? We could probably get one for her—she's not wearing her own jewels this time, is she?"

"Doubt it," Sasha said. "You know how she is."

Helena again touched the chain, as if to verify its reality. "This is old. Quite. A family heirloom. It was my mother's and her mother's before her. Made in Vienna, last century. What made you think it was a reproduction?"

"I . . ." I couldn't think of another way to the truth except by using the truth. "I saw one like it last week. Admired it, is why I remember so vividly. At the library. Logan Square? I mean, the de-tail work—those black stones, framed in gold, the way they're set and all . . ."

Sasha stared at me as if I were a foreign film without subtitles.

"But I must be mistaken, if it's one of a kind." I shook my head, miming a slow mind piecing things out, I hoped. "Unless it was you! It must have been you. I'm afraid I was looking more at the necklace than at its owner."

Helena touched the chain and backed off a step. "I suppose there's more than one, then," she mumbled.

"Thinking about that necklace makes me remember everything that happened that day. Awful. A woman was murdered."

Helena bowed her head slightly and straightened the scarf on her shoulder. I thought she might mention that the dead woman was her sister, but perhaps she was simply being professional in keeping her silence.

"Was that you?" I asked. "In the library?"

She looked peeved. "Possibly," she said. "I have a . . . a friend there. It's a pleasant walk, a bit of exercise, so I frequently join . . . the friend for lunch. Or I look at old books of photos, prints for ideas . . ."

"This was Thursday morning."

She looked at me sharply. "Thursday?" She shook her head. "I don't think so." She actually went in search of a date book and flipped pages. "No," she said.

"Sorry, then. It was somebody else." I made my voice and body language as perky as I dared, tossing out I'm-no-threat vibes like fairy dust to blind her. "And probably a different necklace design altogether. It's just that look, maybe. The big scarf and the chain, but my memory stinks. Anyway, I was in the Rare Book Depart-ment, not the print department or cafeteria, where you'd be."

Her pale skin blanched even more. I plodded on, doing a dumb-blonde routine even though my hair is a fairly intense red-brown. "I remember where I was because . . . because that's where the woman . . ." My voice was down to a whisper. "Where . . . you know.

159

Later in the day, where it happened," I finished lamely. "Right outside it."

Helena tightened her lips and held them that way before she spoke. "A crazy person did it. They should lock them all up. They're ruining the city. They ruin business—nobody wants to crawl over them to get into a store. And now they're killing people."

"Horrible, isn't it?" Sasha held a leather box with straps for closures, one of those things that never had a possible function but looked stunning.

Sasha might keep having a good time with her imaginary assignment, but I'd reached a dead end. Helena had been at the library. She'd admit it, I bet, if asked again. I had nothing beyond a memory of her standing over that case—the visual equivalent of hearsay, so now what? I was desperate enough to try for the truth, or something akin to it. "My sister knew her. My sister was friends with the . . . victim."

"Really?"

I nodded. "Good friends. She was even at a housewarming party for the . . . victim this past weekend."

"Really?" Helena's interest was honest and complete. "I was at that party, too. I might know your sister. Mind my asking what her name is?"

"Beth Wyman." I saw the flash of recognition, thought I saw the irritation, too, but it was quickly stifled.

"Of course," Helena said. "Then you must be the little sister. The schoolteacher. She mentioned she'd been to see you."

"So you are . . . you were a friend of the woman who . . . of hers as well?"

After a long pause, Helena spoke. "I'm her sister," she said.

"I'm so sorry! That's . . ."

She half nodded and brushed away any further commiserations. "My sister was an unlucky woman."

"My brother-in-law works with . . . I guess he's your brother-in-law, then," I said.

"Ray." She managed to get five syllables' worth of disdain into the short name, to make it sound like a curse.

"The boy who they think did it," I said softly. "He's my student. The one you called crazy."

"That's what the TV called him."

I thought they'd used rather less inflammatory terms, but so be it. "I don't think he did it. I think he's innocent. What would his motive possibly be?"

"Crazy people do crazy things." She fingered her necklace, then pulled her hand away, looking worried by her automatic gesture. We'd run out of discussion prospects.

I glanced at my watch. "Sasha, I'm going to have to get to that appointment. Maybe we could come back tomorrow?"

"Actually, I'm closing the store for the day tomorrow," Helena said. "Family matters."

"Then another time," I murmured. "Thank you so much for letting us browse. Again, my condolences. And I'm sorry for the mix-up."

She looked puzzled.

"About the library. Thinking I'd seen you up in the Rare Book Department."

She nodded curtly, then looked at Sasha, who was running a finger over the intricate raised design on a high, narrow chest of drawers. "Anything?" she asked. "Anything you want to consider? Anything I could hold for you? You'd be under no obligation, of course, but this way it would be here, for a reasonable time, while you decide."

It was so loud and clear, despite the soft voice trying to hide it. Her near desperation was deafening. I felt an unwanted pang of sympathy for Helena and her miserable business. Or maybe it was a pang of recognition—of that moment of terror when the future yawns in front of you, a fanged mouth whose bite can be softened only if filled with money.

I wonder what she'd originally thought—perhaps that Emily

and Ray would bail her out, support her, keep her afloat, no matter what happened?

How desperate had she been to be out from under the weight of debt?

Sasha pointed at a silly chest of drawers, the sort of idiosyncratic piece that made no sense to me. Each drawer could hold three pairs of underpants, perhaps. A dozen handkerchiefs. One folded, finely woven T-shirt. Maybe that was its charm—furniture for people who already have all the furniture they need. "This is so interesting," Sasha said. "And it would be just the right height. We'll find something to put on top of it, too. I'll let you know."

Helena scribbled information on a tag, attached it to a drawer pull, and waved us off with renewed cheer.

"I like that nutty chest," Sasha said when we were outside again.

"Do you recall that this is all make-believe? We have no rich client who wants to simulate her own home for a portrait. So why on earth did you put that monstrosity on hold?"

"I consider it my job and duty to spread hope where I can."

"Really?"

She nodded gravely. I invited her for dinner, practically begged her. I needed all the hope she was willing to spread.

Fifteen

FOR once Mackenzie was at home when I arrived. Thank goodness he and Sasha were at peace with each other, because I didn't need to be a camel to believe my back could be broken with a feather's weight more of stress.

Happily, she served as a buffer zone and made the evening ahead feel more comfortable.

Pork stew was in the freezer, and I could fake the rest. This was Sasha, not somebody who provoked my Og-woman dazzle-instincts.

The man's attention was again on a screen—not the small one this time, but the tiny one. "Off in a sec," he said. His ability to focus intently and give something his total attention is incredibly sexy when applied to me, infuriating when applied to electronics. I put the frosty containers in the microwave and pressed the necessary controls. As the food heated I watched C.K. highlight and copy something into a file. I managed to make my table setting involve passing by him, and I saw the word *schizophrenia* at the top of a solid block of text. He was studying up on Adam. Learning what to do when he found him. I couldn't decide if that was good or bad.

I listened to Sasha decide whether she liked our painting of the window looking onto the bucolic scene. "Cows in space," she said, walking back and forth in the middle of the loft across from it. "Airborne bovines. Cowstronauts."

"We think it's funny. Doubly so because we're up here in the city air."

Her expression—now she was being the nonpro with the good eye—made me fear our senses of humor needed tuning. Then she shrugged. "I like it. I don't think I should, but I do." She looked around the loft's walls.

"No use searching for it," I said. "The space is reserved, though. Right over here above the table." She'd done a photograph of fruit that was anything but a still life. It breathed; it was so sensuous it was almost obscene, inviting the touch of fingers, lips. And it still awaited Sasha's attention. I'd offered to have it enlarged elsewhere, but she took that as a personal insult.

"I've been busy," she said. "Having your armpits sniffed takes time."

Mackenzie swiveled around. It was more a matter of having turned off the computer than of Sasha's armpits, but he nonetheless seemed intrigued as he walked over, accepted a glass of wine, and settled in next to me.

"Sasha's been a guinea pig," I said. "At the Chemical Senses Center."

C.K. lifted his glass in a mock toast to her. "To a thrilling-sounding life experience."

"A paid guinea pig," Sasha said. "That's the thrill of it. All I had to do is sweat. Long time back, right here in River City, they found these chemicals that produce odor. Underarm variety. And they also found, separately, that underarm chemicals can influence the menstrual cycle—hope you don't mind this talk of female things, mister. You asked, you know. So anyway, they had a bunch of us involved in three overlapping experiments for a month. Easy money, but not the way to keep friends and influence people. I had to work out—several times—and stay dirty. Other times I had to sit in the third circle of hell and sweat."

I chose not to question why that fragrant month wouldn't therefore have been the perfect time to spend alone in a darkroom, printing the photo. I questioned, instead, the researchers. "So they, ah, actually sniff you?"

Unfortunate timing. Mackenzie had just lifted his glass and was in the very act of inhaling the pale fragrance of the wine. He paused, looked at me, and grinned. "Good thing I'm not big on power of suggestion," he said.

"They sniffed us," Sasha said. "Except when we sweated onto cotton pads under the arm. Then they sniffed them, or put them through tests. Sometimes we worked on getting up a sweat, sometimes they just made us hotter than hell, and sometimes they made us nervous. That was about the antiperspirant component. So don't think there wasn't variety, challenge, and excitement on the job."

"Nervous? Like how?" Mackenzie leaned forward, toward Sasha, who sat in the oversized easy chair at right angles to the sofa.

I had the feeling Mackenzie was hoping for tips for the interrogation room.

"I had to give a speech to the doctors there."

Mackenzie settled back into the cushions, mild disappointment reshaping his mouth. It would be difficult copying the technique. Murderers were reluctant to give speeches. He'd have to make them sweat the old-fashioned way.

"All these people with Ph.D.'s in sciences I'd never heard of—I had to talk about my feelings about body odor," Sasha said. "I knew it was part of the experiment, but even so, I thought it mattered

165

what I'd say in my talk. I got myself into a lather—see? That's exactly what they wanted. God, just thinking about having to speak and I'm beading up on my forehead."

Public speaking. Ahead of death on the great fear list. I thought of the many oral book reports I'd assigned, supposedly to help America's youth and actually just adding to their load of misery. I seemed to do a lot of that lately. "But the sniffers?" I asked. "Who are they?"

She shrugged. "I don't know if they're chemists or what. They're trained, though. Like wine tasters. Professionals. I wish I'd been allowed to take photos. Whole lines of these people, going from one to the next, lifting our arms, sniffing this pit, then that one. . . ."

Strike pit sniffing off the list. It felt good to clear away another possibility. Through the process of elimination, I'd sneak up on the right career.

"What say to a change of subject?" Mackenzie asked. "The winetaster analogy—that pushed it over the edge for me."

"Can I ask just one thing? Do you know if the experiment was a success?"

"I'm not sure what they wanted," Sasha said, refilling her glass. "You know how sometimes they tell you it's one thing, but it's another altogether." She was good at talking and sipping simultaneously. "You know, when they first isolated this chemical, they thought it had to do with schizophrenia—"

Mackenzie turned and checked me out, as if I'd fed the word to Sasha.

How had aimless talk about her bizarre job involved schizophrenia? It was as if we'd entered the room playing the game Don't Drag Adam into This Evening. Rule one: Whatever you say, do not say schizophrenia.

"—because the chemical was in schizophrenics' sweat. They thought they had a major medical breakthrough, but it turned out it's also in the sweat of people who don't have schizophrenia. The point I'm making is, who knows what they wanted this time and whether they got it, found something else accidentally, or what. I just know they now are aware of my feelings about body odor."

Both Mackenzie and I smiled weakly. I tried for more and failed. He seemed to have stopped trying altogether. "He got himself in more trouble today," Mackenzie said.

"I know. I just didn't know if you knew."

"What?" Sasha said.

"Did you arrest him, then?" I asked.

"Who?" Sasha asked.

"No," Mackenzie said. "Hard to find runaways."

"Not fair. You're so—"

"Thanks, guys," Sasha said. "You're making me feel right at home. Or is this a new experiment designed to make me sweat?"

"We'll find him, you know. Soon."

"Won't you even look around first? We were at Emily Fisher's sister's store this afternoon and—"

He shook his head. "That's my job, Amanda. I don' tell you how to teach. Why do you insist on—"

"But she lied. She was in the library Thursday and she's lying about it. And she wears these oversized scarves—"

"I'm going home," Sasha said. "This is downright creepy."

The microwave beeped. I stood up. "You're right, Sash. I apologize. We're being rude." I knew all I wanted about Adam's status now. He was still among the missing. And I knew a little more about Mackenzie's lack of open-mindedness than I wanted to know.

The pork was still frosty in the center, but I thought it was now capable of being transferred to a pot for a slow reheat, which process I then began. Not that transferring bits of meat in a frozen sauce is that engrossing, but it did take me a little too long to realize that the room was suffused in silence. It was as if when Adam was removed as a conversational subject, the remaining option was muteness. I heard Mackenzie offer Sasha more wine, heard her accept, heard him murmur about finding another bottle somewhere. Heard more silence.

"I'll put on music," Mackenzie said, standing. I nodded from where I was, even though nobody was looking my way.

At the same time Sasha must have completed her mental global search for a safe topic. "So," she said in a forced party voice, "what do you think of Mandy's plans? You going to visit us in merry old England? Make it merrier?"

I turned, too late to hurl myself between Sasha's mouth and the sound waves, but in time to see Mackenzie pause for a slice of a second, complete the insertion of the CD into the player, wait until soft Brazilian shusses swirled through the room, adjust the decibel level imperceptibly, and then turn, smiling, in Sasha's direction. He was good. You'd have to know him intimately to be sure he'd heard what Sasha said, let alone digested it, made sense of it, and been upset by it. Unfortunately, I knew him intimately. He was intensely upset.

"Which question you want answered first?" he asked mildly.

Sasha cocked her head. "How about we begin with how you feel about Mandy going to graduate school in England?"

I was heartsick. This was no way to treat a lover, no way to broach the subject, and I wasn't even sure yet that it was seriously a subject to broach. It was an idea to play with, a security blanket, an escape hatch.

"Sasha," I began, "you take everything so seriously! When I said that, I was only—"

"What?" she began, but Mackenzie interrupted, his voice silky, Southern, and suspect. "How'd I feel about those plans? Well, when I first heard, I was stunned, of course." He looked over at me and smiled, as if we were in collusion, even though the time he'd been stunned was approximately one minute earlier. I hadn't realized what a fine actor he was. I didn't know if I liked knowing it now.

"Amanda's always seemed confused—no, that's too harsh . . . *ambivalent* about what precisely she wanted next."

His bayou roots strangled his syllables. *Precisely* was said as imprecisely as possible. Emotion does that to him. When it's sexy emotions, it sounds just right, like auditory dessert. But at that moment, all the hard edges he had sliced off his every slurred word and sentence joined like magnet filings and zigzagged through my bloodstream.

"So to have her make such a drastic plan . . . to go so far in pursuit of . . . well, it took me by surprise, is all. Made me speechless, to tell the truth. But I'm impressed that her thinkin's clear now. That she's willin' to make the necessary adjustments an' all. That she knows what she wants."

At the moment what I wanted was to curl up in a fetal position and stay that way a few years. Instead, I positioned myself behind Mackenzie, where Sasha could see me but he couldn't. It was as close to hiding as I could rationally get, given the situation. I shook my head at Sasha, ran my finger across my throat. She saw it. She got it. She ignored it. I'd upset her when I'd tossed out the idea of my relocating along with her, and she had the rapt expression of a missionary, the zeal of a mediator.

"Won't you miss her?" she asked Mackenzie sweetly. "Or will you be able to spend lots of time over there?"

He sighed. "I'll miss her big-time. She knows that. But unfortunately, the police department's not goin' to change its structure because Amanda's changed her life plans. She knows that, too," he added softly.

"Listen, you guys," I began, "let's not talk about this now. This is making me really uncomfortable. First of all, you're acting like I'm not here—"

"Just practicin', honey," Mackenzie said.

His words, so perfectly aimed, and so deserved, hit me and left me speechless.

"That's what I thought," Sasha said. "You didn't tell him, did you? You didn't even discuss it. Just this one-sided—"

"I really don't think you should be—"

"Right!" It came out close to a snarl. "I'm the one who's supposed to be the goof-off. You're the sane one. I'm the one always screwing up with men. So I should keep my mouth shut and definitely not offer advice, but I'm telling you, sister, we've switched roles, and this is dumber than any dumb thing I've ever done!" She stopped a moment to consider her own words. "And that's saying a lot!"

It was indeed.

"This," she continued, opening her arms until she looked like an evangelical Edwardian princess, "this is pure foolhardy—"

"Sasha, please. You have no right—"

Mackenzie remained immobile, except for his head, which swiveled from the one of us to the other, spectator at the U.S. Open of Girlfriend Spats.

"I do so have the right," she said, one hand on her hip. "I have the right to be your *friend*, you stupid woman! I'm *being* a friend, you dolt! I've known you since before you suspected that boys would be of interest, and that gives me the right, you hear?" She stamped her foot. I knew, and she knew that I knew, that the stamp was in place of a total throttling, as were my clenched fists.

In the decades of our friendship, I didn't think we'd ever been this angry with each other. I was frightened—literally chilled, as if a cold wind had filled me up. I rubbed at my arms and had a moment's happy fantasy that none of this was happening. That this was another bad dream in a bad month.

Then Sasha exhaled loudly, as if she'd been holding her breath for a year. I didn't think people did that in dreams. "Listen," she said in a soft voice. "I'm out of here. This is your chance—better late than never. Talk it through. Work it out. You guys make me really sad."

We both opened our mouths to protest, to explain, to offer something in return, in defense—but I couldn't think of what to say, and apparently neither could Mackenzie. With a rueful wave and a kiss, Sasha was out the door. And then the enormous loft, which so often felt frighteningly large, suddenly felt like the Poe tale where the burning walls move closer and tighter.

Mackenzie shook his head. "England?" he said. "Grad school?

Where? Cambridge? Oxford? London School of Economics? What subject?"

"I . . . it's still kind of . . . I . . ." I could have lied. I knew then I could have whipped something up, something that was so British I had to be there. English literature, for starters. Logic would be on my side, except I couldn't lie. Didn't want to. Wasn't in the habit of doing so, most particularly, especially, with this man.

"Ah," he said. "It isn't about studyin', it's about movin' on an' movin' out, do I have that right?"

"Listen, I didn't mean—when I said that to Sasha, it was a whim, pure speculation, talk, a—"

"Is this because of Adam? I know you're agitated, annoyed with me—and I with you—but to split . . . I had no idea." He sat down on the couch again, heavily. "You could have said something."

"Yes. Right. I would have. No, wait—that makes it sound as if it *is* because of Adam. Or something. It isn't even an *it*!" I sounded like a world-class jackass. And I wasn't making sense, even to myself, so how could I hope to make sense to Mackenzie? "This isn't because of Adam, although I wish—Sometimes your job seems like a third person here, and you're so bullheaded—"

"As opposed to your willingness to listen to the opposite side?"

I ignored that. "I said that about joining her—I said that maybe mostly to hear how it sounded because . . ." I, too, sat down. Balancing on my two feet no longer felt safe or possible. "Because I feel lost. I don't know if I'm a teacher anymore. I don't know if I'm doing anybody any good or harming them. I don't know if I'm going to be employed anymore. I don't know where we are."

"That part at least, that last thing—we could have talked. Could have talked about it all, but definitely about that part. I'd think we owe each other that much."

He was right. I knew he was right even though his words were so slurred by now they were barely English. "Everything's falling apart," I said. "All at once." I had a sudden rush of hope. We could make this better. Look, we were starting to.

171

He looked at me with eyes that suddenly seemed the precise shade of blue that gave its name to sorrowful days and music. "It's not the way you're sayin' it. Not as if it all just happens to you while you do nothin'. You're pushin' things over yourself, it seems to me. Like a little kid who wants to see what'll happen if she topples what she's built."

His voice was practically a whisper, but what I heard were shouts.

"You want to talk now?" I asked.

He stood up. "I want air. Need to walk some. A breather."

He was gone within seconds. I watched the door close behind him and felt my skull fill with words written in thick capitals, words I'd seen on the computer screen before it crashed, words that weighed and pressed and bolted themselves to my brain: FATAL ERROR. FATAL ERROR.

And more softly, like a lament: *You are losing your best friend.*

And then, good English teacher that I was, I edited them, revised them, made them closer to the truth. I wasn't losing anything; Mackenzie was right. I wasn't a little victim girl, standing innocently by as bad things happened to me. Not all the time. Not now, for sure. I'd behaved as if I could opt to leave, unilaterally behaved as if I could have my adventure, follow wherever it took me while Mackenzie and whatever we had was wrapped in plastic and tossed in the deep freeze. As if he didn't matter and didn't count. I wasn't losing my best friend—I was tossing him out with a negligent, dismissive flick of my wrist.

I was hurting everything I touched—first Adam and now Mackenzie. Something was very wrong with me.

My eyes stung from something more than frustrated tears. Smoke and then an acrid stench hit my nostrils. The forgotten pork was burning. Some things are doomed from the git-go.

Sixteen

 SAT in a near stupor. If I let myself think, then I was going to
have to admit the scientific truism that every action has a reaction. Plus the less scientific but equally apt aphorism that I'd
made my bed and had to lie in it. Actually, I wanted to—but it was
too early in the day, although I surely understood why emotionally overcome Victorian women had taken to their beds, sometimes for years.

Besides, I was born in the wrong century, at the wrong time,
with the wrong personality for swoons and neurasthenia. I had to
solve this, but how? And in what way?

I tried to reverse the roles, and honestly didn't know if I would

be willing to forgive if Mackenzie had "forgotten" about me enough
to never mention that he planned to relocate elsewhere, leaving
me behind. Even if he wasn't sure he was going to do so, had only
mentioned it as I had, to test it out, I'd feel hurt and resentful as
hell that he hadn't tested it out on me.

What had I been thinking of? Flirting with the librarian, with
all sorts of destructive ideas. Flirting with disaster.

I tried to sink back into the painless gray-flannel nothingness of
the stupor, but it would have none of me. Just as well, because the
phone rang.

I was sure it was Mackenzie and that this call would move us to
the next stage, whatever that was. I was afraid to lift the receiver,
held my breath.

Let the machine pick up, I decided. Let me hear what sort of
message was forthcoming before I had to do anything. My reac-
tions were off lately. Skewed.

The phone rang again.

Coward. He's making a move. You aren't supposed to duck. I lifted
the receiver. "Hello?" I said, angry with myself for letting my nervousness show.

"Oh . . . I'm . . . oh, I don't know . . . you have to—you said—I
don't know—"

I instinctively pulled back, away from the receiver, as if it could
hurt me. "Adam?" I whispered.

"Yes," a voice whispered back.

"Where are you?"

"Lost."

"Yes. Can you see any—"

"My scarf."

"Lost your scarf. Yes. But are you okay?"

Silence. Not good. Of course he wasn't okay. He was ill, and virtu-
ally abandoned by his parents, who wanted to believe that this would
blow over, that he was safe with his dangerous so-called friend, that
he'd be fine, get into a good college, justify their existence.

"Adam—what do you want? Why have you been calling me? What do you need? Please let me help you." This maybe I could do right. Finally. "Tell me where—"

The phone slammed down.

Nothing, a voice in my head tolled. Nothing works. I can do nothing right. Nothing makes sense.

The phone rang again. He'd changed his mind. I grabbed it. "Adam? Don't hang up this time, I—"

"This is not Adam, Amanda!" The voice was definitely female. "Don't tell me you mean that mentally ill boy, the one who— Please. This is your sister; remember me?"

"Beth?"

"Is there another sibling I don't know about?"

You'd think my mind, already boggled with the turnarounds and miseries of recent days and minutes, would have no room for any more amazement. Wrong. "You—it's just that you seldom phone, and this is dinner hour. The time you told me not to ever call you because things were too hectic there. Are you okay?"

She giggled. "Things probably are hectic there, but I'm around the corner from you."

The city mouse in town—again? The third time recently that I knew of? What was going on?

"Have you eaten yet?"

"No," I said, and the memory of the burned dinner and, worse, the reason for its burning moved my attention away from Beth-amazement and back to my woes.

"Is Mackenzie home?"

"No," I said again. "Not really."

She must have pondered this a moment. Then she returned to her upbeat voice. "Let me treat you to dinner. Girls' night out."

"That's sweet, and usually . . . but I'm not hungry, and I'm really . . . I'm no fun."

"You sound—what's going on?"

"I can't really talk about . . ." Why not? Beth was as close to

175

normal as anybody I knew. Beth was sane. "Remember the other night?" I said. "When you made up that excuse for not going home?"

"You mean about you and Mackenzie?" Her voice was merry. "Oh, gee—you know, I told you that, but—"

"You could use it as an excuse again tonight," I said. "Difference is, this time it's accurate."

"I'll be right over," she said. "Buzz me in." The merriness was so far gone from her voice it was hard to believe it had ever been there. I wanted to tell her about Adam, too. No matter what she thought about him in the abstract—because of how I'd poisoned her mind, she was a mother. She had to care about some other mother's child living on the streets, not able to protect himself.

But she was on her way, sounding like someone who knew things, someone who would solve whatever was wrong. Everything that was wrong. She sounded like a big sister.

She must have been two feet away when she called, because the buzzer sounded before I had a chance to tidy myself up, and according to what I saw in the mirror, my attempts at thinking or avoiding thought both involved raking my hair. When I buzzed her back, brush in hand, I still looked like one of the Three Stooges.

She was wearing her suburban uniform: a blue blazer, white shirt, tailored khaki slacks, and proper low-heeled brown pumps. That, at least, hadn't changed. And she immediately launched into a whole bunch of words, all of them sympathetic, supportive, and encouraging, even before she had the slightest idea what was going on.

Her actions were, in essence, the absolute opposite of mine with regard to Mackenzie. I wasn't sure what Beth was saying, but the message was clear—I care about you, I care about you, I care about you.

Made me want to cry, but that would have provoked more sisterly mothering, so I controlled myself, and instead we exchanged further murmurs. It was a chorale of sorts, or a two-part invention. I was vague and sad and said "I don't know" a whole lot of times, and she was sweet and concerned and performed several variations of "It'll be all right." Finally she stood up and said, "Enough. We're getting nowhere. Brush your hair, put on lipstick, we'll go to dinner and you'll feel better."

There were times when such pronouncements would have either raised my hackles or made me sneer at the sheer banality of my sister's pattern of thought. This was not such a time. I was grateful for her direction and assurance, and I did as told.

I put on a fire-engine-red corduroy jacket that I liked to believe was so loud in its fabric merriment that wearing it made it impossible to be depressed.

Outside, it was all I could do not to search for Mackenzie. He'd needed air, he said, but he hadn't mentioned what air, where. I hoped it was local air. He loved walking, and often tried to think through a case by taking a five- or six-mile walk, up and down the city streets.

That never worked for me. Sounded great, like what people did to work things through. But while I do get some exercise, my thinking takes breaks for window-shopping, passersby, traffic hazards, and noise—and winds up in an even worse tangle than it was in when I left home.

I found myself searching for Adam, too. I had missing men all over town.

"How about crabs?" Beth asked. "Isn't DiNardo's near here?"

"Around the corner. I feel crabby, anyway." Mood-appropriate food, although it didn't matter to me. My appetite had walked out along with the man.

Beth, however, was ravenous. We were seated in a large booth, and in the nautical dark of the restaurant, I watched her neatly dissect and devour half the Chesapeake Bay's output while we did a catch-up on our parents, who'd been oddly quiet this week.

"Mom's writing her memoirs," Beth said. "She read that everybody's selling memoirs these days, even kids in their twenties, so she's hopping or at least crawling on the bandwagon. But apparently she got to a point and noticed that her adventures lacked a certain excitement. That a lot of her adventures are other people's adventures. That which the other people call gossip, I suspect."

True, but only to a point, so I wondered. I knew my mother had secrets she'd never shared with me and I'd never shared with Beth. I wondered if she was going public with those memories, which weren't all that dull. And who knew what else there might be?

"So she's reevaluating every choice she made—and to tell you the truth, every choice I made," Beth said with a rueful shake of her head. "She can call it whatever she likes—I still call it nagging."

"Welcome to the club. She's spent years nagging me to be just like you. But something is definitely up, because this last call she changed her tune. Put the whole marriage machine in reverse." I sighed. "It fed into everything that's gone wrong. She offered to pay for grad school. To subsidize me if I go have adventures of the undomesticated kind."

"Aha," Beth said, again offering me a small, spice-encrusted claw. I shook my head, and she sighed and ate it herself. "Things begin to make more sense. Back in the loft, it was pretty much a jumble, but now I see. . . ."

"Good, because I don't."

She looked at me, cracked yet another claw, and picked out the tender white meat. Then she looked at me again, this time with a smile. We had changed gears in some way. "So just because your life is in a complete shambles now, aren't you going to ask why I called? I have news."

"News?" I moved my mind back into the world. "Have you found out where Ray Buttonwood was that afternoon?"

She grimaced. "Who cares? Not that I didn't try. And Sam reacted completely predictably. The client was late, but then they worked all afternoon, and yes, they took breaks, and no, he didn't follow Ray, and why was I drilling him, anyway. So what can I tell you? He was and wasn't under observation all day, just about. I do know they were taking the deposition one block from the library."

"One block? My God, it'd be . . . What about the will? Did Sam find out how much money Emily was left?"

"Can we drop that subject? It creates problems for me, and I'm positive that a man doesn't take a coffee break to go strangle his wife. It doesn't make sense. And Helena—even if she were desperate about the money—Helena's too . . . too fastidious to do a thing like that." Beth cleared her throat, sighed histrionically, and folded her hands in front of her, behind the plate full of crab shells.

"Sorry," I said. "I can't shake the idea—and unless somebody else admits to killing her, my student is going . . ." My sister was plainly and simply not interested. "Tell me, Beth. What is your news and why are you here in town? Again. At this time of day— dinner, baths, bedtime stories."

She raised her eyebrows skeptically.

"I am interested. Truly. Have you run away from home?"

"Not exactly. I've been working. Scouting locations." She unclasped her hands, lifted a crab claw, smiled, and waited.

"Meaning what?"

"Meaning scouting locations."

"Like for movies? Commercials? I don't get it. Why would you? For whom?"

"I'm starting a business along with two other women. It's called As Needed, and we're supplying total party and event services." Her voice sounded charged as she described what she'd been doing. "We have a stable of experts we can call on, people who can do everything a person might need. We're catering, but we'll provide music of any kind, decorations, flowers, entertainment—the whole shebang. And I've been looking at unusual places to rent. We want to have the best, absolutely most comprehensive—corporations, too, you see—and—"

If I'd been dumbfounded to find my sister in the city again, the idea of her becoming an entrepreneur left me speechless.

Her smile was a mix of smugness and pure glee. "Been working on the idea for a few months, but I didn't want to tell anybody—

except Sam, of course—until I knew it was really going to happen. Look here." She fumbled in her pocketbook, pulled out a slim card case, and presented me with a slick business card with a logo that looked like a shield with a whisk crossed over a note of music. AS NEEDED was in bold print, then a phone number, a fax number, an e-mail address, and the alphabetically-in-order names of three women: Sondra Cruz, Marilyn Goldstein, and Beth Wyman.

"The kids are growing up. Alexander's in a preschool group and Karen's in first grade. And Sam's great about it. I don't know how he'll be when we get rolling—it'll mean nights out and such—but he's really pitching in now with the kids."

"Where did this come from?"

She looked peeved. "I always knew I'd do something. Didn't know what, but did you think I was going to be just like Mom?"

"You seemed so happy—so absolutely contented."

"I was—am. I was lucky; because of Sam's job, I was able to be there for those first few years. But I have this mother I love but do not want to emulate. Did you think that I, too, would use all my energy and brain power to overengineer my kids' lives—and the life of anyone else who'd let me?"

Precisely what I'd thought, but despite my recent record for emotional cruelty, I couldn't bring myself to say so. "I'm amazed. I had no idea. You'll be perfect, too—your parties are always the most thought-through of any I've been to. You're a natural, and it sounds like fun. Hard, but fun. Why didn't you ever say something?"

"Why didn't you ever ask?"

"Man, am I striking out in the human relations department today."

"Not to worry. Now that I've got you feeling guilty, I can bore you to tears with what I'm doing. Like today I looked at five places, including a terrific gallery right here in Old City. I can't say it was an original inspiration, though. Sam's office had a reception honoring some political hopeful there last night."

"Ray Buttonwood?"

She pursed her lips and shook her head. "He hasn't officially said anything, Mandy. He's waiting until . . ."

"Until he's a properly respected, widowed single parent who then becomes engaged to some heiress who'll help him, perhaps?"

"Oh, please." Then she closed her eyes a second and exhaled, opened her eyes and sighed again. "That isn't a bad scenario, actually, but I don't want to think about it."

She was silent long enough for me to think there was something—something about Ray—she was already thinking about. I waited while she idled with another crab claw.

"Actually," she said after silent deliberation, "Sam pooh-poohed this, but you'll understand: Ray Buttonwood was there."

"He's really taking his wife's murder hard, isn't he? Out glad-handing every night and all. He's a natural for politics. No wonder he wants to run."

She shrugged. "The thing is, he frightened me. Went out of his way to tell me that he'd gone back to Emmy's building and verified you weren't a resident."

"I knew you shouldn't have—"

"That isn't the point. He acted like he was sure we'd gone to Emmy's."

"But we did."

"But he wasn't to know. Nobody was to know! And he acted as if he wanted to blackmail me, or at least threaten me, about it." Beth shook her head, affirming her disbelief at the man's actions. "He said—" She cleared her throat and pitched her voice lower, imitating him. " 'I find it interesting how different your regard for the law is than your husband's.' He wasn't making sense to me, and it must have showed, so he leaned very close and said, 'Emily's place. Before the police had a chance at it.'

"I said, 'And you, Ray?' And he said that she was still legally his wife, the mother of his son, so there was nothing odd about it at all, but we had no legal reason for being there. Kept asking what *Sam* would think of my expedition."

"Is Sam going to be upset if this jerk tells him?"

Beth's expression was cryptic—bemused and still a little annoyed. "Why would he be? I told him before I went." I really did not know this woman who was my sister.

"But you said—"

"Oh, that. About making up an excuse for you? About your so-called breakup? That was for your benefit. I thought you'd be more likely to go with me if you thought I was sneaking behind Sam's back."

"Beth." I frowned with disapproval, then couldn't sustain it. She was right. I broke into a grin. I'd never have roused myself for a legal, Sam-approved expedition. "All that aside," I said, "do you think Ray Buttonwood killed his wife? Would there be any reason? I did see that man in the pinstriped suit, and so did Emily."

Beth tilted her head and looked sourly amused. "Reason?" she said. "Sure. Precisely what you intimated. That way, he'd be a sympathetic widower, not a cold-hearted man dumping his wife and leaving her penniless, and stealing her kid. This way, he can marry the money that would help his campaign, plus he can probably run on an antiviolence platform and be a shoo-in. So sure, there are reasons. But Mandy, I'm positive that Sam would testify that he was with him all the time."

"He'd lie? Sam?"

She shook her head. "Never. But he truly believes he was with him, enough of the time to make any side trips for murder impossible. And frankly, so do I. And I can't keep questioning him. He was really annoyed by my suspicions about his friend. He'll clam up if I start acting like the Gestapo, asking for a minute-by-minute breakdown."

I would have to find a way around Sam. "Were they still fighting about money?"

Beth searched for her credit card. "I don't think so. I mean, Emmy was hard up and he was being a creep about it. He makes enough to be a whole lot less creepy. But I think she gave up the battle because her mother left money. Of course, she loaned it to her sister, to open that store, but when Helena paid her back, things wouldn't have been that terrible." The waiter took the gold card and the bill.

That troubled me in several directions. It was likely that Emily would have had money issues for a long time, because I'd seen Helena's store and didn't have much hope for its making a profit—legally—in this lifetime. And that would mean ongoing divorce-money issues. Both Helena and the bland blond Mr. Pinstripe kept their ominous auras.

"Beth, Helena's business is pathetic. It's a fake, whether or not she knows that. She'd never have been able to pay back the loan."

Beth half nodded. "She insists on acting as if she were a rich woman, somebody's pampered wife. I know that. But she told Emmy she was going to be in the money again soon."

"I'm telling you, the store—"

"Not the store. A prospect. A financially affluent prospect."

"A sugar daddy?"

"Haven't heard anybody use that expression for a long while." Beth's tone was neutral. The subject seemed exhausted and she changed it. "You didn't eat a thing, poor baby, but your appetite will be back soon, because this foolishness between the two of you is going to work out, you'll see. You two have too much going for you to let . . . to just . . . Well, you aren't going to listen to your mother for the first time in your life, are you?"

I'd never thought of it that way.

"I promise you, it'll work out."

She almost made me believe it.

Outside, the night felt like silk chiffon on the skin. It was the variety of balmy spring evening that releases endorphins into the air, forcing everyone who breathes to fall in love. Trust me to make it the night I break up.

Beth had parked a few blocks south, so we slowly walked down to Second Street, toward Market. Beth talked about her business, speculated as to how she'd manage family and work, about her partners, about what, perhaps, Ray Buttonwood had hoped to accomplish with his quiet thuggery the night before. I listened, happy for her, but mostly lost in my still impenetrable thoughts.

We passed Christ Church's iron-gated garden and graveyard, a place I like to sit in on fine days. One would think repeated exposure to such reminders of time's passing, of mortality—even the church's ghostly presences of congregants Washington and Franklin and the men who signed the Declaration of Independence and came here to pray—would have given me perspective by now. One would be wrong.

We reached Market with me still surveying all points for Mackenzie and perhaps Adam, listening, more or less, while Beth thought out loud about how she'd arrange her schedule. The light changed to green, we stepped off the curb, and I, still scanning, turned my head just enough to see a set of headlights and a sleek, dark car tearing down Second and turning right, sharply, at top speed. Directly at us.

"No!" I screamed, grabbing and pulling her toward me. We fell together, landing in a heap of arms and legs half on and half off the curb as the car sped by, grazing Beth, who collapsed.

A woman across the street screamed—in tune, it seemed, with the sound of brakes being forced to outperform themselves—"That car! Stop that car!" although I wondered how anybody could stop a car. "Get its plate number! Call an ambulance!" The woman standing next to her watched, gape-mouthed, until she realized the last bellowed instruction had been for her. She got the idea, digested it, nodded, and took a cellular phone out of her pocket just as something—the immovable object of physics lore, judging by the protests of ripped metal, the shrieking brakes, the boom and tinkle of falling glass—did stop the car.

I lay there, my sister half on me. I thought perhaps Beth and I were dead or about to be. I couldn't believe that the worst day of my life was going to be its last as well. I was sick of irony, and now was dying of it.

I tried to right myself, get up on my feet. I could already feel my coccyx protest, and my knees felt wrongly engineered. I was all-over wobbly but alive. I looked at my sister, who was still crumpled. A dark stain was next to her calf, and I could see the cut where her khaki slacks had a gash in them. "Beth! Say something! Oh, my God—"

Things had, impossibly, gotten worse. I lay back down and planned never to get up again.

Seventeen

S HE inhaled. I heard it.

"You're alive!" I nearly sobbed it out. "Oh, Bethie, you're alive."

She started a nod, but cut it short with a wince. "Okay," she gasped.

"Can't breathe?" I looked around wildly. The two women stared from across the street. "Get help!" I said. "Ambulance!" I thought maybe I'd already said it. Or maybe they'd already gotten it, but I couldn't wait to find out. I tried to remember CPR, damned myself for not taking the refresher course, but thought I had some lifesaving techniques still up there.

"Couldn't!" Beth said in a harsh whisper. "Can now. Am. But my head hurts. And my leg—"

Her leg looked bad, bending at not quite the correct angle. And bleeding. But she didn't need to know that yet. "You'll be fine," I said. Until that moment I'd never quite known why people blurt that out, but now I know it's a reflex. A gruff, gut-level request to the gods when there isn't time for lengthy prayer sessions, pleadings, and offerings. "Thank God you're alive," I said. "I don't have to go clean out your rice carton."

She almost smiled. "Noise," she said.

That there was and had been, nonstop, layers upon layers. The brake squeals, the car crash, shouts and screams, male and female, across the street and down and from windows above. The women telling us not to be nervous—so nervous themselves they repeated it endlessly, a tape on continuous play. And maybe me. Maybe a little bit of the noise was me. I'm not saying I was crying, or screaming—but maybe something. Now boil all that down and squeeze it into about three seconds' worth and you'll have it.

I tried to reduce my share of the noise output and leaned closer to Beth.

"Aspirin in my bag," she said, trying once again to lift her head, and immediately giving up.

"Don't—don't move," I said, thinking spinal injury. "Don't do anything. I'll find it." Were you supposed to pop aspirin before a doctor looked at you? Could it hurt?

"Don't be nervous—I called! I had my phone and I called 911!" the woman across the street shouted for the fifth time in a row. She acted as if she were on the other side of a raging river, hallooing us, unable to cross. "Stay calm. An ambulance will be here any minute. I called them on my cell phone."

I wanted to tell that woman, who was barely containing her hysteria, that I loved her, but Beth was so agitated, I had to pay what little attention I had left to her.

"My bag," Beth repeated. "Need my bag."

"Don't worry!" the woman screamed across the street. "I called the police!"

I looked up—my hip didn't feel great, but it didn't seem the time to mention it, only to stay still as long as I could—and saw nothing except that the reason the dark car had been stopped was that it had made another right, into a parked car halfway up the block. I looked more attentively, although clear vision was prevented by a parked off-road vehicle doing its dinosaur thing in center city Philadelphia. The least those damn things could do is get off the roads, as advertised.

The good news was that it wasn't going to be hard getting the dark car's license plate. Literally. That car wasn't going anywhere. Two men on the far side of the street ran toward it. They could have strolled. Backward. The dark car was wedged in at an angle that didn't look forgiving. It was going to be difficult for the passengers to get out, let alone flee.

"Are you sure you had your bag?" I asked, continuing in my acutely stupid mode of meaningless conversation. If there's one accessory a woman knows she's got with her, it's her bag.

Beth tried to push herself up.

"What's the matter with you?"

"My head—"

"No—I mean do not move! Haven't you seen enough movies to know that?" But that always had to do with moving a victim, not yourself. Maybe if your own muscles were working enough to move, you should. Medical training via feature films didn't answer everything, and since what I didn't know could definitely hurt her, I tried to cover all bases by allowing nothing. "No aspirin, either. Thins the blood. The ambulance is coming. Don't worry. Relax." I had now broken all previous records for saying stupid things that didn't make anything better.

"My bag," Beth repeated.

I heard the whine of an approaching ambulance and the siren of a police car. People shouted from down where the dark car was stuck. People shouted back from our corner. My rescuer across the street repeated herself again and again: "Don't be nervous! An ambulance is coming!" A man bellowed, "I was having a goddamn meal in the restaurant when he comes around, and look at my car!" I felt battered by the incoherence of the moment—message overload from sirens and shouts, movement of people around us, near and far, and then over us—and could not imagine how Beth must be feeling except worse. I bent over her and was interrupted by paramedics getting to her; by somebody shouting that somebody else had the guy and he maybe needed a doctor, too; by a policeman checking the scene, moving people back; by the paramedic examining my hand, scraped and slightly raw, to my surprise; and then by a voice. The voice. It cut through everything else—cut through in its own unique way, softly.

"Mandy! Sweet Je—Mandy! You all right? Jesus!" All this said as he ran from the far corner toward me.

I couldn't turn and greet him because the paramedic was checking my eyes, but he told me I was fine just as Mackenzie reached me, barked at the cop that he was one, too, bent down, and took me gingerly in his arms. His blue eyes had a film of moisture over them. "I thought I saw that red jacket from down the street—all the commotion—I thought you were—" And then he paused, took several deep breaths in a row, nodded, and smiled his relief.

I wondered when he'd remember that he was furious with me. I certainly wasn't going to remind him.

"We'll be taking your sister in for some patching and observation," the emergency worker said. "She'll be fine. Bruised up, but fine. You probably want to come in and be checked out, too. Just to be sure."

"I'll phone her husband."

It was the paramedic's turn to nod.

"You want my phone?" The woman who'd been across the street and made the call was now standing about two feet from me. "I have my phone right here. That's how I called the—"

I smiled and shook my head. "I'll call him later. Soon. From home. And thanks. You saved the day."

She balanced her weight on one foot, then the other, searching for a new role in this drama. "I saw that car," she said abruptly. "I saw what happened, and let me tell you—you're lucky to be alive! It was going like a maniac! One second later and everybody would have been dead."

I didn't find her patter cheering. The cop, however, was intrigued. "You're a witness?" he said.

First she nodded enthusiastically, waved her girlfriend over, and said, "We both are." Her friend shook her head. "Didn't actually see anything," she said. "Don't want to get involved."

And then the phone lady reconsidered and half shrugged. "Now that you mention it . . . My memory stinks. Everybody says so. Plus it happened so fast. Scared me to death, it did."

I decided they could find their moral centers without my assistance or interference.

"My bag," Beth said. "My bag!" Her voice was getting stronger. A good sign.

A second patrolman walked toward us and heard Beth. "She mean pocketbook? Maybe brown with a twisted gold lock?"

"Curved," Beth said. "The clasp curves."

"To be honest, I'd call it more like twisted now," the cop said.

"It's my favorite bag," Beth said, and I was surprised to see large tears dribble toward her ears as she lay on her back on the stretcher. I reminded myself again about her having bumped her head. I was going to insist on scans if she was going to carry on about pocketbooks when she'd nearly been killed.

"It died in place of you," I said. "Sacrificed itself. Jumped in front of the car to save you. Think of it that way."

"My bag," Beth repeated, but softly this time.

"I'm sure it was, but now it's evidence, ma'am. It apparently hooked onto the bumper and was dragged down the street."

Beth groaned.

"You in pain? New pain?" the paramedic who was settling her on the gurney asked.

"My bag!" she said. "Everything's in it."

"I know," the patrolman said. "Won't be able to put a new face on for a while."

"No, I mean my list of contacts for my business."

Mackenzie glanced over at me, one eyebrow raised. "Business?" he silently mouthed.

"Her new business. She's minding her own business." In my exhausted, relieved, fatigued state, I thought that was the funniest thing I'd ever heard, let alone said. I sat on the curb, quietly laughing to myself, frightening the hell out of everyone else.

"All my phone numbers," she continued. "My keys, my wallet—all my ID. My date book—how will I know when anything—"

"Dragged, not run over, is what I was told," the patrolman said. "Contents are probably fine. We'll inventory them, and I'm sure you can have your lipstick back. Doesn't seem evidence of much that we'd need at the station."

I stopped laughing. "Her lipstick?" I said. "She's starting a business and all you can think of is—"

Mackenzie gently touched my forearm. "Forgive him. He knows not what he fails to think about," he whispered.

I hoped his whispered confidence signified that we'd jumped the chasm and were on the other side. The same side. That we'd never look back, either, because it was come-home-all-is-forgiven time. I was truly tired of being angry with him or about him or because of him. It had been interesting to try that on for a while, but it got old quickly, and I hoped I hadn't realized too late how poorly it fit.

Nonetheless, I glared at the patrolman—I yam what I yam—but as he was not looking at me, I gave it up. It would have required extensive consciousness raising, anyway, and I wasn't exactly up to it.

Instead, I looked toward the car down the street, from which area now emanated the sounds of an enraged man and a furious woman. I had the sense of having already missed a great deal of a major fight. I also suspected that what had just happened was a slow silencing of the crowd. The quarrelers had become street theater, and all of us were audience.

She screamed: "I told you to keep your hands off! Want to kill me?"

He shouted: "I was trying to avoid—look what happened!"

"Your fault! All your fault! You want me dead, don't you? That has to be it. You want everybody dead."

"If you'd let up, if you'd just for one minute let up—"

"*You* let up! I can't afford to. You nearly—"

"My nose is bleeding. Can't you have a little—"

"Big deal! You keep bleeding me—it serves you right."

"You owe—"

"Go to hell! It's mine. She's dead, it's mine! If this had happened, my mother would have left it all to—"

The damned four-by-four blocked my view of the drama. I didn't want Mackenzie to think I wasn't totally consumed by the nearness of him, but the fact was, I'd nearly been killed, and so a tiny portion of my consciousness was really eager to know who'd done it. I walked a few paces into the street and saw a blond man holding a handkerchief to his nose, and a woman in dark clothing with a pale patterned scarf and dark hair pulled straight back. She looked like a fashion model—she sounded like a fishwife. I knew them. Knew them both.

But I'd never expected to see them together. "Those people," I said. Then I lost confidence. Maybe I was doing another *Turn of the Screw* number, now putting my ghosts together as an evil duo. For there they were, two people, each of whom had carefully mentioned how dreadful the other one was.

"What?" Mackenzie said, suddenly eager to listen to whatever fantasies I might spout. "What people? Those two? What about them?"

I watched while they fought on, although he made a great show of turning his back to her while she screamed about his wanting her dead, too.

I blinked, tried to see as clearly as possible. I no longer trusted my first impressions. "I think that's Emily Fisher's husband—Ray Buttonwood, the one she's divorcing—and her sister, Helena. Is that possible? That he—or she—that they were in the car that hit us? Together?" I started to shake. If that were true . . . if that were possibly true . . . "They tried to kill us," I whispered. "On purpose."

A second patrolman had gone back and forth between the two accident scenes on the street, and once he knew Mackenzie was a cop, he'd pretty much backed off. But as I spoke he looked at me sharply, then at Mackenzie, then back to me. "You know Mr. Buttonwood, ma'am?" he asked.

Then it *was* him. It *was* them. I wasn't crazy, and they'd tried to kill us. One of us or both of us. I nodded in response to the policeman's question before I realized that in truth I did not know the man. I knew his name and occupation. I knew what he'd been doing, in theory, Thursday. A block away from the murder. I had opinions and emotions about him, but I actually didn't know him at all except for having been introduced in front of an elevator. "My sister knows him." I gestured toward the ambulance, where Beth waited while the paramedics tried to get a word in edgewise between Ray Buttonwood and Helena Spurry. It had to be a technicality, to avert a possible lawsuit, because they looked hale enough, in full battle mode, all engines chugging as far as I could see. A bloody nose seemed the only injury, and possibly Helena was having first aid for dishevelment; a cord of her black hair had sprung loose from its tight binding. Ray's posture, despite the nose and the crash, was still that officious-looking military bearing. How hurt could he be?

"My sister knew his wife, the woman who was strangled at the library last week," I said. "Knows him, too. For a long time."

The woman who had not wanted to be a witness gasped. "Oh, my *God*," she said to her companion. "Did you hear that? She knows a woman who was murdered, too."

"My sister, officer," I repeated, "the woman in the ambulance.

She knows him. He's a lawyer and he's in the same firm as my brother-in-law." My hands would not stop trembling. It had been on purpose. Beth and me—one or both. They'd aimed for us.

Mackenzie didn't say a thing. He certainly didn't suggest that I was having another attack of paranoia.

But apparently, having found me basically hale, he lost interest, because without a single syllable of explanation, and never a backward glance, he took off down the street toward the miserable couple.

I squelched my stab of annoyance. "He's on that case," I said out loud, to remind myself of his professional obligations. Despite my aches, despite feeling as if I had a low-grade fever every time I let my mind return to the idea that I'd been a target, I felt a surge of elation at being vindicated. Now even the cop would know that there were other suspects, or at least two others to suspect. To check out. That perhaps one or two of them had just tried to kill my sister, but why? Because she'd seen him taking something from Emmy's apartment? But maybe I was the one he was aiming the car for. Or she was aiming for. Because I'd been snooping around Emmy's apartment and Helena's store, saying I didn't think Adam had killed her sister. Because I'd pushed Beth to ask too many questions about his whereabouts. About the will.

Or maybe I was constructing something out of nothing, just so I'd have a story to explain my bruises. And a story in which I played a major role, wasn't a mere footnote. To not simply have been in the wrong place at the wrong time.

Still, whatever their motive, if Helena was really with Ray, what were they doing together? He'd justified going through his dead wife's apartment by saying Helena would have taken a family heirloom, that she was greedy. And Beth had suggested the same thing in a different context—that Helena was jealous of whatever her sister had.

Helena herself had implied nothing but a vast and permanent disapproval of her brother-in-law. Her sister, she'd said, had been unlucky. Married to a rotten man.

Had they both protested too much, and were they, possibly, romantically involved? Could both have wanted Emily out of the way?

"Don't tell Mom!" Beth called out, breaking through my stupid, circular speculations. "Get my bag—the business stuff." The paramedics closed the ambulance.

"Bethie kept reassuring me, saying everything would work out between us," I murmured to Mackenzie, who'd returned from the far end of the street, his skinny notebook back in his pocket. "I believed her, too. I believed in big-sister hocus-pocus, that she'd find a way to make things better—but I didn't mean for her to do this! This is an extreme way of getting us past the rift, don't you think?" Although, in fact, it had apparently worked. All it required was my getting the stuffing knocked out of me, the fear that my sister was dead, and the appearance of my knight-errant to save me if need be. And just like that . . . peace in our time.

He took both my hands in his. I wanted to ask him about Buttonwood and Spurry. I knew he must have learned something. But he wasn't wearing his detective face, and when he said, "How about we talk?" he definitely didn't sound like a cop.

I nodded. The prospect and all it implied felt terrifying, facing demons and unanswered questions and risking everything all over again.

But it also felt inexpressibly comfortable, like falling back into my life. Of course, as I thought of it, imagined us talking, I remembered again how much ground needed to be covered, how much needed saying.

For the duration of this time on the sidewalk, the other pressures of the week—or most of them—had receded, paled in contrast to imminent death. Now they were back. We had a lot to talk about.

"I have one thing to say—"

"Hold off till we're home," he said. "First I'll take you to the hospital for a look-see, make sure you're fit."

"That'll take forever." I could feel bruises working their way from my insides out. I was going to feel like hell. I didn't need a professional to tell me that.

"We've got time," he said. "An' then we'll go home, and we'll talk. Then. So it's not rushed and cramped and prone to misunderstandin'."

I nodded and followed him to wherever his car was parked. My hip didn't hurt as much as it had, and I knew I'd be fine, and that the hospital would be a legal technicality. For Ray Buttonwood's sake. To prevent a heavy-duty medical claim.

"I really do have one thing to say first," I repeated.

He stopped and looked at me with patient despair. "You'll never change, will you? You are the most bullheaded, stubborn—"

I hated what was ahead. Knew it was the most important thing I was going to do today and tonight, knew it was imperative—for him, for me—but nonetheless hated it.

"Well, then, go ahead," he said. "You're so stubborn you'd let yourself die rather than not say your piece, wouldn't you? What is it you so absolutely have to say first?"

"I'm sorry."

I'd just made history, and the shock of it registered on Mackenzie. Saying that word is not my strong suit, even when I think it and feel it and know it. "I'm sorry," I repeated, trying not to notice as he quickly erased the delight and surprise from his face. "I treated you shabbily and hurt your feelings, and although I didn't mean to do it, I did do it, and I'm very, very sorry."

He seemed ready to say something back, inhaled, closed his mouth, nodded again, and took my hand once more, looking extremely concerned. "We'd better rush you to the hospital," he said. "You've gone into shock."

Before I could protest, he grinned. "I know that was real hard for you to do," he said softly as we slowly walked through the city. "Therefore damn noble and brave. And it's much appreciated. Very much appreciated. But in future, if we have one, let us both work on this. You don' need to stage a war an' nearly get killed, an' I don' need to think you're dead, before we're both scared enough to say the things that need saying. Deal?"

"Deal." We moved on.

Except for somebody having tried to kill me, it had become a fairly decent evening.

Eighteen

O NE thing I have had the chance to learn—over and over again, alas—is that no matter how staggering and stupefying the events of your (okay, my) life may be, it pretty much doesn't matter to the rest of the universe.

And so the next morning, mind abuzz with confusion and questions about what precisely had been going on the night before and why, limping and bruised but declared not in need of hospitalization or medical pampering or even serious mind-altering drugs, I went to work. Had I not needed to, had I not already been in major occupational jeopardy—had I left a decent and current lesson plan—I might have stayed home to spend the day wallowing in self-pity and obsessing about my problems. But I couldn't, and there is nothing quite as efficient as a gaggle of teens to disabuse you of the illusion that you're the center of the universe.

In preparation for this, I attempted to look on the positive side of everything, much as that concept annoys me. But there were positives: primarily, that thanks to a crazed driver, whether or not he—or she—or they—had been trying to kill me or my sister, my love life seemed in a better place than it had for some time. This was good.

Also, because of that same driver, my mother, who had immediately heard about or intuited Beth's accident, was sufficiently distracted by the one daughter's near loss of life that she failed to ask the other daughter what I was doing with the remainder of mine.

End of list. A very short list.

I'd add reprieves. Bad things that hadn't happened. Yet.

The Yet List.

I hadn't been fired. Yet. I had a few weeks more of employment. It was odd how much that meant to me, even though all the while I was deciding whether I even wanted to continue, whether I was still doing a decent job, whether it wasn't time for something altogether new. But as long as I wasn't fired, I could still feel in control of my destiny, and it was a shock to fully realize how basic and profound that need is. I was holding on by my fingernails, true, but that was infinitely better than falling into the abyss—or being pushed there by Havermeyer.

Second, Adam hadn't been found. Yet. I wasn't sure if that was good or bad news for him when I imagined him on the street somewhere, high or sick on whatever drugs he was finding, subject to the whims of the bad company surrounding him, police out searching for him.

But Adam's missing and wanted status had stalled his parents' suit against me. They probably didn't want to attract more attention to him while he was the prime suspect in a murder. So I wasn't being sued. Yet.

The Yet List was underwhelming, too. All it had established was that a lot of bad things were poised, waiting to happen to me when the time was right.

Nonetheless, I was in stasis, carefully balanced, but still in the game. All I had to do was keep Havermeyer's requested low profile, mine and the school's, while I figured out what I wanted and how to get it. There was time and maneuverability. Cowardly Havermeyer wasn't going to do anything publicly.

To my delight, I realized I was, for the most part, okay. My sibling was going to be fine, too, after her torn ligaments healed and her stitches were removed. Until then, her partners could cover for all her ambulatory duties. And I'd promised to pitch in as much as I could. When the term ended, I might wind up working for or with her. Who knew? That might be my next stop. But for now, I was still employed. No permanent damage to either sister.

I was halfway up the staircase, en route to my room, when the Bobbsey twins—Jill and Nancy—barreled down, stopping as soon as they saw me. "There she is!" they told each other.

"Good!" Jill said as Nancy nodded agreement. "We thought we missed you and we had to talk to you?"

"Tell you something," Nancy said.

I suggested we do the telling upstairs because otherwise we risked trampling. It's amazing how resolutely our students push up or down the stairs en route to classrooms they'd rather avoid altogether.

The girls didn't settle down once inside my empty room. Bad sign. Something was off-kilter. Something minor, I decided, or their faces would reflect more. They were the least cryptic of young women.

But I had other worries, so I gave the girls only a third of my attention. The brush with death the night before had prevented my finishing the garbology collection, and I was juggling lesson ideas to see how I could finesse that gap and catch up on lost time with my other classes as well. "What's up?" I asked. "I'm so sorry, but I haven't had time to edit your news story. It will be in the next issue—the end of this month—but I've . . ." No way in hell could I explain the last two days to these innocents.

Instead, it felt acceptable, or at least expedient, to play on their sympathies. "I had an accident last night—sideswiped by a car. Didn't get home from the hospital till late."

The joy in life disappeared from both their faces. "Oh, Miss Pepper," they said in unison, conveying volumes of grief and sympathy in three words.

"I'm fine. Really nothing. I was lucky—only banged up." I liked playing the stoic heroic guy thing—especially when what I said was the whole truth but sounded as if I were underplaying. I was indeed fine. "Now, what's up?" Once again I gestured toward chairs close to my desk, but they stood where they were. So be it. I had work to do, so I sat down at my desk and pulled folders out of my briefcase.

Both of them cleared their throats. "Our parents," Nancy began. "Our parents are really excited about the newspaper article."

"We gave them a copy of the story we wrote?"

Someday I had to edit Jill's punctuation, tell her this questioning vocal tag was a sign of insecurity, a need to seek approval. That men did not speak that way. That she had to purge the habit, speak assertively, fight for verbal equality. Someday. Now I had to find out what was up.

"They're real excited that you've approved the story and that we're going to have our own article in the paper and all."

Pause. No comment from the echo chamber. Big worry signal. I put down a stack of vocabulary quizzes and gave my visitors my full attention.

"The thing is, they say that since it's about an actual illegal crime thing, the school administration has to know about it. I mean, we can't go around knowing about a crime and not reporting it, that's what they said."

"My uncle Josh is a lawyer? He said so."

"And reporting it in the school paper, which is what you're doing, doesn't count?" I asked. It seemed as if it should. Isn't that what actual journalists do? Had Woodward and Bernstein filed a police report first?

"My mother said it wasn't right. That at least the headmaster of the school had to know about it—"

"—sooner than a month from now, which is, like, when it'll be in print? Because it wasn't fair to spring it on him through an article? It's his reputation, too?"

As if I needed reminding of that. Connect the dots into the future, the rest of this term. His school is the viper's nest, the corrupt center of a criminal ring. It could not be worse.

And my profile, promised to be kept low, would jump into the stratosphere. At least it would seem that way to Havermeyer, who would scapegoat me as the troublemaker, she who authorized the story.

The girls' parents were probably right, and although I was sick of doing the right thing and having it boomerang, I reopened my briefcase and extracted their article. They waited as I skimmed over it. I had a memory of what was in it and hoped against hope that my memory was failing me.

But there it was on the second page: names. Students' names, schools' names, the Philly Prep ringleader's name. And not on the page—yet—but as a postscript to what was already written, I also saw expulsions, nongraduations, possible revoking of college admissions, involvement of other schools.

You'll never work in this town again, Amanda.

But the right thing to do. Morally correct. Ethically proper.

And on the other side of the scales of justice, what did I have to offer up as an objection and counterweight?

My convenience.

My comfort level.

My butt.

"Also the police?"

For once, I hoped Jill meant that question mark, that she didn't know if the police needed instant notification.

"Because it's a crime, an actual illegal thing, her uncle Josh says."

"They'll need to investigate? Uncle Josh says just because we wrote this thing doesn't make it true legally for a case? That, like, the kids could sue for libel or something? So there has to be an investigation, like with detectives and everything? Uncle Josh thought maybe me and Nancy—"

"Nancy and I," I said, working by remote control.

"Nancy and I could write the story for the big newspapers, too? Maybe? Maybe the *Inquirer*?"

"Maybe," I murmured. My pulse was going triple-time. The little idea that grew. Any higher profile, I'd have to be on Mount Rushmore.

TOWARD THE END of the day, my seniors were in their circle, working on their movie projects. Adam's absence was no longer physically visible—his chair removed, the circle made whole again, although Troy Bloester came up to my desk to whisper, "Adam's okay. Thought you'd want to know."

"How do you know?"

"He's been around."

"Around where? What do you mean?"

"Around here. This junior saw him early this morning. His mom—the junior's mom—was dropping him off, and they both saw Adam and another guy in the alley behind the school."

That didn't sound so okay to me. Adam was either unaware of being the subject of a manhunt or unaware of everything.

"The mom called the cops, too, but Adam was gone way before they got there. Thought you'd want to know. I was glad he got away, and so was the kid whose mom was going to turn him in. Nobody wants Adam in bigger trouble than he already is. The guy's a weird dude, but . . ."

I waited.

"He's our weird dude."

I found that a rather elegant and suitable philosophy, and thanked Troy for the update.

Sarah Adams, the tiny girl who'd missed the ruckus at the library, had seemed positively infected with her project since that day. Now, having gone back to the library each succeeding day that it was open, she was creating an involved story about a frontier woman whose adventures served as the basis of the books she both wrote and illustrated. Sarah hummed to herself as she drew. Every time I saw her and was again amazed by the transformation of an otherwise lackadaisical pupil, I smiled. With enough time, with enough breathing room to think about the students and to plan, I could . . . I squelched the joyous expansion of my heart— that touchdown feeling that always followed a teaching success, minor though it might be. The optimistic hopes for still more successes.

I had to wean myself of those feelings. They had no future.

A messenger entered with a note. I knew what it was going to say almost before I opened it, and I knew why the ancients used to kill the messenger. I tried not to glare at the hapless kid as I read: *Miss Pepper, stop in the office before leaving school. Dr. Havermeyer needs to talk with you.* Signed by the Office Witch herself, who'd carefully omitted any social pleasantries such as please or thank you. "I'll be there," I told the messenger, who seemed to feel the tension field surrounding the note, and who wheeled around and was immediately gone.

Too soon after, I stood in front of a red-faced Havermeyer, a man so overwhelmed by impossible emotions that he could barely form an unintelligible sentence. "First and foremost," he said, "I regret the necessity of immediately, as of this moment, suspending publication of the *InkWire*."

"The school paper? You aren't going to let the kids print their last issue of the year?" I'm not sure why I found it necessary to ask questions to which I knew the answers, but I did. Just to hear the facts sounded in the land of freedom of the press.

"Miss Pepper, you should have prevented a story of this magnitude—do you even begin to understand the ramifications of what those girls—have you any idea of the negative—I thought I communicated with you to the effect I wanted nothing more than to preserve the integrity of the school's reputation—just when our scores and admissions were . . ." He obviously realized why we were suddenly doing so well, and clamped his mouth shut, but his skin tone could have been made into a crayon color called Stroke Victim.

"They investigated on their own," I said. "They aren't doing this for personal gain. Do you want a crime like this to go unpunished? Do you want me to censor honest inquiry? What they've done is what we hope our students will do. What participants in a democracy would all do."

"No InkWire," he said. "Publication indefinitely suspended."

"Why indefinite? We have only one more issue before the year ends. Those editors will move on."

"Then not indefinite. For the duration of this term," he said. "And next term we will have to have a prior agreement on what constitutes responsible reporting—what is permissible in a school newspaper. This isn't the New York Times. There was no need—"

I was thoroughly incensed. Forget my job. Forget the stupid and petty politics of this wretched school. The baseline was that two tenth-grade girls had shown amazing gumption, done a bang-up job of reporting and putting together a story, and it was now considered an offense, something I should have squelched.

"I think you're making a mistake," I said. "The police—"

"We are delaying informing the police, pending our own investigation," he said. "This school will undertake an inquiry on its own before we involve the entire city and the wider press. The girls' parents and I have come to an agreement that will spare their daughters unnecessary and undesirable exposure and involvement in a criminal proceeding. Until such time as it may prove necessary, of course."

"Who? How?"

"You may put your mind at rest and stop being bothered by that question, because it is no longer a concern of yours," he said. "I have relieved you of that concern by virtue of suspending publication of the paper." He turned his back to me and looked out the window at the street and the square beyond it.

"They tried to do the right thing," I said. "That's all they did."

Outside, our students made their start-and-stop way across the square. I could see them around the silhouetted figure of my headmaster at the window. "I requested a low profile," he said, his back still to me, "and this is anything but. Everything but. I do not feel that ours is a harmonious working relationship, and this insubordination and refusal to honor a modest request on my part, a protective desire for our school—all this leads me to believe that you might definitely find a more compatible working relationship and be happier elsewhere. I hope that such is the case, because I feel obliged to terminate your employment."

"Now? Today?" On a Tuesday in late April? It seemed ridiculous.

"A leave of absence until the end of the year." He finally turned and faced me. "Please leave your substitute your lesson plans and any finals you've prepared, of course. A brief sabbatical. Shall we call it that, then?"

And that was it. The accumulated frustrations of this worst of all weeks—what felt like effort after effort to behave responsibly, to be a good citizen, a good teacher, a good adult—all of it misfiring and winding up here, with nobody trying to do the right thing by me—all of that exploded. Besides, I had absolutely nothing to lose.

"I don't think I'd call it a sabbatical," I said. "I don't think that's the right word at all. I think we should call it being fired for allowing students to enjoy their constitutional right of freedom of speech. I think in fact what you're doing is illegal and deserves a news story of its own. You're not even giving me a chance to say goodbye to my students, are you? I think they deserve to know what's going on."

"No need to humiliate yourself. We'll tell them you're ill. Medical leave. In all honesty, your appearance . . . you might well require such leave."

"I'm not ill." He thought I was. Mentally.

But Adam wasn't, because his parents donated money to the school. "And I'm not humiliated to be fired for such a tawdry reason. I'm proud of it." I stood up. "Is that it, then?"

"Well, but . . . what is it you're going to do?"

"I don't know, Dr. H. I'm going to have to think about it this weekend. I'll let you know."

I was fired. For real this time. No, worse. I'd been banished—told not to darken the doors again. To plead sickness. It sounded like the old Soviet Union, where dissidents were put in so-called hospitals forever.

Well, I'd be damned. I would not go gentle, and that was that. I couldn't have said if this was about me or freedom of the press or simple stubborn stupidity, but as I walked outside, I saw Jill and Nancy, who waved.

"Hey, girl reporters," I said. "I have news. Bad news. The paper's been suspended. There'll be no story for any of us this year."

Both their mouths opened slightly. Their collective *oh, no* was silent, but I heard it.

"And listen, this is awkward, but—I've been fired for having allowed you to think we'd print your story. I'd say I'd see you, but I don't think I'm going to be permitted back in. Not even to say goodbye to anyone."

They were the best of all possible audiences, their faces registering the full spectrum of disbelief and horror at what was going on.

"So—I'll miss you. I hope you get the chance to run with the story—it's an important one, and you've done a great job. Take care."

I walked around to the back of the building, where my car was parked, trusting that after all these years, I knew the power of two animated tenth-grade girls.

News of my expulsion would be universally known within nanoseconds.

It was the most—and least—I could do.

Even if they didn't care about me, they had to care about their story.

Nineteen

IT had been a beautiful day for a firing, sufficiently crisp, green, and springlike—even in the city—to make the prospect of living on the streets not that unpleasant.

Or at least walking on those streets, which was the method of transport Mackenzie and I chose to visit Beth in the hospital. She'd thought she'd be released immediately, but she had bonked her head when she fell, and that necessitated tests, scans, and observations. So far so good, and now she expected to go home the next day, but we thought we'd divert her attention from the fact that she was stuck there for another night. Boy, did those Pepper sisters know how to get attention—one fired, the other incapacitated.

"Let's buy her dinner," I said. "Something suitable for the occasion."

"Unhealth food, for when you're bruised and bummed," Mackenzie suggested.

"Why not? What's less healthy than getting hit by a car?"

So we kept our eyes out for a sign of steak sandwiches en route, hoping we wouldn't have to go all the way to South Street for a suitable one. There was lots of time to talk about things we should have talked about a while back, which we now did, in gingerly fashion, as if each sentence were a carefully placed stitch, mending our ripped edges.

"I feel like a complete failure," I said. "Everything I touch, or even try to touch, gets hurt. I only wanted to help. Didn't want to be a bystander. An 'I could have told you that would happen' kind of person. And look where it's gotten us all. Adam's wandering around, sleeping wherever, in real danger from you guys, from his new best friends, and from himself. And I'm unemployed. Out of work. Mortified."

"I'm not gonna let you live on the streets, you know," he said. "You won't have to be like Adam, looking for shelter."

"Thanks, but it's not all about that. I don't want to be any-body's dependent, the screw-up, your personal charity. It's just that if I was mixed up a week ago about what I wanted to do, which direction I wanted to head in—if any—I'm a thousand times worse off today. I need to be in control of my life, or at least have the illusion that I am."

"Don't let him fire you that way," Mackenzie said.

"What way should I let him fire me?"

"Don't go gentle into that dark night, I meant."

"I was thinking the same thing. Then I remembered—that poem's about dying. I'm fired, not dead."

"Glad you've noticed." His voice was mild, but his message hit me with enormous force. I was alive. Quit-your-bitchin' time.

"He expects you to disappear like a bad smell might. Don't."

I thought about a counterattack as we walked. A legal fight, a taking-it-to-the-press fight. Any sort of fight at all.

There was a general air of merriment on the streets, a new scent and texture, nature promising that winter was absolutely over. As of this evening, spring had arrived in all its infinite power. Mating season was on, and you could sense it on every city block.

This weather could galvanize anybody into action, except, I realized, me. "I'm too tired for a battle," I finally said. "I wasn't sure I wanted to keep going, that teaching was really for me. Maybe this was an effective way of answering that."

He shook his head. "It's wrong, is all." Having made his pronouncement, he walked along slowly, cogitating. Once again I noticed how his multitrack mind worked. He barely looked at the stores we passed—except for two, one selling used books and one stocked with kitchenware. He's into equipment and tools, doesn't matter for what—even if he's lost in thought, his radar will nonetheless spot hardware stores and camera shops and electronics emporiums.

I, on the other hand, tend to get caught up in the displays, imagining them on me or owned by me, and whatever else I've been thinking about gets pushed so far aside, I forget all about it.

"How's this?" he asked a block later. "Say I show up at the school first thing tomorrow, introduce myself as a member of the Philadelphia police force—"

"He knows you are. He knows you're with me, too," I said.

"Think so? I'll bet we all look alike to him. But even so, doesn't matter. I'm not speakin' officially, just professionally, complimentin' Dr. Havermeyer on his exemplary behavior. Which of course, I heard about from a fellow officer."

"Have I been missing something? Has Havermeyer ever in his lifetime done something outstandingly good?"

Mackenzie nodded. "You mean you missed how he was immediately handlin' this sad perversion of academic standards? This travesty being perpetrated on the SAT exams? You missed how he was

211

upholdin' the standards of Philly Prep, settin' a great example for the rest of the city's schools by callin' the police in immediately for a full public investigation."

"Perfect." Havermeyer had many more than two faces and would wear whichever suited the atmosphere around him. It was easy for him—there was nothing behind the mask except another mask. If Mackenzie could convince him that not only did the police already know about the cheating scam, but that they were under the delusion that he'd broken the ring, brought the corruption out into the air, the man would run with it. And with Havermeyer taking bows for his moral leadership, there'd be no point suspending the newspaper and firing me, at least for the moment, would there? Perhaps Mackenzie was right and I could walk out on my own terms.

"My hero," I murmured as he again came to a full halt.

We had not come upon a steak shop. What we had come upon was the rare-book dealer I'd visited just days ago. The beautiful shop where the perfect Mackenzie gift was found and then lost by the imperfect Pepper price tag. It was closed, but it still had its calm and inviting air. "Nice place," I said.

"Bauman's?" He nodded.

"You know it?"

"I go in when I'm in the neighborhood. Ever been inside?"

My turn to nod. I told him about the Daniel Boone poem that he wasn't getting, and he said the thought was what counted, and he loved the idea and was quite as contented with his life without the book as he'd been before he'd heard of it.

"I never cared about anything except what was written in a book," I said. "Never went into that sort of bookstore. But this last month—probably ever since my first trip up to the Rare Book Department, I . . . I really wish I could have those books. They're beautiful. The man in there showed me lots of titles, and I don't care about Americana—this was for you—but really, I wanted them. All of them."

"Careful. Book collectors are an entirely separate world. Very intense. An' I don't know if there's even a twelve-step program for them," Mackenzie said. "I do know that we don't have the disposable income for them. I know, 'cause I've spent lots of time drooling and despairing, too, here an' on the computer. This guy's on the Net." He disengaged from the window. "Think of all the books we aren't going to buy," he said. "Think of those price tags. A thousand dollars here, a thousand there."

"They had books at the library worth a hundred thousand," I said. "More. They have books like the Gutenberg Bible, whose every page is worth fortunes."

"Let's not buy those, either. Think about how much more we're savin'!"

Savin'. The word echoed, touching off vibrations. Savin. Wasn't that the name I kept . . . no. Sabin. The polio guy, only he wasn't. The man at Bauman's. And the stickum at Emily's . . . "Have you ever heard of somebody named Sabin, but not the polio guy? Something to do with rare or antique books?"

"A reference, I believe," he said. "Documents a book. Gives the provenance. The condition of specific editions and printings. Why?"

"Just a thought, but all this talk about their worth made me wonder. Do you think Emily Fisher . . . she said she thought she had a way out of her financial mess. Do you think she could have been . . . would people buy books that were stolen?" I knew it was a stupid question as soon as I'd formed it. People would do anything.

Which is precisely what Mackenzie said.

"How? Through a bookstore?"

"Not one like Bauman's, no. But it's like art—you don't find paintings stolen from museums for sale at the reputable galleries where the provenance of the works is known, but there are always less reputable dealers and unethical collectors, and those paintings disappear into the hands of private collectors who never show them to anyone else. They just have to have them. Collectors are a breed apart from thee and me. Go on the Net and look at the lists of stolen books people are on the lookout for."

I mulled this over, still without any conviction that this made sense. Some logical glue was missing.

"To answer your question," Mackenzie said, "sure, books get stolen, but it can't be easy stealin' them from a library—or one of these stores—without being caught. Emily was barely there long enough to get the drill down."

He spotted another of the aluminum portable kitchens on the corner across from us. This one had a line of people waiting for one of its unhealthy offerings.

I pushed Emily to the back of my mind—still wishing, however, that I knew her way out. Since she wasn't using it, maybe I could.

"Popular spot," he said. "To think we've never dined there before."

Mackenzie bought generously. You never knew who might stop by, he said. Best to have too much rather than not enough. He sounded like my mother.

"Here you go," the man in the instant restaurant said. The voice, I thought. That stonewashed voice.

A bearded man handed Mackenzie the order. "Want drinks?" he asked, sounding as if pebbles lined his throat. He put sodas and bottled water on the sliver of counter, and slowly, like a Polaroid photo coming into life, I recognized the steak-sandwich maven. The Thwart Man. The library—the quarrel with the woman who turned out to be H. Emily Fisher Buttonwood. Who turned out to be dead. "Hi," I said. "Don't I know you from somewhere?"

"Wow," Mackenzie muttered. "Your lines are real original. What next? 'What's your sign?' Or 'What's a nice guy like you doin' in a place like this?' "

"Been here a while now," the steak-sandwich man said.

I shook my head. "No . . . a meeting, maybe? I heard you speak. You're Louie. The advocate for the homeless."

His smile changed his face so much, I wouldn't have recognized him at all had he been serving his sandwiches with that smile. "Louie Louie," he said. "Louis Lewis," he spelled out, "if you must know. You know me, huh?" he asked. "You're in the group, too? I thought I knew all the—"

"No, no. Not yet. Thinking about it," I said. "So you've been here a long time?" Hadn't Terry and I decided he must be a trust-fund baby? How jealous we'd been. How wildly wrong.

"Pays the rent," he said. "Six hours a day so's I don't wind up homeless, too. My uncle owns a bunch of these. Gave me the easiest shift—twelve to six. Don't have to get up too early, don't have to be around after dark."

"You're here every day?"

He held up a finger, as if in warning. "Weekdays only." He looked at me, his head at an angle that was reminiscent of when I'd seen him with Emily Fisher. His stance had subtly become more aggressive. "You're thinking this isn't such a hot job, aren't you?"

"No. Why would you—"

"Don't bother. I know how people feel. But lemme tell you, being outside, like I am—it's healthier. I haven't been sick a single day since I started. Ask my uncle—I never missed one day of work. Tell me that's true of inside jobs."

"No," I agreed. "Always getting head colds or worse. You're right, that's amazing—a perfect attendance record. Congratulations."

"You are one cordial customer, Miz Pepper," Mackenzie said as we walked away. "Unless he was an old friend. Or beau."

"I saw him quarreling with Emily Fisher the day she was killed."

"I remember now. You were pushin' him as somebody to watch. The homeless advocate. Right. Because you decided that, against all logic, it was a part-time cheesesteak salesman who did her in, not a schizophrenic student who felt she dissed him."

I kept my eyes on the pavement. Frankly, I was disappointed to lose Louis Lewis as a suspect. He'd been my favorite, and not just

215

because of his ridiculous name. Until five minutes before, I'd known nothing about him aside from that name, and he had no humanity, no identity except his anger, which I'd witnessed. It would have been so easy and remote if he'd have been the murderer, but with his unbroken attendance record at the steak kiosk, he was out, and the field narrowed ever more tightly around Adam, yet I was increasingly sure he hadn't done it. Money was too involved with Helena and with Ray Buttonwood to be irrelevant. Money was a strong motive for what seemed a premeditated act. Adam had no motive, was not a violent person, and couldn't have planned something that no one would see or hear, the way this murderer had.

"Hope not," Mackenzie said as we entered Jefferson Hospital.

"Not what?" My thoughts were still tangled around Louie.

"Sleuthing. You. I really hope not. You're in enough trouble without interfering with a—"

"Thanks. I know the drill." I didn't want to be annoyed with him. Not now. "Only thing I'm interfering with—*we're* interfering with—is hospital routine." I smiled. So did he. The moment was defused.

I hated how Beth looked. All sorts of bruises had found their way to the surface overnight. "You're doing your face in autumn colors in spring?" I said. "How daring."

She grimaced. I thought it was supposed to be a funny expression, although along with her multihued face, it made her look still more horrifying.

Her leg was straight out and encased at the knee. She looked understandably unhappy and uncomfortable, and it all felt my fault—my city, my streets, my fault. But maybe she hadn't noticed that, so I chose not to mention it.

"Look at it this way," I told my older sister. "Life in the big city is full of adventures. Like this one. Frankly, when's the last time you slept with a stranger?" To her credit, Beth pretended to do the calculations. The woman she was rooming with, a grim creature who'd had foot surgery, did not adjudge my remark to be funny. Nor did she want us to think we'd get away with smuggling in cheesesteaks.

"Against the rules," she said. "Not permitted. I'm calling the nurse."

"Some people bring chocolates," I said.

"Chocolates don't smell the way those things do," she said. "It's already making me sick. I'm calling the nurse."

Mackenzie was about to speak, but I put a hand on his forearm and smiled an I-can-handle-this at him.

"I'm so sorry," I said. "They are fragrant, aren't they? I'll just open this window a crack, and that should do it." I stood down-wind, salivating in the fumes. I was ready to eat even the paper they were wrapped in.

"I'm ringing the nurse. Your sister is supposed to stick to the special, individualized hospital menu the dietician has worked out for her." She'd memorized the damn puff piece the hospital provided. "She's to behave the same way the rest of us do."

We explained that Beth found cheesesteaks psychologically heal-ing, and she did not need to eat hospital food in order for her lac-erations or ligaments to heal.

The woman said, "Rules are rules." Her thumb was on the buzzer that brings the nurse.

"That's true," I said, "but isn't it also a truism that rules are made to be broken?"

"Not hospital rules. Not rules in my room. And to have all of you—like a dinner party—sitting around and planning to munch and chew . . ."

"We'll be so quiet and well-mannered, you'll never—"

"You disrupt the entire hospital and endanger sick people with your—"

I gave her my sandwich and said I wasn't hungry and wouldn't she please, please try it.

Her moral scruples were never heard from again. Nor was she.

Not even a thank-you. One small burp, and she didn't follow it with so much as an "excuse me."

I tried to find the moral center of that small episode, to make it a learning experience, since it certainly wasn't a culinary one, but all I heard from my inner self were stomach grumbles until Mackenzie, having a good laugh about my persuasive powers, shared his steak. As did Beth. "And what would you have done differently?" I asked.

"Drawn my gun," Mackenzie said. "Blown her away."

Beth was full of plans for how she was going to manage her unborn business despite being on crutches for a while.

"I'll help," I promised. "I'll be your legs. I'll carry you around like Tiny Tim. Don't you worry about a thing." I didn't have a chance to tell her how possible that was, now that I had all the time in the world, because Sam, neatly tailored and carrying his briefcase, entered at that point. I'd expected him. That's why I hadn't tapped the fourth cheesesteak.

"Didn't expect you tonight," Beth said, her face lit with joy. Sam's such a dry and methodical man, such a predictable and, frankly, unsexy, forgettable man, I'm always shocked to be reminded of the charge that runs between Beth and him.

He put a small bouquet on the night table next to her. There were five enormous baskets and floral arrangements lined up on the windowsill. Beth's friends moved speedily. "I can't stay long. My folks can only baby-sit till seven. . . . You've gone Technicolor, Beth. Your poor face!" His words were light, but he looked as if he might cry.

"Doesn't hurt. Just looks disgusting. It's a shame it isn't Halloween," she said.

"We're having dinner," Mackenzie said. "Join us. There's a place set for you." He handed Sam the final white-paper-wrapped cheesesteak. Sam sighed, shook his head, said how really bad the combo of steak, cheese, and fried onions was for him, then quietly ate the whole thing.

I wondered what Sam really thought of me. To him, I was always the troublemaker, and now I must have seemed even more of a screw-up and the cause or x factor in the accident.

I wondered if he was right.

"What about Ray?" Beth asked. "What about Helena? What's going to happen to them?" Her swollen lips were set in that stern line that tolerated no nonsense. I got the sense she'd like to see them hang. Me too.

"They released Ray last night. His nose is broken."

Which might make him more interesting-looking. Finally something had happened to his face.

"I don't care about his nose. How about arresting him for reckless driving?"

"He wasn't driving the car. Helena Spurry was. It was her car."

I don't know why that should have so surprised me, but it did. Even the dog-faced woman in the next bed stopped chewing and looked over, as if also startled.

"And Helena's still in the hospital. This one, one floor up. Turns out she had a couple of broken ribs and possible internal damage."

"You aren't representing her, are you?" Beth's voice had edged toward the shrill. "That isn't why you know those details, is it?"

"I refused," he said softly. "I can't imagine why she asked me in the first place, given that my wife was her victim."

"Because you're a good lawyer, that's why," Beth snapped. "And she is going to need one!"

"There's nothing to collect, though," I said sadly. "No money there." So no great settlement was going to pad my brand-new retirement, either. "Wish she'd married her sugar daddy, whoever he was, before going for her joy ride. Which reminds me—what were they doing together? Is Ray Helena's secret love? That 'prospect' of hers?"

Sam looked horrified. "He's—he was—married to her sister!"

"Like that never happens?"

"No," Sam said. "No. He . . . no."

"Trust the man," Beth said. "The truth is, Sam knows who Ray *is* involved with."

"Beth," Sam said sadly.

"What does it matter? Emily's dead. And she knew. We all knew."

Mackenzie's beeper buzzed. Everybody was saved by the buzzer. Mackenzie excused himself to make a call, and we chatted about tiny, noncontroversial things—the quality of the food, the calls from the children, how my minor bumps and aches were coming along, and the like.

Then my guy reappeared. "This is either good or bad news, but there's just been a—the thing is, a witness we've been tryin' to reach for weeks is upstairs here, just brought in, an' I need to interview her as soon as possible. Very convenient and serendipitous, but sorry, Mandy. You get to go home in a taxi. Alone."

"I'll take her home," Sam said. "It's almost on the way. I'll get on the expressway from there."

I felt mild apprehension, for no obvious reason. Of course Sam would make the offer, and indeed, the Vine Street Expressway was seconds from my house; he'd have offered even if that were not so. But I felt it nonetheless, and after we finished the cursory chitchat and promised to be in touch the next day, Sam and I left, and I felt it still.

Sam's approach to life is straight on. If I had to draw mental charts, or diagrams of attention, most would look like the spiky mountains and valleys an electrocardiogram produces. Mackenzie's would look like that—in duplicate, or triplicate, mountains doing a do-si-do with valleys, and all points tracking. But I envision Sam's as a straight line. Perhaps several parallel straight lines, but they move inexorably from A to Z, with not a zig or zag en route.

Halfway to my place, which wasn't far away at all, I was aware of that straight line again. "Amanda," he said in his formal manner, "I know that you've been upset on behalf of your student, and you've been trying to find other solutions to the identity of poor Emily's murderer. I know this because Beth is now involved, and she asked me a great many questions about Ray Buttonwood's whereabouts this past Thursday. And believe it or not, last night, at the hospital, she asked more."

"Because of the accident. Because it felt like he—whoever—aimed the car at us."

Sam sighed. "I gather they were fighting about a loan. They'd been taking care of preparations for a memorial service, neither of them willing to allow the other to plan it, and wound up fighting about money Emily had loaned Helena. Of course, that missing money is part of Emily's estate, and her husband would inherit . . . or at least her son, and so it's all a mess. The business is not a success, and unless there's a miracle—"

"Well, this would hardly be a miracle, but there's supposedly a man on the horizon, a future husband." I didn't try to contain the contempt in my voice.

"She mentioned him," Sam said, "although not by name. She's optimistic, and feels that then she could settle out this debt. But may I emphasize that the gentleman in question is most assuredly not Ray Buttonwood. I myself believe that it's not anybody. Or rather, it's somebody who has no idea he's being auditioned as husband number two, or that there's an outstanding large debt, let alone one he's expected to pay off."

I wondered if Emily's financial solution had been as illogical and unlikely as her sister's.

Sam cleared his throat. "Let me reemphasize that I was with Ray on that . . . tragic day. We were taking a deposition. He was barely gone from my sight until we were finished, well after the . . . sad event. There's no rational way to think he could have done that. Or would have. He's a good lawyer. That makes him seem fierce or unpalatable to you and Beth, and so be it. He'd argue to the death—but that's the only way he'd kill anybody.

"I'm sorry, Amanda, for dashing your hopes, and I'm sorry for the boy, but there is every indication, and no doubt in my mind, that your student is the perpetrator. I just hope they find him soon, and that they keep him somewhere that's safe for him—and safe for the rest of us, too. Mostly for you. You're too close to a disturbed young man who has already killed. Much, much too close."

Twenty

ONE happy thought about being fired: I didn't have papers to mark. Or, more accurately, I didn't have to mark the papers I still had.

I didn't have calls to return, either. The answering machine was a blank.

I could watch TV, rent a video, read a book, scrub the floors, polish my nails. Do absolutely nothing. Whatever I wanted.

Odd that it didn't make me happier. And odd that, having all options available, I couldn't choose one. It was a replay of my paralysis about what I'd do if I could do anything, and where I'd live if I could live anywhere.

I found myself behaving as if this were an ordinary Tuesday evening. I emptied my briefcase, stared at its contents, and realized as soon as I saw the worn paperback of *Turn of the Screw* that I'd never had the conference with Lia about her adaptation. Havermeyer be damned. I'd go back to tie up loose ends. I wasn't walking out on Lia.

Good. I'd done something. I'd made a decision.

Now what? There was nothing I had to do. I put everything back in the case. And fidgeted.

Adam. I should have made him talk longer when he'd called. Had the phone tapped. I should have ensnared him, tricked him, trapped him, allowed the police to take him in—to protect him. From me. Instead, I'd helped make him a fugitive. With a little more of my help, he was sure to land on *America's Most Wanted.* But there was nothing I could do about him now.

What should I do, then? Something different. Something I normally never had time to do. Something to signify a new, unemployed era.

A bubble bath. The very image of leisure. A long soak in the tub. That was what I'd do with my first night of freedom. Or was that my first night of an aimless, purposeless life?

I undressed and then considered my sweater and slacks, which had, as the day progressed, begun to feel too woolly. The wrong texture against the skin. The season had turned, and I probably wouldn't wear them again till autumn. Time to wash and put away the sweater, have the slacks cleaned. I checked my pockets, lest I lose something for the next two seasons. Nothing, except the predictable unused, disintegrating tissue, one paper clip, and a crumpled piece of paper. I started to toss the lot until I realized what the paper was and where I'd found it: *Bauman/Sabin: AL: CDPP—17K, EAPMS95K* . . . Numbers, letters, more of the same. I remembered asking Beth if she knew what it meant. Neither of us had had a clue, and we'd renewed our search for the love letters. I must have absentmindedly stuck it in my pocket.

I stared at it again. Five days had not improved my comprehension except for the Bauman and Sabin parts. But knowing that made it probable the rest of the symbols were also about books. And money. *17K. 95K.* Seventeen thousand, ninety-five thousand dollars—it had to be. Her solution? Her way out—way, way out I thought, looking again at that *95K*.

Bauman was a reference, a way to find out worth even though the actual sales would be elsewhere, to unethical collectors, mad to own something no matter its origins. How would she find them?

Emily told my sister that books were what she cared about, almost exclusively. Reading them. Working with them. Saving them. Selling them. My wild speculation had been right.

I had nowhere in particular I had to be for the rest of my life, so that bath could wait. Instead, I sat down half clothed and logged onto the Net, searching for rare books. Mackenzie window-shopped on-line. Maybe doing the same would clarify something for me.

I found a page of dealers, with easy access to their websites, and the first I came to had his catalogue divided alphabetically. I looked at the scrap of paper and pressed the section that said *C-D*.

Charles Dickens. Of course. I felt like an idiot. And the PP, *Pickwick Papers.* The CDDC—*David Copperfield.* ED—*Edwin Drood.* The abbreviation—*il*—for *illustrated.* Emily's stickums had been so full of *CD*s, I'd thought they were certificates of deposit. Or music disks. But they were works by Charles Dickens, one of the library's specialties, and next to them, prices she'd gotten from catalogues for comparison's sake.

Now, with a sense of her coding, I looked at the *EAPMS*. Earlier I'd focused on the *PMS* part of it and wondered. Now, knowing this was about books, I recognized *MS* as *manuscript*, and Poe's initials practically popped out at me. Ninety-five thousand dollars' worth of manuscript. And the man wrote short stories.

The other initials obviously referred to other books. Manuscripts, incunabula. Irreplaceable volumes for which enormous sums would be paid.

I saw descriptions mentioning a book's "leaf" or "gutters" and realized how off I'd been in their interpretation. I'd thought Emily was concerned with her household maintenance.

Here was Emily's solution, as incredible and dreadful as it sounded: stealing and selling the rare books she was supposedly saving.

I waited for the heady eureka bubbles to elate me—I'd solved a puzzle, after all. But they never became airborne. There were weights in those bubbles, and one by one they ruptured. The truth was, my solution didn't work.

If Emily was the bad actor, selling off rare books, why had somebody felt a need to kill her? Aside from moral scruples, there were practical ones: What would be gained? If someone knew and was horrified by the act, why not turn her in, expose her? Become a hero, not a murderer.

The jolt of the phone's bell annoyed me. I was—almost—on to something. Right there—almost. But . . .

I pressed the talk button on the phone.

"Good. You're there. I had to tell somebody, and Mr. Propriety, to whom I'm married, needs to be told such things gently," Beth said. "It may not have been prudent, but I went and saw her. Confronted her."

Beth could only get so far on crutches, so I knew who "her" had to be. "Helena?" And indeed, in the light of any future lawsuits, a visit would appall Sam.

"I went there to be the voice of doom, the avenging angel, the—I have no idea what, but tough, at least that. And furious. But she was pathetic. Cried the second she saw me, apologized over and over, said they had been making memorial service arrangements, carpooled, but Ray badgered her. Said he was taking her store and her apartment because of the debt, because he legally could, because he'd never liked her. She wasn't looking. She was screaming and crying and just wanted to get him back to his car, get him out of hers."

"So you wound up new best friends." Money again. Even Beth's tears and stitches and bruises had been caused by a quarrel about money. Everything kept being about money, often the same money going round and round.

And Emily the librarian had somehow been sucked into the whirl of it. Money . . . Whatever happened to sex, ambition, and drugs as driving forces? "I gather you were less than tough. Or avenging. And, in fact, you've changed your mind about hauling her into court, haven't you?" I wondered whether I should tell Beth my suspicions about her murdered friend, or keep them to myself until they were proven either right or wrong.

Another sigh. "She's got nothing."

"You're un-American. Don't you know to sue the hell out of anybody and anything that happens to you?"

"If Ray calls her debt, she'll have less than nothing."

"Why doesn't she get herself an actual job?" I snapped with the righteous indignation of the unemployed.

"She's like those displaced Romanovs after the revolution, absolutely unable to realize that the glory days are over. Now her lost glories include her car. She's just clinging to the hope of marriage to this man."

"Poor jerk. Should we warn him her intentions are impure?"

"They're pure enough. Purely material. They met on a luxury liner en route to France, can you believe that?"

"Not about a penniless person like Helena." It makes me crazy that people like her exist and get away with their grasshopper lives. Surely some of her fare had been paid for by her sister's loan. Or she needed the loan because she blew her inheritance on a deluxe trip to Europe.

"She, of course, was on a buying trip for the store she had in mind at the time."

So I was right. She took her inheritance and sailed to Europe like a grande dame of a century ago.

"This guy used her scouting talents, and she's provided pieces for his beach house and his place in New York. She has high expectations of moving beyond designer status to wifehood. Only she told me it became awkward because Emily then got herself a job in the same place where he works, and she was always afraid of running into her sister. Afraid Emily might go after him, too."

Wait a minute. "Mr. Big Bucks works at the library?" Helena was further out of touch with reality than I had thought. But she had said there was somebody there she visited. I'd assumed it was her sister. Once again I was wrong.

"As a hobby, she thinks. To have something to do."

Money again. Lots of it. Money to be relocated from the librarian to Helena to Ray, except that money is something libraries need, not something they provide, and the idea of a gentleman librarian . . . It wasn't the best fit I'd ever heard of. It wasn't an as-if occupation, the way Helena's was. It was hard work and lots of it.

Still. A rich librarian.

Emily afraid of something, asking Beth to clean things up. Emily afraid, yet having a plan that would bail her out.

The money. The books. The scraps of paper checking out worth.

A rich librarian.

Somebody had been stealing, but not Emily. She knew about somebody else's stealing. That person killed her because she knew. Odd that the balloons and trumpets still didn't rise in triumph.

I had to do more thinking. It wasn't right yet. Emily had told Beth she had a plan. An economic plan. Like her sister, she'd thought she had a way out. But she hadn't said what it was. Didn't that hint at something less than ethical? If you were going to get a second job, sell an asset, win the lottery—anything that was socially acceptable—wouldn't you tell your good friend?

Whistle-blowing was out. It was socially acceptable but it didn't bring in bucks. Could not have been Emily's secret plan. Emily was involved. Co-thief? Perhaps. Or blackmailing the real thief. Probably the latter, because she was still researching the probable worth of the books, didn't know that on her own. I didn't think she was the one stealing or selling them. But blackmail was just as bad, and more dangerous.

Or maybe there really was a rich guy working at the library simply because he wanted to. I put the reins on my runaway thoughts and looked at the crumpled slip of paper again. *Bauman/Sabin:AL.* "Was the boyfriend's name Al?"

Mackenzie could find out what was true and what was not. He'd believe me on this one, wouldn't he? At least find it worth pursuing.

Call waiting beeped. "Beth," I said, "hold on there—I have to take this. It might be Mackenzie." I clicked and answered.

"Pepper?" an unfamiliar voice said.

"Who is this?"

"Your name's in Adam's pocket."

"Is he all right? Where is he?"

"Where he is is on my nerves. I don't need this—I have my own problems."

"Try—tell me where he is, what he wants. Who you are."

"We've been hanging. He's no trouble. Wasn't. But he's like . . . he's gone really weird. Thinks he needs his scarf, but he needs a lot more than that."

"Again? The scarf? Where is Adam?"

I don't know how you can hear a kiss-off without the kiss, but I had the definite impression I just had. "He says the library kept it, and he wants it back, which is where he was headed. Tried to call you but he said his fingers weren't working anymore, he couldn't press phone keys. Couldn't read the numbers, either. See what I mean? So, well, I did this because I'm out of here. I can't take no more. Somebody better get him."

"But is he—when did he—" The connection ended. Adam sounded like he was having a full-fledged psychotic break. I clicked back to Beth.

"Was it Mackenzie?" Beth asked.

"No. It . . ." What should I do?

"You know," Beth said, "about Helena's rich boyfriend's name. All I remember is something like a wine. His last name. Chardonnay? Burgundy?"

It was barely seven o'clock. The library was open for two more hours.

"Blanc? Rosé?"

I knew. The library's Rare Book Department. A name very much like a wine. Like Bordeaux? Could there be more than one person with that kind of name there? A Frank Champagne, or Claude Merlot?

"Wait," Beth said. "I remember that he was going to France because that's where his family was from—half his family. The other half was Scots. Lots of jokes about cheap wine." Her yawn was audible.

Scots. Cheap-wine jokes. Short for Alastair, Terry had said.

Terry. Alastair Labordeaux. AL on the crumpled paper. At the library, where Adam was headed—Adam who'd found Emily, not murdered her. Adam, about whom Terry had questioned me, had offered to help find. Sweet God—

". . . a little tired, actually," Beth was saying. "I should—"

"Absolutely. Right away."

"If I get this tired walking one corridor and riding one elevator—"

"We'll talk tomorrow." I pressed the disconnect button before I finished my sentence. Mackenzie had to listen to me this time. I punched in his page number and felt a flash of understanding and then a flush of embarrassment. Labordeaux hadn't been coming on to me, and he hadn't been upset because I had another romantic involvement. He'd been upset because I was asking too many questions. Because I hadn't known where Adam was or what he knew, and he needed to know what Adam had or hadn't seen.

That boy, he'd said. *That crazy boy who did it—where is he? Do you know? Is he in touch with you?*

That boy was walking into big trouble, worse trouble now than ever before, and there was no way he could anticipate it.

No return call from Mackenzie despite a second page with a 911 hooked on to make it clear this was an emergency. I watched the clock change, move forward a minute at a time, a dot on the side of the face pulsing with each second, each of which I felt along with the cumulative pressure of the past week, the impact of meaning well and doing poorly.

This was my last chance to help Adam.

To do it right this time.

I looked wistfully at the silent telephone, then at the clock.

To do it myself.

Now.

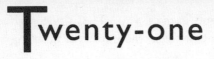Twenty-one

MOVIES have ruined real life, made it feel sluggish and damned near impossible, with countless irrelevancies demanding space between hither and yon. In a movie, if I had to get from Old City to the library, I would have done it in the blink of a scene change. Instead, I had to live all the intervening molasses moments, from riding the sluggish elevator down to getting to my car, to having somebody double-parked beside it, to finally getting free, to being stuck in traffic (which never, ever happens in movies—instead, they have wild, high-speed chases right through town), to not being able to find a parking space within dreaming distance of my destination, to the walk-jog, finally, to the library itself.

And with all that time and intervening garbage, you'd have thought I would have thought—anybody with a brain would have thought—about what I was going to do once I arrived at the place.

Goes to show you . . . I'd gotten as far as *get Adam*. Without a clue as to how to do that, or what I'd do if I found him, I speeded by the ever-present sullen smokers out on the front steps and into the lobby, which, to my amazement, was densely populated. I caught a glimpse of a poster with SOLD OUT on a banner across it. A special event, a lecture by somebody famous. More people. Too many people.

I looked around, sure that Adam would not be a part of the crowd. People were not his favorite things, and being touched frightened him. I worked my way through the crowd, slowly, with many "excuse me's."

Maybe having a lot of people around was good. Nobody would act out with an audience. I could find Adam, and keep him away from Labordeaux, and . . . The librarian's questions about my student echoed in me, as did his controlled anger at my questions about the case, about my asking for details, when I opted to revisit the scene of the crime. I could see his face as he held the elevator door, trying to look natural and only partially succeeding. How abruptly, angrily, he'd withdrawn his hand from the door, setting the elevator back to work.

The elevator. I suddenly saw it for what it was—for that minor moment when I didn't know if Terry Labordeaux would allow me to go to the Rare Book Department. When I was in a small box and he guarded the exit.

It wasn't only a perfect scene for a crime, but the only possible way the crime had happened. Why hadn't I thought of it before? It was the only place a murder could be committed without anyone observing it in that fishbowl of a balcony.

The elevator. Of course. He'd been upstairs at the cafeteria, he said—and who knew if that was true? Maybe they'd both been. Ten seconds, Mackenzie had told me. Ten seconds to unconsciousness. Hold the elevator. Keep it out of action just a bit longer, then open the door and push the body out, to the right, around the corner, away. Reset the button and return to the cafeteria, probably without anybody's having noticed your absence at all.

So easy. So dreadfully easy. A life in ten seconds. Then Adam had come out of the actual department, seen Emily's body, cried out, called for help in his disorganized way, heard his own voice, tossed his scarf over the balcony like a summons—that scarf was close to his alter ego—then run, setting off the alarm as he pulled back the wrought-iron doors to the staircase.

By this time I'd maneuvered my way through the clumps of people and reached the foot of the great staircase.

Labordeaux had become a terrifying figure to me, a terrible, heartless danger to Adam. The best thing he could do for himself would be to further incriminate Adam—or eliminate him, if he could make it look like an accident or self-defense against a crazed and crazy killer.

I needed to get to Adam first, take him home, wait for Mackenzie, make sure he got psychiatric help. Perhaps the saddest idea was that he'd be safer with the law than with his parents. At least he'd be evaluated and treated in the legal system.

The people in the lobby swirled aimlessly. The auditorium probably hadn't opened yet. I scanned again for Adam, then looked up, toward the statue of Dr. Pepper. I wondered if Adam might be upstairs, looking for his scarf. Not in the Rare Book Department. It was closed for the night, as I'd realized, and the elevators were programmed so that they would not stop on that floor.

Which meant Adam wasn't there.

Which also meant Terry Labordeaux's workday had ended two hours earlier, and he was gone. Adam was not in as much danger as I'd feared. Relieved, I reconsidered my options.

Upstairs, perhaps, at the statue?

Altogether gone? Gone as soon as he couldn't find his scarf? Gone long before I'd inched my way here?

I stood at the bottom of the staircase, my bronzed nonancestor looking magisterial and dour above me, and admittedly late in the game to do so, I considered my course of action.

"Amanda! Is that you?"

I turned so quickly I nearly gave myself whiplash. He wasn't supposed to be there—wasn't supposed to see me. But he was, beaming, dressed in fine but rumpled clothing, his silk tie skewed. I'd found that endearing a few days ago.

"I thought that was you!" he exclaimed, as if we were best friends, not people who barely knew each other and who'd parted awkwardly. Not people who were both profoundly suspicious of each other. "You here for the lecture?"

"I—no. I'm doing research. I have to find something." I managed a semisocial smile. "I won't keep you," I said, "and I'm in a bit of a rush myself. Library hours and all, I need to . . . I was just heading up."

He glanced at his watch. "I've got five minutes before they open the doors to the auditorium. I'll walk you, to be sociable, and then I'll bid you adieu. What is it you're looking up?"

I wanted to say, Back off! I wanted to say, I know what you did. I don't have the details yet, but I know you did it, and I'm going to convince the police you did it, too. I wanted to say, You're lying. Every sentence you've ever said in my presence was a lie. Except maybe in the Elkins Library. Maybe what you said in there about the place was true. But even then, I realized. Even then he was angry with Emily Fisher. I'd thought because she was usurping his role, but now I remembered. Linda had asked about the value of the books, and Emily had said something to the effect that these books were not for sale. Had said it emphatically. The message had been for this man, who'd gotten it, loud and clear. He'd been silent— resentful, I'd thought, of her speaking up when it was his turn. But it was much more than that. It was a warning given and received.

And she was dead by that afternoon.

I said none of this. I did nothing except walk briskly up the staircase.

"What is it you're researching?" he asked pleasantly. "Still involved with Henry James?"

I shook my head. "No. This time it's . . . *Crime and Punishment.*" I didn't veer my sight line from straight ahead—and that very second I saw Adam on the landing, pacing near the statue, staring at it as if it might return his long-gone scarf.

"Hey!" Labordeaux shouted. "You!"

Adam looked without recognition.

"It's him!" Labordeaux shouted. "The kid who killed the librarian!" He took two steps. I grabbed him, screamed. "Run, Adam!"

Luckily, the library-goers on the landing couldn't decide who was the actual crazy one—the shouting man, the bruised woman, or the boy who looked panic-stricken. No one moved.

"You crazy?" Labordeaux said, shrugging me off as if I were no more than an annoyance. "You nuts? You've got a killer here—again."

"No—no, I don't. No, you don't. And you don't have a victim here—again." I pushed him, and he slipped, went down on one knee, but was up in a second, behind me, and we both raced.

Adam wasn't on the landing anymore.

I saw a flash of black sweater in the social sciences room. It could have been anybody, but I had to hope it was Adam. "Adam," I called, "stop! I'll—"

I ran through a sea of gaping expressions, of librarians standing up from where they'd been, ready to warn me, to stop Adam—and Labordeaux was right behind, shouting to get that kid! Get that killer kid!

Adam wasn't in sight. Not anywhere. I glared at Labordeaux, half furious, half relieved.

"I'm getting the guards," he said. "Call the police," he told the librarian. "We'll need them in a few minutes. He's in here. They'll get him." He turned and ran down the stairs.

I wheeled around, scanning the large room with its high, book-lined walls, the stacks midfloor, the wrought-iron balcony ringing the room one story up. No sign of Adam, who had to feel like a hunted animal now.

Who was a hunted animal now. The librarian left to summon help, and in that second I saw him—he'd been behind the nearest stack, and now he darted into an open doorway behind the desk and was gone.

I followed immediately, before the librarian was back and would stop me, for surely this was off-limits.

It absolutely was. I went through the doorway and maneuvered down a narrow circular staircase, feeling like Alice—where the devil was I going? "Adam," I whisper-shouted. "Adam, it's me. To help you. Where are you?"

Nothing. No one. Except a shout from above I could still hear: "In there! Get the guard!"

We'd been seen. I reached the bottom of the winding staircase and was relieved I wasn't in the basement or a frightening dark space. I was in a small, bookcase-lined room, or corridor, or series of rooms that were strung ahead of me as far as I could see. What was this? "Adam?" I called out. I couldn't hear any noise from above anymore, and I felt safe calling for him. "Adam!"

I heard steps ahead, labored breathing, and I followed the sound. The corridor's contents changed—a computer, a desk, more and more and more books in stacks on shelves. A parallel corridor, glass doors, shelves in the middle and along the sides. Dividers and sections and I ran, and ran.

Adam was gone. Disappeared down one of the alternative "roads"?

I suddenly remembered the maintenance man in the basement telling me there were hidden passageways between the floors. He'd said not to bother looking for Adam there because it was a maze. Impossible. A person could be lost there for weeks.

I told myself I wasn't lost. I'd come along a straight path—I thought—and I could go back the same way. I was not lost in passages that honeycombed the library between floors.

I wasn't alone. That much was for sure. I heard a thunk and a bang. Something overturned, a guttural curse. "Adam!" I shouted again.

I reached the dead end of the passage, looked to a hallway running sideways from it, but he was nowhere.

I had no choice. I had to turn back, to summon help, to hope someone would believe me when I said the real menace was not Adam but the gentle-looking librarian.

I turned and hurried and only slowly became aware of a change in my surroundings. I hadn't noticed the old-fashioned library catalogue cases. Maybe I'd been too intent on finding Adam. I simply hadn't noticed. If I kept walking, I had to reach the glassed-in cases, the staircase, the social sciences room.

Except that nothing was familiar—nothing was right, and there was no opening at the end of the passageway, no spiral staircase. The light felt as if it had dimmed. It wasn't bright enough, it was a trap, and I was lost. I was somewhere else altogether, and I had no idea how I'd moved off track, where I was.

The maintenance man had called these passageways a maze. He'd been right. I was turned around in my head, surrounded by muffled corridors, and the only other human being I knew to be down here had disappeared.

I could be here forever. How could anybody find me? *I* couldn't find me!

I had to calm down. Had to stop this. Of course I would be found. There had to be people who knew how to claim the books stacked and stored here, the equipment. People who used the glass-paned cubicles. I would be found. Eventually. I stood still and took a deep breath, and then another, calming myself. I'd be fine. By morning, by next day—by tonight, if anyone had listened to the person who'd spotted us—somebody would form a posse and find me. Mackenzie would. The police had been called. I wasn't in trouble, just in corridors and storage spaces I hadn't known about. This wasn't a frightening place—simply new and unknown.

I was finding it increasingly difficult to listen to my stupid reassurances, but every time I imagined the enormous library and these narrow paths, like an ant colony beneath the departments, between those soaring double- or triple-height stories—every time I saw myself inside them, a dot in a maze, I found it difficult to breathe.

"Adam!" I shouted. "Adam, where are you?"

Nothing. It was as if my voice were absorbed by the walls, by the sighs and rustles of all the books waiting to be read, by all the words already written and said.

And then I heard a step, a bump, a low curse. Behind, not in front of me. "Adam?" I said, but cautiously. He could have wound up behind me in this crazy-house, but I didn't know how. I didn't even know for sure which direction *was* behind me. I listened.

I heard the shuffle of a shoe. A man's dress shoe, not a sneaker. Not Adam.

Calm down, I told myself again. It's the guard. It's the security person he summoned. "Hello?" I said.

Nothing. Nothing and more nothing. A guard would call out, a guard would say "Halt" or whatever they said. I turned to run—but where? Best bet was to wait and see where these footsteps came from.

There. Closer. Closer still. And still in silence. I looked around, realized there weren't many choices left. Only toward or away from.

I saw the shoe come around a stack. Dark blue slacks. Then him, his face, his jacket, his white shirt.

I ran like hell. Away.

What I'd seen caught up with me around the next bend.

White shirt—no tie! Tie off—I hadn't seen it, but I did now, in my mind, ends wrapped around his hands, ready for another quick garroting. Ten seconds—why had Mackenzie ever told me that?

I knocked over a box of something, left the clatter behind me.

"For Christ's sake!" He was panting between words. "Why are you running? Help me find him, that's all!"

Lies. Liar. We weren't on the same side, and he had nothing to lose except a suspicious snoop by adding me to Adam's supposed list of crimes. I said nothing. I didn't have to help him locate me by telling him I wasn't going to help him. I liked my neck, liked my life. I apologized to the cosmos for thinking of changing a thing. The status quo was perfect. Breathing was good. I wanted it.

Suddenly dark. Thick, impenetrable dark. He'd turned the lights off. I lost my last bit of orientation, and lost hope as well. I was completely and totally lost, and there was no way out.

I knew how Adam must have felt all these past days.

"Don't panic," he said. "I wanted to slow you down, to help you. You're in danger from him. The police are on their way, Amanda. Let them find Adam. You never will. These corridors are endless. They stretch the entire city block, one side to the other, back and forth. But I know my way around them—I know these passageways. That's all I'm trying to do, help you get out of here."

He hadn't added the magic word: out of here *alive*. All right, then. I could be hopeless—but not inert. I felt my way around a stack, hit my side on a desk, my head on the bookshelf itself, felt the jolt of this new pain plus a fiery surge of every reactivated ache of the night before. My ragged breath was as good as a flashlight for locating me, but I couldn't stop it, couldn't hush it.

I was underground, a blind and panicked subterranean creature, nothing more.

I tripped.

He was on me in a second, grabbing my shoulder.

I screamed, loud as I could. Screamed and screamed, and thought somewhere, too far to matter, I heard a murmured response. "Help!" I screamed again, but the only response was the heat of him, his fury.

He tried for my hands, grabbed them, but I grabbed faster, pulling the flesh of his cheek, up to his eyes—I scratched, clawed, gave way to being the animal in a trap, the animal who would free myself by gnawing off my own hands if I had to.

He couldn't hold his tie and me at the same time. Couldn't strangle me efficiently the way he had Emily, from behind, by surprise. He didn't want to strangle from the front—Mackenzie had told me that, too. A struggle would mark him, make his story obviously a lie. I marked him now—hurt him however I could—no thought, pure fury, pulling hair, tearing skin, biting—and squirmed until I was free of him. I leaped up, turned, and ran—to what, I didn't know. Where, I didn't know. To wherever I found a glimmer of light. Ahead. Around.

I heard him behind me. Bites and scratches were not nearly enough for anything except evidence after I was dead. I saw a yellow glow ahead, turned to the light. Another book-crowded space. I could throw books at him, arm myself with a stack, but I had to break the glass, get into the cabinets—

An old-fashioned pale wood catalogue case stood by the wall. How Helena would have coveted that for her store.

Half its drawers were missing. Only half.

Labordeaux came toward me. His silence terrified me more than anything he might have said.

"Get back," I said.

He took another step toward me. As I'd hoped. My upper body strength was not the best. I needed him close.

He didn't see what I held, or he didn't care. Maybe he thought I was doing my research down here, but the moment he was near enough, I lifted the drawer I'd removed from the cabinet and hurled it, cards and center rod and metal pull and all. Hurled it at his face.

It was all sharp edges, metal and wood, with enough heft and speed to reach him as he froze, confused, for a second too long. It hit the side of his head and threw him off balance; he grabbed a bookcase next to him, and both of them went down.

I didn't stay to survey the wreckage. I still couldn't see an exit, but that murmured sound sporadically recurred. Voices, people, were somewhere near. I hadn't imagined it, and I moved toward it. And saw light—a half circle of it—but in the wrong place. The wrong shape for a doorway. It was to the left of me, down a new corridor, and a half circle of light down here made no sense, but it was all I had.

I was suddenly on metal flooring. A balcony, enclosed, with more stacks, and then there—the light, the murmurs.

And Labordeaux, bleeding but unbowed. "Don't be an ass," he called out. "Don't be—I didn't mean to—come back here, I'll show you the way—"

I heard the scrape of something he'd grabbed, heard his dress shoes advance, and I looked at the semicircle of light.

I was on a balcony above a room, but not the one I'd left. I saw bright book jackets, an arrangement I remembered. The fiction room, the lending library below me. I was in the stacks and the high oval opening from below ended at about eye level, where a soffit almost shut it off. A plain iron railing blocked more than half of the opening, leaving a small space.

But enough.

A small space with nowhere to go, except down, a story or more, to marble floors that were almost as terrifying as Terry Labordeaux.

I pulled back, dizzy at the idea of the plummet.

And heard him. "Amanda," he said in that weary, overly patient voice. "Stop being a child. Nobody's going to—come here. That's not safe—"

Three steps away. I had no choice. I pulled myself up and half over, keeping my head low, below the curved ceiling. I crawled to the outside, perched on the railing, and screamed. "Help! Help me!" Maybe they'd have a mattress ready, a net—maybe they'd all lie down and catch me. Save me.

People stopped where they were, looked around, up, and sideways. Finally a few saw me, but instead of rushing, instead of coming up with an inspired plan, they stood gape-mouthed, as if they'd never seen a screaming woman hanging from an iron rail above their heads in the lending library.

Maybe he'd back off if he knew he'd be observed. Maybe I

didn't have to jump at all; I could crawl back to what now felt like safety. Real floors instead of space beneath my feet.

Wrong. He was there, pushing me from behind. Pushing from the shadows behind me while shouting, "Don't jump!" as if he were my rescuer. Pulling my fingers off the rail, breaking my hold. Pushing.

"You're going to die," he whispered as he pushed. "Your smart brains, your questioning mind—it's going to be all over that floor. Thanks for doing the job for me."

I was, very literally, in no position to respond. With each push, my center of gravity shifted forward until—I looked, I clenched muscles, I prayed for an agility I'd never possessed, I aimed, and I jumped, screaming as I descended.

Screaming as I landed, on my back. The first thing I saw after I realized I was still alive and my brains were still inside my skull was a man in a vest. His face was upside down, staring. I was sprawled atop a stack. An orange and blue lettered sign saying NEW FICTION lay next to my face. I lifted one arm and tried to point. "Up there," I said. "There's a . . . get the police to go up there . . ." I could see the opening, but nothing within it. The man swiveled his stare in that direction, then returned it to me.

A crowd gathered. The librarian—I assumed that's who it was— shouted up. "Are you all right? Are you hurt? Can you move your head? Can you sit up or get down from there?"

I didn't know. I was afraid to find out. "Police," I repeated.

"They're here," she said. "Hold on a second."

And then I heard a joyous burst of sound. "She's there! She's there!"

"Adam," I whispered. I tested my neck—it worked. I could lift my head. I could see him, black hair ragged and wild, over in a corner, waving, and with him, two uniformed officers and a third, who was approaching me. "Adam," I whispered again. "He's okay."

"The boy came down the stairs, lady," the gaper said. "Why didn't you? Those stairs over there lead right down here—you were maybe ten feet from them. He found them—why didn't you? And, lady, he's supposed to be the crazy one."

I closed my eyes. I was delighted to be alive and safe, but I wasn't quite ready for irony.

Twenty-two

I FELT a little like a kid on the first day of school as I limped beside Mackenzie, en route to the principal's office to praise him for deeds undone, to shame him into doing them. I was sure the ploy would work and, with Mackenzie's gentle suggestions of spin—making Philly Prep's headmaster the heroic seeker of justice—the school would emerge a winner.

But it wasn't my first day of school, it was my last. One day, in fact, beyond my last. I wasn't supposed to darken those doors again, but I needed to get Lia's book back to her, to return papers. To clear my desk.

After months of wondering whether I was a burnout case, whether anything I did here mattered, whether I wanted to stay after all that dithering, all those unanswered questions about what I'd be when I grew up had been answered, abruptly and finally, by Maurice Havermeyer, of all people.

But surprisingly, my sudden freedom did not gladden my heart. My classroom beckoned, as did the smell and noise and tempo of a school day. What was wrong with me? Was I perverse—take something from me I was going to give away and I immediately want it back?

"You done good, kiddo," Mackenzie said as we walked. "Sorry my pager went on the fritz, or I could have been there for the finale, too. I kind of wish I'd seen that leap." Labordeaux was being held. I'd told the police about Emily's notebook, and I'd explained the stickums that seemed a guide to missing library treasures. The dentist Adam had robbed said he wouldn't press charges if the boy got help. Even Adam's parents reluctantly conceded that psychiatry and medications were better than jail for their son. I had hopes for him and didn't regret my intervention.

Turned out I was a semi–Good Samaritan.

Helena Spurry was in mourning, of course. Not for her sister but for her lost hopes. Her "prospect's" only prospect was a long spell in prison. And I was sure that as soon as Mackenzie spoke to Havermeyer, the *InkWire* would be resuscitated along with Nancy and Jill's piece, the scandal exposed and made better. So things were falling into place.

And speaking of falling, I was in one piece, except for a bump on the back of my head, assorted bruises from my falls in the back passageways, an "insulted" coccyx that complained about its slam onto the book bay with each step, a bandaged cut above my eyebrow, and a bruised ego. "You aren't angry, then, that I . . . interfered, sleuthed, whatever?"

"I've been thinking," he said. "I don't know how it is a schoolteacher keeps involvin' herself in these things, but Lord knows you do. Maybe you were itchy about everything—me, your job—because it had been too long a stretch of ordinary time. Crimeless time. So maybe it's good if you get your minimum daily requirement of adrenaline from other people's problems. Maybe we're a matched pair, and maybe it saves us grief."

It was a theory, all right. Of course, I would no longer be a schoolteacher who slid into crime. Just a . . . I didn't know what.

We reached the corner of the school. "Okay, now," Mackenzie said. "I'm going in. I give him seven minutes max before he reverses himself on every point. Including you. But I'd prefer you didn't think of it as the strong arm of the law used on a spineless jerk. Think of it—think of me—as your knight in shinin' armor, chargin' the dragon to rescue the damsel in distress."

"We damsels take care of ourselves these days." Limp, limp, wince. Mackenzie did his one-eyebrow lift. "I'm alive," I reminded him.

"Maybe an exception just this once," he said. "For old times' sake."

"Really old times, like the Middle Ages?"

"You have somethin' against the Middle Ages?"

We turned the corner. And stopped in our tracks.

The sidewalk was lined with students—my students—carrying signs that read IF SHE'S OUT, WE'RE OUT! They made a slow circle on the pavement in front of the school—in front of my apoplectic former headmaster, who stood at the entryway, sputtering and flailing his arms. At the head of the line Nancy and Jill, twin cheerleaders, set the brisk pace. "Look at that," I murmured. "Look at that. Look what they're doing."

"They're your kids," he said softly.

"Maybe it's an excuse to get the day off."

"Maybe. But it gives you pause, doesn't it?"

"Mackenzie, I've just had the most amazing thought. What if I *am* grown-up already? What if this is what I'm going to be?"

"Deserves consideration." He surveyed the marchers. "Kind of eliminates the need for the shinin' armor bit. You've got yourself a damsel brigade."

"The dragon still needs taming," I said. "Use all the strong arms of the law you've got. And thanks, Cisco."

"You're welcome, and you're wrong."

The warning bell rang. Another school day was about to begin. The kids marched, their signs held high, ignoring the warning. Nobody spoke a word.

I stood there, beaming at them. Silently they waved at me. Their images swam and blurred as I blinked hard.

Havermeyer's sigh broke the silence. "You'll be late," he said. "All of you." His glance reluctantly but definitely left the students and moved to me. I was a part of that *all*.

Mackenzie gave my arm a gentle squeeze. "One last thing, okay? Should it happen again that you don' know what job you want," he whispered, "contact a career counselor. It's a lot easier and more efficient than getting involved in a murder, being fired from your job, nearly getting killed a few times, and stirring the student population out of its spring apathy in order to reach a decision."

I'd consider it. If there was a next time. Right now, I had to hurry. The late bell would ring in a few seconds.

Feeling like a benign Pied Piper, I nodded back at Havermeyer, and led my kids and myself back to where we belonged. Together.